THE CAESAR FILE

CAMERON

Ordering Information:

Prime Seven Media
518 Landmann St.
Tomah City, WI 54660

Printed in the United States of America

TABLE OF CONTENTS

ACKNOWLEDGMENT

This book would not have been possible without the support, encouragement, and inspiration of many people.

First and foremost, I am deeply grateful to my friends and family for their unwavering support, patience, and faith throughout this journey. Your love and encouragement carried me through the toughest chapters.

To my editor, John 'Digger' Buxton, thank you for your insight, your guidance, and your dedication to helping this book become the best version of itself.

To my readers—past, present, and future—thank you for giving my words a home.

Finally, to everyone who shared their wisdom, offered feedback, or simply asked, "How's the book going?"—thank you. Every gesture mattered.

CHAPTER 1

$\mathcal{S}$aturday morning was running slow for Pat, she was on the backwash of another case. She had just made some toast covered with chunky marmalade, when suddenly, there was a knock on the door. Pat put down her coffee, peeped through the spy hole and recognised her new friend. She opened the door and greeted her. "Hello Sophia, what can I do for you?"

"Tea would nice babes," came the reply, "Oh and if you want, I am here in the role of Cupid, that's if you want to play the game." She confidently stomped into the hallway and into the kitchen with Pat.

"I have been pestered by, well I don't mean pestered, I should say been approached or had to beat of inquiries....."

Pat interrupted, "Sophia I am sure the desk Sergeant can help you file a stalking report."

"Ah, aha, no honey, I am here in the guise of Cupid meets Mercury." She was smiling and almost bursting being the one that knew her message may change someone's destiny.

"Do you recall a tall chap coming over to chat to us and then disappearing?"

"Yes vaguely, why?"

"His name is Brian and he has asked me to ask you .... Oh, this so delicious, he would like to meet up with you and has asked me see if you would like to meet up with him."

"Sophia I was undercover with a false identity! I can't get involved."

By now she had made Sophia a cup of tea as requested. They moved into the living room and sat opposite each other, Sophia on the sofa and Pat in her favourite chair.

"Look hun, he is a biker but he isn't part the Local MC, like Andrew and myself we are all independents. We just go there because it has the right sort of music and booze and we keep away from the biker politics. If I thought there was a problem for you, I would never have suggested him to you and Andrew also vetted him, so now it is down to you."

"It isn't as simple as that; I was all over the news not so long ago."

"Don't worry about that, firstly as those that took an interest in that event didn't see you here, and secondly, those that did, can't place you here and besides, you cleared us, not condemned us bikers and that makes a big difference."

There was a pause, Sophia drank some of her tea and then tried a different tack.

"Pat I ain't here to push one way or another. I get it you have a position which you have to protect and if you get it wrong then it goes belly up,"

Pat nodded in agreement, "but then the fact that you are single and a Gran means you can enjoy yourself without going through the stupid games we played as kids and you can keep control of what you are doing without getting drunk and stupid."

"With Brian?"

"Look, Brian is considered quite tall and enigmatic and good looking to boot but that will be your loss if you walk away."

"Loss? What do you mean Loss?"

"Hun, you have a great place here and you have the right to keep it as you want, but let's face it you slept on your own and that is sad. He may not be your Mr Right but unless you give it a try you will never know."

"Sophia you ain't going to let this go are you?"

"Look hun, just like the last time, me and Andy will be there by your side and play chaperone and if you choose no he will back off. We will be there and besides because it was a while ago, you can reinvent yourself and no one will know what was said or just tell them you're a home grandmother or a driving instructor, true?"

"I suppose."

"Hun, I saw how you looked at him and your jaw hit the floor so don't tell me you didn't think about it."

"Sophia stop." By now Pat was unusually blushing which was matching her strawberry blonde hair. She took a draught of coffee and looked at her tormentor's beautiful beaming face and new she was beaten.

"You'd better keep a close eye on me then."

"YES!" Sophia fist pumped on the success of her mission.

They continued their chatting into the afternoon and Sophia left agreeing to meet up with her later on outside the clubhouse and Pat undergoing the preparation for the evening events.

Later that evening the detective pulled up outside The Cold Harbour in her silver Beetle. She waited there until she got a text message. "You coming up?" She approached the door girl and paid her two pounds with a smile to both her and the doorman. With a thank you she was allowed to go up the stairs and into the darkened room.

Detecting the Norman's, she walked over and they exchanged greetings.

Andy got up quietly and asked Pat what would she like to drink. Looking nervously, she muttered, "I am driving so a full fat coke with a slice of lemon and ice please," she paused, "but what I would really like is a bottle of Gin with splash of tonic."

Sophia stood up a gave Pat a cuddle and calmly reassured her everything would be alright. They both sat down and Pat noticed that it was still the same as she remembered from before as Andy returned to the table with his beer and two cokes as ordered.

Soon were they lost in conversation, it was meaningless chat mainly about the television and suddenly Sophia noticed a tall six-foot two inches gentleman standing at the bar wearing black leather trousers, a plain waistcoat, a white cotton shirt and a black Australian style hat.

She gave Pat a subtle tap on her leg under the table and with a wink they observed the leather clad chap's advance to their table.

Andrew stood up, shook his hand, turned and said, "Ladies, may I introduce Brian he would like to join us for a drink, this is my wife and her friend Pat."

He smiled and took off his hat and sat down slightly embarrassed with the short introduction.

"Hello ladies it is nice to join you."

"Nice hat" chipped in Sophia.

"Yes, I brought it down under last year," came the reply.

Pat showed an interest. "Whereabouts in OZ where you?"

"Queensland, a place called Cairns have you heard of it?"

"Yes, I was there in 2009."

"Cool, did you go out to the barrier reef?"

"Yes, I went in one of those glass-bottom boats, it was awesome. We saw a really big blue Wrasse called Napoleon and I also went into the rainforest by train and back by cable car and you?"

"I was working for a year driving the land trains into town."

"You scuba, do you?" enquired Andy.

Brian replied, "Yes mate, do you?"

"Yes, got me licence in the RAF – BSAC"

"Oh, I just have PADI open which I got when I was in the Med., it is just enough to get my feet wet and play. I have to admit I can't handle the deep stuff and I am heavy on air as well but then the reef was well worth it."

"Yes, me too, been down to thirty metres but that was on a slow descent on a wall dive."

"That sounds really cool, did you see much?"

"Yes, sharks up close and personal."

"Apart from your work do you get to travel around the place like Port Douglas?" Pat interrupted.

"Yes, my boss had a lodge there, it was a canny place and a great little market, did you get there?"

"I went a couple of times and even got to drink some Sugar Cane juice, it had a kind a grassy taste to it and wasn't as sweet as I thought it would be."

"Well, it needs to be concentrated during the refining process I suppose for that to happen."

Soon the conversation deepened enough for them to lose track of time. Then the last orders bell rang and Andy looked at his watch, turning to his wife, "Darling, fancy a curry?"

She thought about it for a second replying, "No babes but could certainly use a Chinese. Pat, would you like to join us?"

"Er, no thanks Sophia, as much as I would enjoy your company, I think I need to go home."

Brian, then feeling some kind of moment, "Pat may I escort you home?"

"No but can you walk me to the car park where I am parked."

With that they rose from their chairs and descended the stairs. Pat's mind was tying her in knots as she hadn't been in this situation for a long time and was starting to sweat.

"I am in the silver Beetle." So, they walked over to the car. Brian too was starting to show signs of nerves.

"Pat, I would like to…..err, I have enjoyed your company tonight and hope you will like to spend some more time with me, if that is ok with you?"

She automatically handed over her phone number, which he dialled and let ring a couple of times.

"It's a strange thing for me. I have been single for quite a while. I don't think of you as a throw away pleasure, but more an evocative quest." He gently held both her hands together and kissed on top of her hands. She was taken aback as she slipped elegantly into her car.

Driving back to Westerhope, after that evening's finale, left her in a trance. She was used to male company always hitting on her, that was normal, but he made her feel uncomfortably nice. She had even had a few villains trying it on after they had been arrested. This was the first time someone had backed off and made her wonder why he hadn't kissed her on the mouth or cheek.

She was still intrigued the following morning when her daughter Michelle called around for her Sunday get together and family in tow, they knew her well enough to know that something was up. At first they thought it was work related so didn't ask but then finally Pat confessed to her daughter what was troubling her.

"Michelle, I'm not looking to replace your dad, that could never happen but I like the look of this chap and he seems easy going what do you think?"

"Mum," came the reply, "it's ok, I trust you and it is about time there was someone. I know dad would want you to, I just hope he is good enough for you."

"Look, nothing has happened yet I first saw him last year while on a case but he asked to meet me last night. Then when we left, I gave him my number but he didn't kiss me, so I am not sure yet what is happening."

"Will work be ok with that?"

"I will have to wait to see if it goes anywhere and if it does, I will speak to the Gov."

Just then Pat heard her text message tone go ping. She went over and saw an unnamed number with the message *'Good afternoon, I hope all is well? This is Brian and I hope this text finds you well?'*

"Is that him mum? It is, isn't it?"

"Ssh don't tell the bloody world will you." Pat was beetroot red by her daughter's onslaught.

"Mum go for it, just do it, if you like him then go for it."

So duly Pat returned the text, *'Yes thank you kind sir and how may I be of help?'*

'At your convenience a mid-week evening out might be the order of the day, or do you have a better idea?'

'I could be available to the right offer.'

"Oh my god, you tart!" Michelle exclaimed and with that she grabbed her mum's phone and while wrestling with her she tapped into the phone, *'Tuesday.'*

Pat shouted out, "Tom! Here! Now! Sort your wife out she is trying to pimp her mum out."

Tom came rushing in and started laughing "Sort yourself out as I ain't getting in between either of you two and what's happening anyway?"

He grabbed the phone and looked at the message "Well good for you Pat, it's time you got out and found someone."

The next message came through *'How about bowling on Tuesday?'*

Michelle tapped in the phone, *'Fine.'*

"Now mum it's up to you play nice and you might not be so lonely."

"Babes I am not lonely."

"Yes mum I believe you." So, with the conversation that afternoon set, Pat laid the table for her extended family and they had their roast chicken dinner.

The following day at work Pat was trawling through miles of footage taken at certain shops in the Metro Centre. There had been a spate of shop lifting and the police were working hard on solving the crimes.

Chief Inspector John Haddon came up to Pat and spoke. "How is it going Pat doing your important part for the community?"

"Yes boss I am good. By the way, there is a pattern to what we think the timings are from the shoplifting."

"Have you got the suspects yet?"

"No boss but I think it might be around 9-10am when the parents have dropped the kids off, so it will be just a question of targeting the CCTV, which is what I was doing at present."

"And your friend, sorry Sergeant, er Jane?"

"She is out briefing the Metro Centre security team about the patterns we think we may have, just to keep them on their toes. They are targeting high-end electricals and branded clothing, clearly easy to sell on, no doubt via the internet or dark web."

When Jane reappeared from the shopping centre the talk in the canteen wasn't about work but about the impending date as she and Jane had been close friends for thirty years.

Jane had been to Uni, studied as a journalist and was persuaded by Pat to migrate north as she had joined the Tyneside police force and undertook a law degree. After the death of her husband, Pat's coping mechanism with her grief was through work, which made her quite formidable and enabled her to raise through the ranks.

Where Jane was quite capable for promotion, she had met her husband and focused more on her family, hence only making sergeant. The two ladies were very close as a result and many believed or joked that they were twins or sisters or even Lesbian lovers but this was mainly rejected by potential suitors who hated the rejection. Their friendship even impacted on both their families as the kids had grown up together and were equally as close.

Even though Sophia was beautiful and energetic she could never impose on what Jane and Pat had and this meant that Jane didn't feel threatened with the new names that were being brought into the conversation.

But Brian and his origins of their meeting while on ops did concern her, she tried desperately to persuade Pat to register the liaison with their boss.

Pat quite sensibly replied that she would if there was something to report but at this stage there wasn't as only text messages had been exchanged.

Besides, that investigation was a blind alley leading nowhere and the investigation has been closed for over a year ago but then she promised Jane that if it did then go anywhere then she would speak to the chief about it.

Just then Pat's phone buzzed into life with the text message, *'Where do you want me to pick you up from?'*

So she texted him her address and returned to the CCTV, watching shoppers going around the alleys. At twice the speed it made it easy to spot unnatural behaviour for the those trying to hide what they were doing. For Pat, Monday melded into Tuesday, which to her was more of the same and with no breakthrough to speak of, all that Pat had to look forward to was the evening of escapism that was to be provided by Brian at the bowling alley.

At seven o'clock Pat's doorbell rang. When she opened the door it was Brian dressed in black jeans, tee shirt and trainers. "Madam your chariot awaits" and he held his hand to her as she locked her front door.

Taking his hand she allowed him to escort her to the light metallic blue MG convertible. He opened the door and allowed her to glide into passenger seat.

It wasn't long before they arrived at the Bowling alley and booked in. Brian arrived with the drinks order. They took up station at the number 6 lane and the two started playing the game.

Pat was now into police mode questioning as she wanted to find out from Brian how he came to be. Throughout the evening he told her his tale.

He had left school without much and little hope so he joined the army as a driver in the Royal Corps of Transport, the RCT, but then this had been merged into the Royal Logistics Corps. He had got all four classes of driving licences when his wife insisted that he leave, which he did, but that hadn't stopped her from leaving him.

Fortunately, the chances of a baby hadn't gone full term and also increased friction in their relationship, meaning when they did split up, children, weren't an issue. He had difficulty in coping with the split and it had left a mark on him.

Then he drifted into driving articulated lorries for a living and that had suited him. He had developed a dislike for mixing with people and with driving lorries and motorbikes he was able to keep his distance from those he allowed and already deemed acceptable into his social life.

He had a number a ladies interested in him but none had lasted any reasonable length of time and he was ok with that, as he didn't want a full -time partner.

It wasn't the commitment which he objected to; it was the domination of his life. After he left the army and spilt from his wife, he swore that he would never be told what to do, ever again. But with Pat there was something intriguing and strange about her and he hadn't been able to shake her out of his mind. He was girl-shy and the more beautiful she was, the more difficult it was for him to hold a conversation.

This accounted for the way he wasn't able to give a simple kiss to Pat.

In fact, he couldn't understand how he was able to speak to her, normally he would just nod and move away. On the biking he also told her that he had been approach on quite a few occasions to prospect but had turned them down as it wasn't what he wanted. He enjoyed being independent but he wouldn't disrespect them. He had also been approached by a national motorcycle club that recruited from the those who had served in the armed forces and once again he wasn't interested, too many rules.

He enjoyed his freedom from club rules and tried to avoid the club politics that was ever present. It just happened that he was a personal friend to a lot of club members because of his quiet nature and was one of their go to people to solve problems that arise. He a had his own old boy network mainly made up from those he knew, who he had served with and would readily lend a hand.

He went on to tell her, "I had a dream once and it kinda stayed with me. Circumstances had meant that I was doing a lot for the Local MC and was invited to prospect. I told them that I would think it over but that was more politeness than anything as I didn't want it. Then that night I had the dream and that was about joining up. *'We were working or prospecting from the top of a double decker bus. I told them I was not wanting to patch. Then I turned around and saw a skeleton made of pure white paper with black holes in the eye sockets and red dot for the eyes that appeared angry that I had rejected them. The wraith turned to my cut with the Prospect badge on it, set fire to it with a single look and then pronounced I would never be a 1%er. Then the spectre followed me out of the bus and I was set on fire."*

He kept his direct involvement to a minimum and didn't like regular club contact. He was just happy to do his own thing but he couldn't hide the pleasure he got from a good ride out with fellow bikers and especially enjoyed the festival of lights when the bikers light up their bikes in convoy with lights as they drove in convoy along the Whitley Bay seafront as the sight was awesome. Especially when one looked at them from a distance.

He also had a secret interest in history, visiting historical sites and of course, the wall was a main interest as he was fascinated from an early age with this monument. He had also had weekend breaks to Rome to see Trajan's column and the other monuments such as the Colosseum or as he pointed out the original title the amphitheatre d' Vespasian. That was when he was shocked to find out the original forum still existed and so was the site of the funeral pyre of Gaius Julius Caesar.

He had Pat enthralled at this moment. Pat confessed to him that she was mainly ignorant about history as her job was mainly chasing the present and discovering the ills of modern man. She told him that during the last case she was working on, the victim was into his Roman history and had loads of books written by Caesar and Plutarch and a chap called Cicero.

Then as she discovered this, there was a discussion programme about him. She was intrigued and found that his letters were still in print. His personal slave was credited with inventing shorthand which still was in use today although more refined versions now existed.

It surprised her that much of today was down to the Roman personalities from the time of Caesar. Cicero was the first and last non-aristocratic Consul of Rome and introduced the written law.

So the conversation went on and the evening came to a close.

Brian escorted her to his car and he opened the door to let her in.

When they returned to Pat's house he got out to help her out of the car.

It gave him the opportunity to hold her by the waist and that was when Pat looked at him and said, "Are you going to kiss me?" The invitation was answered as they embraced each other. Brian walked up to the front door, once again they kissed and he asked if he could keep on seeing her.

She agreed but when she invited him in for a drink, he politely declined saying that his car needed fuelling up and he had an early start for work.

Pat looked at him shocked. Seeing this Brian drew her closer, "I think you're a gorgeous woman. If you want, I can pick you up Saturday evening and we can go to the club." He turned away and then back to face her, "Don't go picking up strange men in the meantime, it isn't fair to cheat on your boyfriend before you've got to know him."

This made Pat laugh, but once she walked through her door she stopped did he really say that - boyfriend!

The following day at the police station she was about to wade through hundreds of miles of CCTV footage when Chief Inspector John Haydon walked past.

"Gov!" he stopped and turned to face Pat.

"Yes Pat, how can I can help?"

"Sir, er John we are mates as well aren't we?"

"Yes Pat, what's up?"

"Remember the ops I did last year at the bikers club?"

"Yes, that was a surprise, bikers being found innocent."

"Boss that's not fair, besides there has been a development in that quarter."

"Oh, what do you mean?"

"I was approached by a chap and I ignored it as flirting. You know Andy Norman, the mortician who escorted me?"

John Nodded, "Yes, well what of it?"

"This chap knew Andy and got him to ask me out on a date. Which I went on. I like him and I am going to take it further."

"The case is closed and he wasn't a witness or a suspect. He isn't involved in any crime is he?"

"No boss! He is an ex-squaddie and now a lorry driver. He has nothing to do with the Local MC biker gang. Andy seems to think he is ok."

"Then thank you for telling me, I will make a note and for God's sake keep it quiet."

"Why!"

"I don't have that many counsellors to mend the broken hearts including mine."

She smiled back at John, "What would your wife think?"

"She'd be glad of a clean house." He laughed as he walked away.

Jane then arrived "Boss, I want to show you something."

Jane scrolled through the footage on the memory stick. "Look, the girl in the posh red jacket and guy with his back to the camera, they just pick the Blu-ray player and walk out the door as if they already own it."

"Good work Jane, let us see if there is a pattern in their offending other than timing, now we know who to look for."

During the morning Pat brought Jane up to speed about the date night at the bowling alley and told her she had spoken to the chief, who had given his blessing.

For Pat, Jane was more than a friend and colleague, closer than a sister, with whom she was dependant on all matters and together they were a dominant force in the police.

"Jane, notice how they are targeting high value electrical goods, cameras and technology and only the branded names in the last month. I think this is the best picture. They have taken about four grands worth of goods and they are good at it. Clearly, they are avoiding all the cameras."

"You mean they may have inside knowledge? I hadn't thought of that but now you mention it, I think you may have a valid point. Can we find out who got hold of this information and draw a list of the stores that have been targeted and the companies they use for security."

Pat continued, "Then run it through the Police National Computer and see if it throws anything up as these are professional in the thieving craft. The way they avoid the cameras and their disguises are designed to look normal at ground level but avoid detection from the high ground."

It wasn't long before the search results arrived and almost immediately the names of a well-known couple sprang up. Both Danny and Sarah Mildred were well-known shoplifters in the past, but had been inactive for a couple of years. So Pat and Jane put together a plan to trap for them, they had to catch them in the act. The CCTV was good enough to monitor their activity but their big problem was that the tech savvy couple knew how to restrict their exposure and in the end the CCTV was vital in directing the resources. Pat knew it was going to be difficult not to spook them, so she decided to isolate the shop being targeted using both shop staff and the Metro Centre resources.

She had a hunch that it was going to be a department store as they had a launch of beauty products going on and it would be a big distraction from the electrical section.

So, she put a plan together and went to present it to Chief Inspector John Haydon. After a few phone calls he gave it his seal of approval.

That evening the store's boss arrived. Jack Cheetal was five-foot eleven and had a little middle age spread. Despite his demeanour he was a very shrewd boss, kind and compassionate but not afraid to be ruthless.

He had been in the retail trade as soon as he had left university and worked his way to regional manager but kept his eye on the shop floor on a regular basis just to keep in touch with his client base and more importantly his staff. He knew one of his biggest drains on his company's resources was unauthorised withdrawal of stock.

Pat put together a short film presentation and then the plan.

It started with the surveillance phase around the first two hours after the school run and then with extra cameras around key areas of the products being targeted. At a signal, the security provided from the Metro Centre would take control of the doors and the undercover police would then emerge from strategic points around the shop as they would be posing in as civvies and finally uniform come in to make the arrest just as they step outside the shop.

Jack saw the merits of the operation and offered the stores full cooperation and allow the IT forensic police access to secrete the camera after the shop was closed. The plan came to together and in the morning all that needed to happen was the couple to come in to undertake their unauthorised allocation of goods.

Pat and Jane sat in the shop's office watching in anticipation of the forthcoming events. "Red coat and brown hoody.", came over the radio. True enough the two approached the valued high-end goods and with both amazing stealth and brazen theatrics secreted the valuable cameras into their bags. Pat gave the code word and the doors became manned and the undercover police closed in. Suddenly everyone in the door way, was part of the sting operation and finally the uniformed officer stepped forward and stopped the couple just outside the shop doors, they were trapped with nowhere to run.

They were searched and two £2000 cameras were removed. When they couldn't provide a receipt Jane, (who was now with the couple), read them their rights. Within a couple of minutes it was over and the man and woman were bundled into the waiting police van, handcuffed. Eventually the crowd dispersed.

Back at the town centre police station the couple were separated by the desk sergeant who questioned them about their needs and gave them a grey track suit each to change into, then they were led away to the police cells.

The Mildred's had been through the system so many times as well-seasoned shoplifters that they didn't mess around, giving a full confession. Trying to plead innocent with their track record was pointless especially as they were caught with the goods still in their boxes and no receipt. The only thing that intrigued Pat was why the two-year break? The answer was provided by Danny and later confirmed by Sarah that that was their intention having been diverted with Danny's dying mother.

Pat organised a search of their home where a large number of goods were found that hadn't been fenced.

Both Danny and Sarah became very vague when it came to items that they couldn't be nailed 100% down on. They did mention that the break in activity was funded by a fence called Caesar who was paying over the odds for the electricals and jewellery but was no longer active, everyone thought he been caught. There was a rumour the stuff was bound for eastern Europe.

Pat decided that they had enough information and evidence for a conviction, so the Mildred's were charged and bailed to appear at the magistrate's court at a later date and allowed to go home in time to be there for their kids.

"Just another day at the office." Pat described the events to her Chief when he came down and gave her a well done.

"Pat last year while you were playing doctors and nurses there was a missing person report came through; Victor Gayle picked the case up but went nowhere and had retired at Christmas."

"Your point being boss?"

"There was a middle-aged woman last seen going to the High Force Falls area and was never seen again," he continued, "your case is now wrapped up pending the court case."

"Yes boss, little bit of paper work but most of it is tidied up with a confession, nice dealing with professionals."

"Yes, well I am going to give you and Jane this case. Oh, and your friend Andy Norman might be able to help you with the next part."

"Why?"

"He has a body of a woman matching her description and in the right area. Can you take it forward and see what the score is? Tomorrow will be fine as speed is essential on this one, being a cold case that is."

"Yes boss."

Pat finished off her paperwork and then her and Jane work complete, retired for the evening ready for a new day and new case. Well at least they knew what it would be about.

Joyce Grey was a forty-five old, quietly attractive woman when she disappeared in 2019. She was a tiny five foot five and bespectacled woman.

She had an inquisitive mind and had trained as a state enrolled nurse. But because of her nervous disposition she was working as a health carer in a nursing home. She was deeply religious and tried to follow the Bible. She was also working part-time in her local church as a Church Warden.

She had told her mother, with whom she lived, that she was going out for a walk in the High Force Falls area as she wanted to see the waterfall there because the recent rain meant there would be plenty of water, making a spectacular scene to photograph.

She wasn't expecting to meet anyone there and just fancied a bit of space.

She drove there in an old light blue Fiat 500 which she had bought second-hand and was beat up but functional. This was later found at a nearby car park next to a hotel. The CCTV from the hotel car park showed her briefly leaving her car and going for her walk.

She was never seen alive again. At the time the police searched along the river banks and had the divers in the river but nothing was found.

Joyce was listed as missing and the file left open. She was last seen wearing blues jeans and plain blue top with a fleece type jacket and trainers, carrying a camera over her shoulder.

The car had been subject to the forensic service and showed no signs of foul play. She had never been in touch at work or church and her credit and bank cards have never been used since the morning of her disappearance.

Her mother had called around desperate to find out information but there was nothing new the police could tell her.

The notes stated that she was quiet and mouse like and would only cross the road at a crossing point. She hadn't any boyfriends and only socialised with her church group on official functions.

Pat finished reading the file of Victor's notes, then the initial forensic report that was handed to her separately.

In May 2020, a group of canoeists had made the grim discovery, a mile down from the Falls, the body was trapped in some trees above the water line. So presumably the body was lodged there while the river was in full flood. The cold probably reduced the rate of decomposition and the number of creatures that could get at the body to eat it. Even so, over a year had taken its toll and nothing was recognisable as a human.

She took herself over to the Mortuary and there saw the familiar face of her new friend Andrew. He smiled when he saw her, "Hello Pat, how can I help?"

"The new remains from High Force, where are we in the identification and cause of death?"

He flipped through the chart, "We are dealing with her this afternoon. We are waiting for her dental records, then we can make a comparison and we have already sent off a DNA sample and have a potential match from her mother, which was recorded when the victim went missing."

"So we are working on the victim being Joyce?"

"Yes, er Pat let the science do the work. By the way how did Saturday go for you?"

"We connected; it took a little work. I didn't realise that he was quietly on the shy side. but yes

"So, Sophia did okay for you."

Pat blushed now. "Andy, we will see but yes, we have met up again since Saturday it was Tuesday. We went bowling and we are also planning to meet again. We did kiss on Tuesday but I think gently does it is the watchword."

"Pat, just as long as you're ok and careful, but who cares, enjoy yourself and if it doesn't feel right end it. There is no right or wrong just as long as you are both ok about it. Brian is a good chap I know him from the Legion. There are quite a few of us who are Legion Riders and drink at the Cold Harbour club. Let's face it, we are bikers and that's why we drink there because there are few places where we feel comfortable. Does he know your true work?"

"Yes, I told him and if he remembers I said something different, I will tell him he is confused and or just remembers it wrong. Besides I don't think he going to blab to the rest of the pub, do you?"

Andy agreed with Pat's summing up of the situation and then confessed that Sophia would be unbearable now as she would be flushed with success on her matchmaking skills.

"I guess we will be socialising a bit more Andy" Pat smiled at him.

"I will ring you when we have something to report, ok Pat."

With that Pat gave him a side hug and left to return to her office. When Jane arrived with two coffees, Pat brought her up-to-date. Strangely for the first time, this involved both the case and the new developments on the personal front. Jane was secretly excited to hear Pat's news. She had quite regularly been approached by a few males, even a female colleague seeking the personal attention of DI Nottage and without exception and under Standing Orders she told them not to bother and thanked them for their interest.

After their coffee they went through the documents that related to the case and discussed a plan of action. They decided not to put the lD on the press release but withheld the details until the body has been checked for ID. They also want the mother to be the first to the hear the news.

They didn't wait long as the phone call came and invited them over to the Forensics office. Jane walked over, picked up the documents and brought them back for Pat to read.

"Looks like we can confirm the identity as dental records are matching up for Joyce. That just leaves the DNA results which should be a day or two. Looks like we have a visit to make."

Just then Pat's office phone rang and Jane gave a look of alarm when Pat exclaimed "Christ she is here! Ok I will come down and speak to her.

Are Family Liaison to hand?" Jane quickly picked up the phone. Dialling the number she got the answerphone message saying they were out for the rest of the day. She told Pat.

"Shit what a crap way to find out" Pat muttered angrily.

She went down the stairs, into the public forum and saw an elderly woman, small in stature, with a thin physique. It was clear she had been crying and consoled by a man, similar age and physique to the woman. Pat guessed that was Joyce's father.

The woman noticed the detective walking towards her and stood up, "Where's Victor? He is my detective; he is looking for my Joyce."

"Mrs Grey, Mr Grey?" They both replied yes together.

"Please come with me I am Detective Inspector Pat Nottage." and with that she beckoned them past the security door and into one of the set aside interview rooms.

Pat look intently at Mrs Grey. "Mrs Grey…."

"Louise please," she interrupted.

"Louise, this is my colleague, Jane," pointing to Jane, who had just caught up her, "Victor retired at Christmas and I've been assigned to look after you. We normally like to discuss these matters at home with you with specialist police officers with us. Sadly, you have pre-empted this and Family liaison are out on another case."

"Please is it her? The girl on the radio, is it Joyce?"

"I am so sorry but initially the dental records suggest that it is, but we are also waiting for DNA confirmation as due to the advanced decomposition the condition of the remains makes it difficult to recognise as a person."

Jane took over the conversation. "Louise, if I may," she nodded "I have just come from the mortuary, where they are looking after her as we speak. She is being cared for there and they are looking for any clues as to what happened, but it is going to be difficult. As soon as we can we will let you have her for burial. I believe she was a devout Christian, so you can, if you choose give her a fitting funeral and you can grieve properly knowing where she is."

"Would you like to discuss anything while you are here?" Pat asked. The door opened and a gentleman brought in four cups with the teas and coffees requested a few minutes earlier. Pat was interested in finding out a bit more about the deceased. Her mother knew Joyce's story well and wanted it told. So the conservation ended and Pat promised that she wouldn't rest till she found out what had happened. She asked Louise if she could call around at their home address to see Joyce's room. She checked it was still at Alexandria Road and after they had a hug the couple distraught as they were left for home. Dennis, her husband promised to take it easy on the roads.

Jane escorted them out through the security area and then returned to meet up with Pat. "God that was emotional."

Pat agreed, "Can't argue with that, but at least we are not looking at an abduction, just a straight accident." With that Pat winked at Jane, "Home time." and they too left the building.

The following day the two detectives received the forensic report and although there were signs of bruised bones, including her skull, which were consistent with a fall or being taken by the river and hitting the boulders.

It was impossible to know the exact cause of death due to the degradation of the cadaver. Limited evidence would suggest that the victim fell and either drowned straight away and her body travelled down river colliding with river debris causing injury or she was knocked unconscious and then drowned. It was impossible to rule out foul play but the lack of evidence from the victim's profile suggested this is nothing more than a tragic accident.

This time the Family Liaison team were available and met up with Pat and Jane prior to the visit. Pat was able to brief Karen with the past events.

Fortunately, she knew the case and had worked with Victor, so knew Louise Grey.

They drove to Cramlington in two cars, Pat and Jane in Pat's silver Beetle and Karen in her red Ibiza.

Karen was thirty, a little larger than she would like to be, but was curvy enough to turn a few heads. She met her husband not long after she had joined the police force. She had trained as a social worker at Northumbria University and then specialised in forensic social working. When she saw the Police advertisement for a Family Liaison Officer, she joined up making a tremendous contribution and now was the department lead with her compassion and tough leadership.

As they walked from the cars to the front door, as if by magic it opened and Dennis was standing there, "Hello Karen, hello officers please come in."

The three walked into a spotless room that could have come straight out of a magazine. There were family photos all around the room including a few of Joyce. Louise came in from the kitchen and after greeting them, offered them a hot drink. She took their orders, returning shortly with them on a tray.

Karen started the conversation up with introductions and filling in the background. Then she handed over to Pat.

"As you know Louise, there have been developments to your daughter's disappearance. Yesterday you heard on the radio a body had been found further down the river, about midway between Middleton and Newbiggin, in the Barnard Castle area. From both dental and DNA records we can confirm that the human remains are that of your daughter, I am so sorry." Despite the news lacking any surprise, it was still upsetting for the couple to hear it and they both broke down comforted by each other.

Pat continued, "The pathology report was inconclusive and following the complete lack of evidence and motive against Joyce and her life choices, it means she simply and tragically tripped or fell and drowned."

Karen then spoke, "I know it is sad and you are upset but this was a tragic accident and not as a result of criminal activity be it abduction or mugging. There will still be an inquest but we wanted to confirm to you what we know at this moment, so there will be no surprises for you. Can you do me a favour please Mrs Grey?"

"It all depends, how can I help?"

"I would like to see Joyce's room please."

Louise looked at Dennis. He got up. "Please follow me, this way."

He led them up the mahogany banister lined staircase. There were more pictures of the family and happier days decorating the walls. They ascended the stairs covered in a deep pile dark blue carpet with brown Fleur-de-lis clips to stop the carpet from slipping. Pat was the first to approach the bedroom door, the bathroom was to her right and the master bedroom to her left. Through the door she spied a clean room with a fully made single bed. Against the wall was a work desk and computer.

"Is that her laptop?" Dennis replied that it was. "Apart from the laundry this is the same as she left it. Lou cleans it once a week as we were always hoping she would return home, but I don't know what we will do now."

Pat looked around. "The photographs on the wall, friends?"

"Sort of, they are people she knew at church. I think they would go on trips together; she called them pilgrimages and I suppose to her they were."

"Are you religious Dennis?"

He shook his head "No, I don't know where she got it from. I was forced to go to church at school, we had our own school chapel. I couldn't stand it. I used to do goldfish impressions during the singing and read comics during prayers. Fifteen minutes every day, Monday to Saturday and two hours on flipping bloody boring Sunday. Boarding school for you."

"Do you know any of them?"

"No, not really I wasn't really interested but I respect what she was doing only because she was happy doing it, Daniel is one name, Jennifer another we were hoping that she might settle with someone from the church if only for her to be happy and maybe even a grandchild." He broke at that and excused himself from the light pink room and Pat heard him blowing his nose. A few minutes later he returned with his face swollen from crying.

"It shouldn't be our job to bury our daughter, it should be her job to bury us. That is the natural order of life."

"What church is she with?"

"Oh, around the corner, not the Catholic one but the one further down the road by the junction. I think it is called the Parish Church of St Michael and all Angels. They seemed to be very active in the community, always doing stuff like fates and barbecues, that sort of thing."

"She was church warden there wasn't she?"

"Yes, it was a part time job thing she did and she was loved doing it she got the job when the previous warden died of a heart attack. The Reverend Sam Hunt gave her the chance to fill in a few years ago. She did a great job and he admired her for her enthusiasm with which she approached her role. She was happy doing God's work but he didn't help much with the rent money so she lived with us, not that that was a problem," bemoaned her father. Her last holiday was even with the church. They went for a week in the Lakes starting with a few days in Kent so they could go to Canterbury Cathedral for prayers. We were planning to go to Benidorm before she didn't come home."

Louise went over to the chest of drawers and picked up a photo album. She showed the three police officers the pictures that Joyce had taken while on holiday including a few group photographs. They passed them around making a few courteous oo's and ah's and nods of approval. They were mainly of the groups active with the church and people involved at the time. Some were taken by other people as Joyce was included. Lots of four to five people, arms locked providing a pose for the camera. They then watched some video footage of a summer party. It helped to bring this unfortunate lady to life. It reminded Pat that this was a person whose life they were looking into, but it was also the mother and father telling the state official about their cherished daughter. It was as much important as it was for Pat to collect evidence for the coroner.

Jane summed up their feelings as they left the Grey's mews. "If that is the way that God looks after his own then I don't want any of it. Collecting his devoted is one thing but then leaving them to rot in a river in obscurity without the proper services and prayers from her family is something different, even Jesus got that and they crucified him, yet she just went for a walk in a beauty spot, no trouble to anyone."

"Talking of which Jane, we'd better go to the church to meet some of the flipping flock just to cover the bases and make sure what is, is just that."

"Yes boss, when?"

"No rush Jane, we will it sort out tomorrow, besides, I wanna go home on time tonight. Let's go home, it's time."

That evening Pat was enjoying her chicken salad and a glass of white Prosecco, when her phone erupted into life. The flashing light signalling that she had just received a text message.

'Hi Pat I am thinking of you at this very moment what are you doing?'

She replied *'Oh me, just soaking in the bath.'*

'Sorry need photographic proof' came a swift reply. He's hooked she thought.

'Sorry, against regulations and what are you doing?'

Just then her phone burst in life indicating an incoming phone call. She giggled at the prompt response. "Hello Brian, how can I help you? Was it something I said?"

He laughingly retorted "If I was driving my truck I would have crashed."

"If you were texting and driving, I would have had you arrested."

"Well, it is just as well I was parked up waiting to be tipped then. I thought I would check to see if we are still good for the weekend?"

"Well that all depends what you have in mind tiger."

"The Harbour might be part of it and we see about anything else closer to the day but in the meantime how do you feel about going pillion with me to Holy Island?"

"Do you know what, I have never been there, so Yes I would like that."

"Do you have a lid, er crash hat? Tell you what, you don't need to buy, I have a spare and also a jacket, it might be a bit baggy but it should protect you."

"Okay, are you sure?"

"It isn't a problem. I don't get rid of my old stuff so I'll just wash it down first. Then I can get you kitted out and if you like it you can see about sorting your own personal get up. In the meantime, it won't cost you money, just in case you don't like it. You won't have lost anything as motorbiking isn't for everybody. Oh, by the way, the tidal crossing times are one to four and it takes an hour to get there from here."

"Sounds like a plan Hun." They continued for a few more minutes chatting and eventually ringing off when Brian announced he had to check the back of the wagon as he was being tipped. Suddenly Pat was starting to look forward to embarking on a new adventure on a motorcycle, something she had promised she would never do!

The following morning both Pat and Jane drove to Joyce's church. It was a twenty-minute drive from the Police station and the conversation centred main around the weekend's coming bike ride.

"Here we are," announced Jane "congregation of the bleeding hearts."

"Jane!" Pat glared. As they turned the corner, they were presented with a fairly modern box shaped building next to the traditional church with the lower part of the tower and adjoining porch in coursed limestone. The roof was slate, with some old stone slates and asbestos slates still visible. The Nave and south porch and north aisle had been much restored. A short west tower, with the windows Perpendicular to the aisle and the north door was evidently blocked in. It had the appearance of having been built around the early Victorian era but a moulded stone announced being built 1818, that confirmed it.

The Reverend Sam Hunt was in the entrance talking to one of his parishioners. He was dressed in a purple shirt with the obligatory dog collar and black trousers. He was in his mid-forties and a married man, indicated with a wedding band. He had short cropped hair and stood six foot in black shoes. He was talking to a slightly younger man who was also smaller in stature with a ginger moustache and beard, dressed in a black tee shirt, black jeans with a black leather waist coat and a prominent white Christian cross on the back. They shook hands and the younger man left in a smart car. The Detective Inspector and Sergeant emerged from their car and approached the vicar.

"Hello, are you the Reverend Sam Hunt?"

He nodded replying "Yes"

Pat produced her warrant card. "I am Detective Inspector Nottage and this is Detective Sergeant Richards can we talk, somewhere a bit more private?"

"Of course, how can I help?" He showed them into the church and sat in one of the pews indicating for the police detectives to follow suit.

"We are looking into the death of one your parishioners and former Church Warden, Joyce Grey."

"Ah, yes that was a sad affair, we miss her all here, she was our little whirlwind, how can I help?"

"We are just looking into her background since her disappearance and finding what was left of her body. May I ask, who did she socialise with and when was the last time you saw her?"

"That would be the day before she disappeared, she was here organising the cleaners as she wanted to give a little sparkle to the old building before the garden fete that was planned. She had also planned to arrange a pilgrimage. We weren't sure where to. We were thinking of going to Salisbury Cathedral by bus at the time but we weren't sure. It came to nowt as it was cancelled last year out of respect for Joyce, instead we held a prayer meeting at High Force, where she was last seen."

"Where else have you been?"

"York, Durham, Westminster and Wells, as well as Canterbury again and Lincoln. This year we are going to Winchester, home to Alfred the great. You know, it all started with Harry Potter. As it was filmed there some of the younger flock wanted to go to Durham Cathedral. Joyce organised it as it was local but everyone had such a good time it became a bit of an annual event. Joyce was the back bone and I had the tough decision to get a new Church warden, in fact that was him you have just seen with me, he is biker, they do quite a lot for us. So he brings quite a lot to the table. His bike club support us and we return the favour."

"How long did she work for you as a church warden?"

"Just short of five years, she was blessing, sadly no more."

"In fact, I had just been appointed here and in turn she was my first appointment. I was so very proud of her and what she was doing. Considering she was a very meek person she truly did inherit the world as she was a very quiet powerhouse."

"How did she work the trips to the cathedrals,"

"She would work out the costing and then ask around. I would announce it on Sundays and those that fancied going would pay in advance. She would do the booking."

"You said something about a small group wanting to return, were they the same group?"

"By and large yes they were, but the number increased every year, so we went from six to the current eighteen, but we have lost two of them since we started, one to road accident, the other took his own life sadly and Joyce makes the third."

"What! Three? That's a bit much isn't it? I mean for a small group of people."

"Well, you guys investigated them and weren't worried or connected so I don't think so."

"Ok, I see you have a fete on this weekend?"

"Yes, this one is in honour of Joyce. In fact, we are going to get her a fitting memorial with the money raised but I think with the current news that might be modified, we are going to speak with her parents."

Pat paused for a moment as in thought, then she thanked the Reverend and led Jane back to the car. When they got in, she turned to Jane, "Got any plans this weekend Jane?"

"No Pat, why?"

"I am on a second date with Brian and we are going to Holy Island for the day on his motorbike but I would really like a snoop around here at the fete see who turns up and says what! Perhaps even take a few family snaps and of any personalities that might be of interest."

"Oh, I see, I am the fall guy."

"You got it and at the same time you can take the family out and do that family thing you like to do with Shelly."

"Overtime boss?"

"Get real, you are taking the family out. What do you want overtime for?"

They went back to their office and wrote up their notes for the day. While they were doing that Jane turned to Pat, "You're suspicious aren't you? Why?"

"I don't know, Jane. I can't work it out. It is a straight forward open and shut case of misadventure. I am happy about that but then there is this little voice screaming in the back of mind and I wonder if there is something to connect the deaths or is it just a plain case of a simple coincidence that three parishioners have come to a premature end and knew each other."

"Well, I'll pull the files Pat and have a read."

"Ha, well volunteered my dear friend but do it softly and independently Monday morning." She paused for thought, "I don't want anyone to get the wrong idea that we don't trust their work or we have gone off on one and are trying to make a meal out of something or nothing."

"Ok Pat, softly, softly does it and not Z cars."

With that they left for home and the weekend events that were now laid out before them.

CHAPTER 2

$\mathcal{S}$aturday. Pat was nervously eyeing the clock as it declared the time eleven o'clock. It had seemed like five hours since she had last seen it and not the five minutes that had just passed. Yet Pat was still getting anxious as a schoolgirl waiting for the day out. She put on some old jeans again and was ready with a few extra layers for the bike ride, she still didn't know what to expect. She was listening to the radio when the engine noise started to vibrate the windows. Then as suddenly as it had started, it stopped and Pat went to the window to see a black motorbike parked on the road in front of her house. Brian was dressed in black leather boots, trousers and black Kevlar jacket, her escort for the day. He cocked and flipped his leg over the bike to separate himself from it. Suddenly Pat was a schoolgirl for a minute as the excitement of a ride out beckoned. Brian coolly strolled to her front door and knocked. She opened the door and he offered his hand. Noticing her look of wonder he said, "Hello Alice, welcome to wonderland." He handed her a lightweight jacket which had wires hanging from it and a heavy jacket and helmet with some oversize gloves, which she dutifully put on.

"Why the two jackets Bri?"

"I am glad you asked me that, you see this wire?" pointing to the plug, "If you get cold, I can plug it into the bike and it will warm you up. Oh, and the blue flashing light on the helmet that means we can talk to each other while on the road. It works just like a mobile phone but via Bluetooth. I have paired them up last night, it took ages." Pointing to the large button he continued, "Press once until it bleeps once and then you can talk, but if you do just remember to let me concentrate during any tricky situations for both our sakes."

Pat locked her door, slung her leather handbag over her shoulder and slipped into her helmet and gloves. "Ready," she announced to Brian.

He got on the bike, taking control and kicked the footrest off. He beckoned to her to climb on pointing to the footrests.

The bike was a Triumph Rocket coming fully equipped with everything Brian could think of, he had spared no expense. Radio and satellite navigation, cruise control, feet forward controls, panniers and a top box big enough for two helmets on the back. With the world's largest production motorcycle engine at 2,500cc, it has more power than the average car.

She climbed onto the back of the bike and shuffled a bit, "What do I do now?"

Via the microphone he replied, "Just relax and follow me when I lean, you can put your hands either behind you or wrap them around me." She elected to put her hands around Brian's waist, which made him smile and so the two adventurers set off.

It was a few minutes before they were on the A1M and heading northward. They were riding on the inside lane when they approached a lorry. It was travelling at fifty-six miles an hour so Brian jumped into a space behind the lead car, a black Volvo, but on seeing that there was a bike behind him he slowed from seventy to sixty and then continued to maintain that sixty miles per hour. Brian was now alerted to something was going to happen. "Careful babes we have an idiot that wants to play, I'll try to clear him as quickly and safely as possible."

The black Volvo had now passed the articulated Lorry but was still maintaining the self-imposed speed limit with the traffic building up behind them.

Not to be fazed Brian changed back into the inside lane and was about to accelerate when the Volvo rapidly changed lanes and stopped in front of him. Brian braked the Rocket 3 to a stop, there was hardly any air between the front wheel and the car's number plate. Still, Brian's experience kicked in and the bike being momentary still upright he knocked the gear lever down and accelerated forward around the car which was now picking up speed from his own manoeuvre.

Brian was quick to react but to stop it from happening again he whacked the driver's side wing mirror. He wasn't sure if it was broken or not but it worked, as he pulled forward the Volvo wasn't in pursuit. The noise and shock of Brian's attack had shaken the driver's nerve.

Pat insisted over the mic, "Brian, you can slow down now, BRIAN SLOW DOWN." He noticed the speedometer reading one hundred and fifteen miles per hour, so he backed off the revs.

"Sorry babes are you alright?" he was really concerned.

"Yer, I am okay now that you have slowed down." It was just in time as they passed a speed camera. Pat knew the road quite well and relaxed a bit as the traffic emptied from the road. Once again, the road became single file, she was admiring the views, something she hadn't been able to do before as she was often the driver.

She recognised the services and Esso garage she had used as a timing marker to Berwick. Brian started to brake and slow down and once passed the island in the road he indicated and turned right. Now instead of speeding he rode at a steady thirty miles per hour as he wound his way down the country lane. He shouted "Mind your teeth," as the bike rattled over the railway tracks, "that's the main Newcastle to Edinburgh line." Further down the road he turned left into a small carpark and beckoned Pat to dismount from the bike. Then he put the footrest down and in turn he now dismounted from the bike.

"You ok Pat?"

"Yer, I am now but that was a right prat in the Volvo, does that happen often?"

"Mercifully no, but even then, there are rare cases, which is still too often. I don't get what they want to achieve. Are you ok Pat? It hasn't put you off me or more importantly bikes yet, has it."

"No. I'm made of thicker stuff but it is still nearly an hour before we can cross the causeway."

"I know but I thought that before getting on the island you might want to enjoy the view."

"Brian that is very sweet. That Volvo, I had to investigate a planned murder when two nurses targeted a biker by doing just that - stopping in front of him and he ended up drowned in the Tyne."

"Pat, there are a lot of ignorant drivers out there that will succumb to road rage over anything with little or no reason. I have even had morons try it on with my HGV. So don't worry, they were only amateurs, they got off lightly. I didn't want to frighten you off either me or the bike, when we are only just starting to get to know each other."

"Bri, is there a café nearby?"

"Coffee," she nodded, "and would madame like a sea view?" she nodded again but started to get suspicious.

"Verandas?"

She slowly answered, "Yes."

"Filtered or instant?" came the next question.

"Filtered of course," she replied thinking that there may be gag involved.

He pointed to the concrete blocks that had formed part of the world-war two defences against a German invasion. "I will bring it over to madame." Taken aback she sat on the block and then noticed he pulled off the bike pannier two cups and placed a tea bag in one and a coffee bag in the other. Then he pulled out a jet boiler and a litre bottle of water, within two minutes, he poured the boiling water into the cups. She directed him to the milk and sugar and he brought the drinks over. She laughed at this, "You know all that is missing, is one of those fancy biscuits that come with coffees."

"What like these?" and pulled a plastic container out and offered her one.

That was the way it was. As the two watched the sea become lakes, then rivers and then puddles while they sipped their drinks occasionally pointing out landmarks or features and creatures that inhabit the causeway.

Some of the cars were now queueing further down on the Causeway waiting for the larger puddles to disappear. Brian stood up next to Pat and helped her off the huge concrete block. "Suit up darling," and with that they both put on their jackets, helmets and gloves. Brian brought his bike to facing the way out and after Pat mounted the bike, they joined the queue of cars which was now slowly moving forward.

Pat found it relatively bizarre riding a bike on a road that didn't exist an hour before. She remembered the day when the roads were flooded by rain ten years earlier. The traffic cops were advising staff not to travel as they couldn't see the road and didn't know what was there, potholes or debris so she was very weary and expected to see a squished crab or fish on the road.

It wasn't long before the bike picked up a little speed. Pat felt it was a bit more stable, so she relaxed for the short sprint. She noticed a tower part way over, a safety refuge for the fool hardy. She was unsure when they connected to the island, it seemed a long ride before they were riding along the length of the island. She had seen a map of it and new it was tear dropped shaped and that the road and the thin line of sand dunes were the width of the island at this part. Eventually they got to the right turn that led up to the entrance to the main car park where all the cars peeled off, but Brian kept the bike moving into the village. Here he turned left and a few short hundred yards brought him into the coach park. After beckoning Pat to dismount he parked up. The gloves and helmets went into the top boxes. Brian threaded a thin chain through the outer jacket's arms and through the rear bike wheel while the inner Jackets went into the panniers.

Pat watched and was impressed with the routine and care which Brian was taking in securing the bike and clothing. Finally, he threaded a heavy-duty chain made of rollers through the rear wheel and over the seat.

"Come on young lady let's explore the island," and with that he gently took hold of her hand. They walked up the road and past the few cafés that were open for the public, one even had a VW Beetle covered in hedge row forming the same shape. That impressed Pat. In one garden there was a Bird of Prey exhibition with an owl performing for various meaty treats and the odd photo opportunity. Then came the main attraction the grand Priory. Brian paid the admission at the kiosk. They both entered this ancient wonderland that was more fitting in a Gothic horror film than a quaint island or shore.

"Pat, you beginning to grow an interest in history?"

"Yes," she replied.

"Well, this is the place of the very first Viking attack on a monastery in Britain, everyone was slaughtered, if not sold into slavery and the Priory plundered. The Vikings got so much wealth here that they returned and kept on returning mounting raids up and down the country. Saints Cuthbert and Bede worked here."

Pat took out her mobile phone and started taking pictures. She even got Brian to take one of her with the iconic window frame in the background, then a photo with the both of them in the same frame from by a passing lady. After about half an hour they moved on and found a large building that was full of gifts. One half was full of jewellery and the other had different wines and food products. Here they found a shelf with small samples offering a taste of Lindisfarne Mead. "Oh, that is nice Bri, try one of these." Pat had already tried a couple before she handed one of the samples of the golden liquid to Brian. "I take it you like it?"

"Me like," came the reply. Minutes later she had purchased a couple of miniatures to take back with her.

They walked over to the island's edge were there was a coastguard station and sat for a while staring out to sea. Brian laid on his back and turning to Pat said, "Have you ever been kissed in the dunes before?"

"No, is it painful?"

"Only if you sit on a thistle," he quipped but as she looked at him she saw a sun beam lighting up his face, she rolled on top of him and gave him a kiss fully on his mouth, and that was how it was for the next couple of minutes. Eventually the embrace was interrupted by a black Labrador looking through the dunes for a recently thrown stick.

Brian lovingly and carefully swept the sand off of Pat's face and dusted her down. She did the same with Brian, carefully brushing him down.

"Come on Pat, there are plenty of cafés, let's see what's on offer."

After a cup of tea, they decided to return to the bike and get suited up. Taking control of the bike Brian gave a wink for Pat to mount the bike. As soon as she was on, she tapped his shoulder and he rode the bike onto the road and the Causeway. They stopped at a pub just off the A1 and ordered a chicken dinner each with the afternoon being the centre of conversation.

Brian paid the bill and once again they returned to the bike and set off back home. Unlike the journey earlier, this one was uneventful and it felt like only a few minutes before they had returned to Pat's house. "You still want to go to the harbour tonight or have you had enough?"

"God no, I haven't had so much fun in years and really would like it if you came around."

"Ok, see you in a couple of hours." With that he pulled off and left Pat to return inside her home, which suddenly seemed a bare and missing something, something she had never noticed for a long time, it was quiet. She put on her favourite Ultravox album and had a long soak in the bath.

Around eight, Brian turned up in his MG. Pat noticed as she went to meet him that he had changed and was now wearing leather jeans, a waist coat and a white shirt. She could hardly contain her excitement as she walked over and kissed him. "Come on Bri, let's go to the Harbour."

At the Harbour, they paid their entry fee, entered the bar room and noticing Andrew and Sophia walked over to their area.

"May we join you or are we crowding in?" Pat asked sitting down, while Brian went to the bar.

"Wow!" exclaimed Sophia, "now don't you look like the cat that got the cream." This had the effect of making Pat blush.

"We have just been up to Holy Island, that's all, on his bike."

"Oooooh!" Sophia teased, "so is it going anywhere then?"

"Day by day, shall we say." Pat looked nervously at the bar but she couldn't see Brian. She noticed that he was over in the 'patched' area talking to one of the Local MC. After a few minutes he went over to the bar and by now his drinks had been poured. He paid for them and returned to the table. As he handed Pat her beer she asked coldly, "What do they want?"

"Oh, nothing much really, one of their regular contractors has pulled out from their bike show and they know I have contacts. They want some stall holders for their bike show next month. A burger van and a mystic stall. I can line two up for them, if my mates play ball."

"Does it involve you, in any way?" Pat enquired as it was all new for her.

"No, just a phone call, which I know won't be appreciated until the morning. Like I told you darling, I am just a middle man and believe me babes it's only to help my mates not the 1%er patch."

"Good, because as it stands don't ever put me in a position between you and my career and the law, you might not like what will happen!"

"So be warned Brian," Andy quipped.

It was around about now the twins turned up and immediately demanded on being brought up to date with the blossoming romance between Pat and Brian, with all the subtleness of a tornado.

As the chat flowed and finally broke up with the call of time, the partisans at the table all made their way to the outside taxi rank for the cars to carry them home.

Brian drove Pat home. Pat turned to him and said, "I hope you are coming in for a coffee as it would be rude not to." He nodded in reply and followed Pat into her house.

The morning sun beamed its warmth into Pat's bedroom. She turned to see the empty bed and was disappointed that Brian hadn't stayed the night. Brian was a little shy and she thought he was about to turn tail and walk away. It had been a long time for her, as the job had imposed a certain behaviour code and with her career taking off, she had looked away from possible suitors. It would be easy in that environment for one or two work relationships to fail and office talk would label her as the station bike. She had seen it happen to other colleagues.

As she began to wake up, she decided to emerge and put on her satin dressing gown, looking at the clock she noted the time as being only eight thirty, "Oh no," she groaned. Circling her bed she exited the bedroom, descended down the stairs and glided into the kitchen to make herself a coffee. As she made her drink, she placed two pieces of bread into the toaster. These were subsequently dressed in butter and marmalade.

Pat went into the her living room and picked up her laptop to check her emails. She saw a brief note from Jane saying that she had been to the church fete and would report to her on Monday. Also her daughter had included a few pictures of the family from Whitley Bay.

Monday morning brought the two detectives together over a cup of Latte each.

"So Jane, forget the gold fish and the spider plant, what else did you find out at the village fete?"

"Cheek! Nothing much it seems that there was a click of about four to five people. The group was one girl, our dearly departed, and four chaps. I think one or two of them were hoping to catch her favours."

"Oh really, well I suppose even Christians are young at some point and feel the need to sin even at the Parish Church of St Michael and all the Angels."

"According to the village gossip they all hung out together, even worked together. Apparently three of the lads were conductors on the railways as well as devout Christians and lived in the same area of Cramlington. The two that died in 2018, one was a large chap called Carl Mills the other was a Cameron Wood. Cameron strung a wire around a pole and hung himself in the stairwell after drinking a bottle of whisky. Carl died, when he was knocked over crossing a road, while stoned on dope and six times over the drink drive limit, had he been driving. Both died after Joyce's disappearance and before she was found. The other two in the group were bikers, one call Andy Reid. He was also known as 'Cy' short for Cyclops due to him having a squiffy eye. The other biker was called Darren Hilton, nicknamed 'Animal' due to the teeth he had embossed on his motorcycle helmet in the style of the Motorhead motif.

Darren seemed to have a bit of mystique about him, due to being in the Army. He had served on Op Banner but was given a medical discharge after an Irish bomb left him with a fractured back, although his spinal cord remained undamaged. Once healed, he was discharged and so he joined the railways. Both Cy and Carl had originated from Skipton, a town in Yorkshire. Darren was local and within the group he was the one with the Jesus like power of knowledge and looks, having a jet-black beard, long flowing black hair, with crystal blue eyes adding to the effect."

"Jane, what we are saying is that out of a small social group, bonded together by Christianity, three out of the five have died in a short period of time; each have died differently, two are misadventure and one suicide. Is it me or does this seems fishy to you Jane?"

"Boss, if there is something wrong then where do we go with this? If we go to the Chief Inspector without evidence, he will laugh at us; if we ignore it then we could be seeing another two people die before their time. All three deaths have been investigated separately and nothing suspicious has been detected."

"You make a good point Jane, but then my spidery senses are still tingling and we're running out of time."

"Would the Chief allow a cold case review, you know, just to be on the safe side, like just flag it up as a distant concern? If nothing happens, fine but then if there is an incident involving any member of the group we now know better from the start."

"I think you are close to the point Jane; I will discuss it with him and see how he wants to play it, then at least we are covered."

Pat got up and walked around to see her boss, Chief inspector John Haydon. Outside the office she confidently knocked on the door. Responding to his call she walked in and sat on the black leather swivel chair.

"Hello Pat how can I help today?"

"Boss, I am faced with a number of coincidences that don't add up. The Joyce Grey case, who disappeared and then reappeared badly decomposed, wasn't the only one. What I have found is that out of a small social group that are bonded together by Christianity, three out of five have died in short period of time and have died differently, two are misadventure and one suicide." John gestured for her to continue but now he listened with a bit more interest.

"Joyce died, she slipped and fell and drowned, sad, but there is no evidence of foul play and if there was, then the evidence would have vanished with the floods; but then we looked into her social group who did everything together and within a year three out of five have died. Cameron Wood strung a wire around a pole, using it as a brace, and hung himself in the stairwell after drinking a bottle of whisky, and shortly after Carl died, when he was run over, trying to cross a road, while stoned on dope. Both died after the Joyce's disappearance and before she was found. Both were investigated by experienced detectives and both weren't considered of further interest to us; and to be fair boss, anyone looking to the incidents separately I would say the same and so would any decent copper."

"So what's the problem Pat, why are we talking?"

"It's just too much of a coincidence and the hairs on the back of my neck are tingling. I just want to be sure we aren't missing anything."

"Ok Pat, where are we with Joyce?"

"That is just it boss, again misadventure." She paused, "Sir, I don't know if they saw something or did something, three deaths in a group doesn't seem right but I honestly can't put my finger on it."

"Ok Pat, here is the deal. It is Monday today; you have until the end of the week to come up with a viable theory to justify continuing. It is our duty to follow the evidence. We will review any thoughts or suspicions and take it from there. Is that fair enough?"

"Yes, John. Thank you for listening."

"Friday," he reaffirmed.

With that Pat returned to see Jane who was sat in the office typing up her report. She looked up at her friend. "Well?"

"End of the week to see if we can unearth anything, basically it's the put up or shut up call."

"Fair enough Pat, you can't expect more than that on a hunch, but then that means we will have to work hard to get the evidence to continue this case."

"Yes I know dear friend, but I fear it would be easier to shove cooked spaghetti up a cat's arse!"

Jane gave her a weird look as if to say, what did you just say? "Is that biker talk?" came her retort.

"No babes, but come on let's get on with it, you follow one and report back to me. You take on Cameron Wood and I will take on Carl Mills. If there is any significant event then it will be insignificant on its own as I don't believe it wouldn't have been flagged up by our esteemed colleagues."

"Well boss, we know the three hung out together, the lads worked for the local train company but not the Metro."

"Yes Jane, also attended the same church. The two lads moved up from Yorkshire, so I guess they may have shared the same flat or house together, while Joyce lived at home. So we have work to do at their homes and church, together with friends still alive."

"That will be Cy and Darren."

"Ok Jane, let's go back to the church, then Cy and Darren, and then see if the national train company can shed any light on their professional behaviour."

The two detectives prepared themselves to leave. Once done, they left the office, walked through the synchronised locked doors and into the car park. Jane shouted, "Your car or mine?" She was drowned out by a passing train and its wheels squealing against the rails and its curve. Pat gave Jane a knowing look, Jane guessing it meant the train company first, she nodded saying, "You fancying a short walk first?" Pat smiled.

They left the car park, walked up the hill and under the railway bridge.

The conversation was light and the time passed quickly as the distance between the two different stations was short. They entered the station and saw two transport police officers on duty by the main entrance to the concourse of Newcastle station. Pat approached them. After introducing herself and showing her ID, she asked them where she and Jane could contact the station master.

After a quick chatter over the radio and a smile from the transport constable, a middle-aged man, with balding light brown hair and he had middle-age spread that befitted an office dweller.

"Hello, my name is Malcolm Ryme, I am the station manager here, I understand you wish to speak to me. How can I help officers er ladies?"

Malcolm Ryme was a timed served driver, starting on diesels and then electrics; born and bred in Newcastle and like a lot of people he had dreamt of being a driver. He had worked hard to become a train driver during the turbulent days of British Rail when the government of the eighties had set course for privatisation of the railways and the rundown of services, he saw the way things were going to be and was determined to be a part of the new look and not be side lined.

So, with hard work and going to college to advance himself with management courses, he found himself moving into supervision and

a management role, finally taking on a small station then recently the home station of Newcastle. He was a family man with two daughters, Emily and Barbara. He had married a young lady called Sharon. He knew his station inside and out and had shares in the station which was helping towards an early retirement.

He took the two detectives upstairs into the back office where he worked, they sat on the offered chairs. The office had an outer chamber with plenty of space and to the left sat his secretary, busy on the computer. The front desk formed a barrier for them to walk through. He lifted the flap and escorted the two ladies passed.

The walls were decorated with pictures of trains both modern and from yesteryear. The carpet was deep blue patterned with the old British rail symbol. The carpet extended into the manager's office and the theme of wall decoration. Behind the desk were some group pictures of various courses and events that Malcolm had attended through his life.

"What brings you here and how can I help you?" he offered.

"We are interested in some of your employees Mr Ryme, how can we get to find out about them?"

"Well since privatisation and the fragmentation it is a bit difficult. For instant I now work for Network Rail, as do the platform staff but the train crews work for their respective companies. Here we have five including the Metro line but who are you talking about?"

"Mainly at the moment I am interested in Carl Mills, have you come across him?"

"Well yes, it was a while ago, joined as a Guard in the old days and I believe after privatisation he came into contact with the Transport Police. I was asked to take him on in a non-frontline duty and closely monitor his progress. As for why, I wasn't told but I had a vacancy in the stores as an assistant store keeper. The last I heard he died in a hit and run a few years ago but for more details you will have to speak to the Transport Police as I believe they had involvement in his case."

"Do you know who his friends were?" This time it was Jane asking the question.

"Well, I know he had a close friend call Andy Reid. Andy worked here. He started off as a guard then became a driver and then supervisor. What he is doing at the moment I don't know, or which company he works for. I am unsure, we can easily find out for you but the best place to … tell you what! They have a manager's office at the end of the corridor come with me and I can arrange an introduction."

After a quick phone call he announced, "We're on!"

He escorted the two detectives to the door of the other manager's office. Greeting them was a smartly uniformed middle-aged gentleman from a Caribbean background. "Hello, I am Superintendent John Oyelowo, how can I help?"

Pat took the lead. "Hello sir, I am Detective Inspector Pat Nottage and this my Sergeant Jane Richardson from the Northumbrian Police. I am doing a little background research into one of your employees and I believe you have investigated him."

"Please ladies, come into my office." He turned to the station manager, "Thank you Mr Ryme, I will look after them now." Taking his cue, he smiled, turned and left.

The superintendent led them into his office. The difference from the station manager's office couldn't be clearer, as the symbols of trains changed to law enforcement and became comfortably familiar to what the detectives were used to seeing back at their own depot.

John Oyelowo was thirty-seven, six foot five with African ancestry but born in Jarrow. He had worked hard and had a degree in law which he had studied for at Newcastle University. He joined the British Army with a short-term officer's commission and then saw infantry action in Afghanistan, coming into contact with the Taliban. He led an attack which saw no British casualties, seven Taliban dead and five captured. This also led to gaining a huge amount of intelligence and weaponry. He then left the army and on discharge was successfully appointed to the Transport Police who were having a recruiting drive. He rose very quickly through the ranks to become a Superintendent. He was well-liked and had an easy demeanour about him and drew people into their confidence.

"Now we are in private, we can talk a bit better, how can I help our colleagues?"

"Sir, we are looking into the activities of Carl Mills. He died last year and although we have no evidence of foul play we are looking into a number of coincidental events. We have been made aware that your service has come into contact with him and we are hoping you can help."

"Sure, let's see." With that he tapped on the computer keyboard.

"Ah yes, just as I thought. Operation Walton, from the family show and referring to his home." The two friends stole a quick glance at each other.

"Yes, we were getting a lot of rumours that the go to place for cannabis was at Carl's home address. We were observing his home address in Cramlington, to gather enough evidence for a raid, but we were thwarted by him turning up at work. His supervisor suspected he was under the influence of drugs. Unaware of our interest, he was passed over to us. He cut a deal that he was to give us all his names he supplied to and scored from. He sang like a canary and his reward was to keep his job, but he also was to be removed from front line service permanently. He gave us seven names which he supplied to and two names he scored from. The two were just small-time same as himself and known to both your side as well as our own.

Of the seven names he supplied us with, five tested positive and were sacked on the spot with no criminal action taken against them. The other two tested negative, no further action was taken against them."

The superintendent sent the printer into a whirl of noise and handed over the print with the last known names and addresses of the seven that were brought to his attention.

"I see Andy Reid was one of those who passed the drug test, do we know where he works?"

"Yes, he is now a station master at Durham."

"Great, and Darren Hilton I see he is a guard on the local line from here, any other issues with him?"

"No, he was clean and of course they are tested regularly as per company policy. He is honest as far as we can find or expect but for the rest that were sacked, we have no record of them once they left our employment. Whether or not they had issues with your lot is a different matter." He took the prints and put them in a folder, returning them to the detectives. "Is there anything else I can help you with detectives?"

"Er, no sir, thank you."

"Let me show you out and please if I can help in any other way then don't hesitate to ask." With that, he opened the door and the two ladies left his office and the station.

Pat turned to Jane, "Bugger, that is just what wasn't in the script."

Jane looked her boss, "Just been handed five possible candidates, all with one motive in mind, revenge! And all over a cup of coffee and a soggy railway biccy."

"Jane, I fear we have just scratched the top off of a lot of religious bunkum and hypocrisy. Next time I have hunch, tell me shut the fuckup."

They continued walking back to their own station under the familiar bridge, turning right into the car park.

"Forget what I said about splitting up our interviews Jane, we need to speak to the Drugs Squad, and also, I think we should go and speak to Mr Reid first, as I suspect that he would be easy to get hold of."

"Durham's not too far away, let's do it Pat." They both climbed into the silver Beetle and Pat drove to Durham. The station was built in 1857 with part of the platform stretching over the north road, overlooking the Bridge Inn public house which told the detectives they were near to the station. On arrival, they had to wait a moment for the surge of passengers, who had just arrived by train, to disperse. Once this had happened the two detectives emerged from the Beetle just like larva from its egg. Although the station was Victorian built, a recent face lift had given the entrance a fresh look. Inside the appearance would put any modern station to shame with it having stainless steel turnstiles and clean glass ceilings.

They got to the turnstiles and waited to make contact with one of the platform staff. "Excuse me," Pat projected her voice to a uniformed lady walking passed. Turning, she walked up to Pat and politely asked, "Ma'am can I help?"

"Yes, I am DI Nottage and this DS Richardson, is it possible to see Andy Reid the station master here?"

"Give me a minute please and let me check," came the reply from the young lady dressed in a day glow jacket, who disappeared, returning a moment later saying, "This way please detectives."

So once again that day they were led to offices at the back of a station.

Greeting them was the station manager Andy Reid. He was in his forties and slim in build. He wore a smart grey suit with the company trademark embossed into it. He had a close-cropped beard and long hair tied back. His right eye was offset to his left eye. This feature didn't affect his visual acuity but had led to him being known by everyone as Cy. He used to say it was a proper name and in honour of Cy Enfield the director of Zulu.

"Hello, I am Andy, how can I be of assistance?"

"Well, actually we are looking into the disappearance and death of a friend of yours, Joyce Grey."

"Ah yes, poor Joyce. She was such a lovely girl and very serious when it came to God." He beckoned them to sit down in his office. "Please, what would like to know officers?"

Pat opened with her questions, "What was your relation with her?"

"I knew her at church in Cramlington, she was very quiet but passionate about Jesus, she even became a church warden. We were good friends and she was in our social group. When she disappeared, we searched everywhere for her. When she didn't appear we assumed she had met someone and moved on, but then that appeared out of character for her. I suppose we couldn't bear to think that anything horrible had happened to her. She definitely didn't deserve to die the way she did."

"Who was in your social group?"

"Joyce, as you know, and then there was also Daz Hilton, me and for a short time Carl and also Cameron." He paused for thought, "They were good times and I miss them, still, I have my faith to help."

"I was led to believe you considered yourselves as a militant branch, what do you mean by that?"

Andy laughed. "Yes, it was in joke. Despite it being not so long ago we were young compared to the rest of the church and all devoted to Christianity but we weren't just happy to sing and pray, we wanted to explore and challenge and learn about the deep history and anything up to the Roman period."

"What happened with you and Carl, it isn't important but it has just come into the frame and I would like your take on what happened and the effect."

"Look, me and Carl went to school together back in Yorkshire and we were into trains but not trainspotters, we were into riding them and noting the different sounds and features. We also did the same with beer and music. He was the one that took on the concept of the wall from Pink Floyd being like a wall and alienation. A load of rubbish but then I was visiting York on my motorbike, I saw this statue of Constantine on the spot where he was, by public adulation, pronounced Emperor Caesar on the death his father and this sideswiped me. It was my road to Damascus, Constantine brought Christianity to the world and it metaphorically spoke to me in a way that turned religion from faith into something real. I needed to know more and not just the written Bible. I also wanted to investigate the real holy events. So I went to the Vatican and the Roman forum and even Milan to see the Last Supper. While I was waiting, I came across the remains of Constantine's palace where he signed the Edict of Milan, which legalised Christianity. I brought this to our group at church and they wanted a bit of that, so we made a point of visiting religious significant events around Britain and easily reachable places in Europe including the lance, called Spear of Destiny, which was found in 1098 during the First Crusade at Antioch. The claim is that it is the lance that pierced the side of Christ at the Crucifixion and is currently displayed in Vienna. That is a bit pricey to do, but is a must. As is a visit to Bethlehem. We mainly go around the big cathedrals and significant small churches. With all this going on, me and Carl decided to buy a house in Cramlington, about the back end of the nineties, as we couldn't get a mortgage separately so we got one jointly and it became a hub and a meeting place for all our friends. We were all railway workers. Some of us went to the same church as well, it was a brilliant time. We got drunk and also smoked a little of Mother Nature and had a special time. After a couple of years, Carl had gone into work stoned and stinking of weed. The whole group was rounded up and requested to do a drugs test.

I was no longer a guard but a driver on the electric trains and was clean. So when I went, I naturally had passed the test but some of my friends didn't and were sacked on the spot. It was obvious that he had grassed everyone up to save his own skin and even worse than that I found out we were being evicted as he spent the mortgage money. In fact, we owed nearly twelve thousand pounds, which was the tune of his drug taking and yes, he did a lot of damage. Then he had the cheek to deny it even after he was caught bang to rights.

He had made it abundantly clear he would spill the beans if he was ever caught. It took a long time to pay that debt off, as the building society sold the house at auction for thirty thousand pound leaving fifty-three thousand owing and I had to pay it. I am ok now I am sorted but I do believe that even Judas was remorseful and paid the price of deceit, so did Carl. I forgave him but I will never forget the harm he caused, so he was ostracized. As Christians, we gave him a chance to redeem himself."

"So you heard of his death then?"

"Oh yes, he was now on the fringe of the group, almost abandoned to reflect on his sins but no one wished death on him. They did want him to atone for the hurt he had caused."

"Sorry Andy, that is the risk you take when you get involved with drugs and what about his suppliers, what happened there?"

"I am not sure: but God was watching and he exacted a heavy price. God's court sat in judgement and there was no remission or parole sadly, even his tools are sometimes brutal but no one want it. Carl was my friend but then he destroyed a lot of lives and a community through his own weakness."

"They didn't find the culprits how do you feel about that Andy?" Jane interjected.

"Why? We all believed it was God's work and not man's. If it had man's work, I think our trusted police would have found him."

"Andy, you said you travelled in groups to investigate your new-found faith. Where do you go and who organised the trips?"

"I would take myself off as would others but we would take it in turns to organise trips. The majority are UK based but one was Europe, well we just had to do Rome and the Vatican even though we are not Papist. It was the spiritual home second only to the original, as the Church which was founded in Antioch by Peter, Christ's apostle. Rome may have become a rival, made easier by the Roman Empire going back to Constantine.

Antioch provided one of three bishops that were recognized at the First Council of Nicaea in AD 325. Sadly, the area is too violent to visit at the moment, but to answer your question, Joyce. She organised us all to go along to Durham Cathedral and a close inspection of the Magna Carta, all six surviving copies. It was over a couple of Days in 2015. It was awesome, we stayed in digs. It was the last time Carl was invited along but this was a sort of mistake as he brought a bit of tension to the group. The vicar had asked, as a favour to him, to try and bring him back into the fold but then he caused more problems than he solved, just Carl being Carl."

"What do you mean, "just Carl being Carl?" Jane burst in.

"Oh, I believe it was something to do with drugs. We told him to leave but it was mute as he missed the last public transport, so we let him return with us till we got home and then the gap was too far apart for it to be bridged."

"Was that it?" Jane enquired.

"Pretty much, we couldn't risk the damage he was doing to our lives. We attended his funeral with more sadness due to his lost chance to make amends to the friendship he broke."

"Did he have any other friends or family?" Jane continued.

"No. All his friends left him. We hadn't spoken to him for years but for all the harm he caused I couldn't see him buried alone." He paused for thought.

"Is there anything else you would like to mention?" He shook his head rather downhearted.

Pat took the lead. She had been observing Andy throughout Jane's interrogation. "Here are my contact details, anything you think may help please let me know. Thank you for your time." She glanced at Jane and the two ladies stood up. Pat turned to Andy, "Andy are you alright?"

He nodded and replied, "Yes thanks, just unearthed a ton of suppressed memories."

They left the office and got back into the car. "Jane, nothing concerns me more than the friends of the Lord, but then I think it is always sad when drugs are factored into the equation."

Jane agreed "We will have to see if the Drug Squad know anything about the case."

"Yes Jane, assuming we have a case. By the way, do you need your car tonight?"

"Not really, why?"

"Let me drop you off at home and I will pick you up in the morning. I'm a bit drained at the moment and I have a few things to think about."

"Fine, you're the boss, so long as my hours are right, I am game."

"Thanks Jane."

In the morning the two ladies were in the canteen having a coffee. Seeing their target, they walked over to see the detective in charge of the Serious Organised Crime Agency, (SOCA), sat at the canteen table drinking tea. This was Chief inspector Mark Glover. He was an amiable man with over twenty year's experience in the job. A family man, six foot tall with an African ancestry, he had a degree in law.

"Sir, can I have a quick word please?"

With a smile he looked up and said, "Of course detective, how can I help?"

"Do you have any 'intell' on a chap called Carl Mills, died a couple of years ago in hit and run? He came into contact with the Transport Police but no real follow up after he was sussed out for drugs. He turned Queen's evidence but the thinking is he continued, mainly with Cannabis but there may have been other drugs. He was a small-time dealer, mainly friends. Thank you for letting us interrupt your break, sir."

Pat and Jane went and sat down at their own table. "Jane!" Jane looked up. Pat continued, "We need to go back to the church and see what is happening.

Jane, here is the thing, if you convince an ordinary person that he is doing good, then you can get him to do extraordinary things like many ordinary people in the last two world wars became leaders and heroes. It's the same with murder for instance, Dennis Neilson, a mass murderer by night and a civil servant at a job centre by day. Harold Shipman quietly murdering hundreds in a sleepy village."

"So what you are thinking is it might a close associate?"

"There is a strong case but then that doesn't account for the others, if they are linked, which we have no evidence for. Yet there is one thing for certain, there is nothing frightens me more than friends of the Almighty."

"Why?" Jane looked puzzled.

"How many people have been killed or harmed because God disapproved of a certain feature of that person."

"Well, yes I agree with that."

The detectives finished their breakfast coffee and then drove to the parish church of St Michael and all the Angels in Cramlington. The Reverend Sam Hunt was walking into the church grounds with a bag of groceries when the silver Beetle pulled up outside the arched gate. He turned to see them and smiled. "Good morning, detectives, it's a lovely morning and nice to see you."

"Good morning, Reverend, is it possible to have a few minutes of your time?"

"Yes, of course, what about."

"Just what you know about Carl Mills and his gang."

"Well, I would hardly have called them a gang, more a coterie. They brought a lot of life to the church. I saw they were really engaging in the Word of the Lord and went to everything. They weren't just happy to polish the pews on a Sunday morning, but go out and find the truth for themselves. It was inspirational to me and my other parishioners. They see this and some have joined in with them."

By now they were in the house, entering the kitchen, with the Reverend putting his milk and groceries in the fridge. He continued talking, "Carl had got himself involved with drugs and of course, for his own sake, we were prepared to support him back to health but on all accounts, he was out of control. It was a blessing, we thought, him being caught but then he turned on his friends. I believe the name they used was Judas Iscariot. Strong stuff, they ignored him and I had to appeal to them to soften their stance against him but this didn't really happen. He had caused a lot of pain. Maybe in time the group would have relaxed but he would have had to work hard to regain their trust and friendship."

"Did they attend the funeral and why?"

"We are Christians and no one truly believed he deserved to meet the end the way he did, so it was seen as an act of forgiveness, which was the Christian thing to do. I am proud of my congregation that they endorsed this view and when it came to his funeral, they all turned up to pay their respects which was so beautiful to see."

"So, there was no animosity towards him Reverend?"

"I didn't say that detective, I said my congregation sought solace in his early demise, at worst, saw it as a lost opportunity of redemption."

"Did you have any control over the days or weekends out?"

"No. They asked for guidance that was all. I wasn't asked for funding or sanctioning, they all paid their own way and contributed to the group, as their own talents permitted. Although, they did ask me for advice. I think Joyce would set herself a target and then bring everyone along with her. Her passion, that was like her super power."

"What sort of advice did they ask for?"

"A lot of the advice I gave was historic in nature, where and when significant events happened in the UK and how to go about visiting the locations. For example, they were going down to Canterbury on their first trip, so I suggested they visit the Villa at Lullingstone, near Dartford. That was a really good example of the transition from Roman Pagan Gods to the true God of Christ. It also marked the evolution from the home worship of their Gods to the stability and safety of the church, plus there are some really cool mosaics."

This made the ladies smile.

"I also suggested, as a bit of light relief, that they take an interest in Richborough Castle, a Roman fort near Sandwich, which was the first and last point of the Roman occupation. I also suggested that Rochester Castle might be on the itinerary. It was the site of the pinnacle battle after King John was forced to sign the Magna Carta. He spent the rest of his time chasing down the Baron's who had forced his hand. The Pope also rescinded Magna Carta as it meant repercussions for the church and their leadership at the time."

"So, it was a waste of time?" Jane chipped in.

"Yes, pretty much. It was revised a couple of times but despite being the basis of law in many countries, not ours and even the monument at Runnymede is American."

"Right, ok Reverend, is that all?" Pat was ready to move on.

"Yes, sorry I got a bit carried away. I am just so lucky that I have such an enthusiastic congregation."

Pat and Jane thanked the Reverend for his help and returned to Pat's car.

Pat summed up the situation. "So, we have a rogue gang member who everyone tried to forgive and couldn't until he was dead, but nobody wanted to put him there. We have hit a blind alley this time, let's see if SOCO can come up with an answer."

Jane turned to Pat and with a smirk said, "How is the spidery sense now boss?"

Pat thought for a moment, "Confused, I still feel something is wrong but I don't know what. Normally I read a case like a book. The trouble is, at the moment, some of the key pages are gummed together."

"Well, there is no great shame on reporting no crime Pat."

"You're right Jane, when religion and or drugs are involved then any bizarre logic can manifest itself, but if there is no crime, we can move on to something more straight forward."

Just then Jane's mobile phone buzzed to say she had a text message which she read out loud. "A Mr Darren Hilton is at the Newcastle station on a late shift. He is on the reserve shift so he could be hanging around the railway station all day."

"Well, if he is available, we'll tick that box asap. We will call in at the train station then call it a day, ok Jane?"

"Yes Pat, sounds like a plan."

The traffic was starting to build up so it took slightly longer than they had hoped but they were able to park at the dropping off point at the station.

This time they knew where to go and found the rest room for the guards with ease. It wasn't until they were almost near the entrance that they were challenged. It was the supervisor for the guards. "Can I help you ladies?" came the call.

Pat turned, produced her warrant card and announced, "Police. We're looking for one of your conductors, Darren Hilton."

"They aren't called Conductors these days officers, but luckily he has just come back from covering a local trip, so he has some time for you to talk to him, assuming that is, he isn't under arrest."

"No, we are just wanting some information, it shouldn't take too long."

"It won't take too long as we are due to finish our shift soon," Jane quipped sarcastically but quietly to Pat. Pat retaliated with an elbow in Janes ribs and a glare.

"Let me show the way," offered the supervisor. He opened the door and looked at one of the three people in the room, "Daz, these two ladies want a word with you, the office next door is free."

"Yer, sure." Daz turned and stood up. He was a goodlooking lad and stood with a confident but relax look about him. Pat judged him to be five foot eleven, he also had long black wavy hair, piercing blue eyes, a thick close-cropped beard, and a wiry chin. Jane noticed on his arm he had a military style tattoo. Indeed, he had served in the Rifles intending to be in the army for life. He had seen action in Northern Ireland on Op Banner and come back safely but he had been involved in a climbing accident where he had fallen a hundred feet and broken some of the lower bones in his back. Sadly, for him this meant, a medical discharge. He had been in for eight years and another year learning to walk again. When his discharge finally came through, he was gutted, and more than that he hadn't got any direction to go.

Then at a Job fare he saw a recruiting stand for the railways. When asked what skills he had he simply said, "I can kill a person in fifty-two different ways." He also said he had a liking for travel, hence the army and so he signed up.

It was about this time he met Tina, his long-term girlfriend. She was a Christian and a friend of Joyce. She introduced him to the social set, along with other rail staff in the area. The group formed a bond and they looked to him for direction as he was seen to be really cool with a wise answer to everything, which left the group in compete awe of him. He also had a way with him that meant he gave really provocative answers and just got away with it. His real passion was motorbikes and had modified his helmet to appear like the motif of the heavy rock band Motorhead, gold resin teeth with enlarged canines on a black helmet. These were arranged on the chin protector with Viking style horns painted on the side of the helmet and spikes in the centre forming a Mohican front to back. This had given rise to his nickname Animal, which he wore with pride. Strangely this public image was the opposite to his reality but only added to his mystic.

"Hi I am DI Pat Nottage and my colleague is DS Jane Richardson. We would like to talk to you about Carl Mills, is that ok?"

"Yer, sure ladies, ask away."

"Tell me how did you come to be part of the group and their travels?"

"Well, it started with my partner Tina, we shared our bike travels and she had a friend Joyce. She disappeared, then was tragically found a year later, but at the time they were besties at church. I am not as religious as Joyce or Tina but I was in tow and I really wanted to make a go of it with Tina. There were a few lads from the railway we used to hang out with and we met prior to privatisation and destruction of the railways. Carl and Cy were there, we got on while we were at work and as I said we were hanging out together. It is no secret, at the time I used to get a like bit of blow from Carl up to the time I started dating Tina. I promised to stop which I did. The lads had a house between them and it was a good place to hang out. It became a mini centre where everyone was able to get together and chat, have a few drinks and enjoy each other's company.

Cy and Joyce were mini powerhouses for the visits. Joyce was infectious with her zeal and Cy was able to be the ideas man for the group. They looked to me to give them a sense of direction, which I was happy to advise them. We went to some great places and still do, but it's not the same since we lost Joyce."

"Sorry Daz, but we are here to talk about Carl and his drug use."

"Sorry, Carl, as it is widely known now, he was a supplier of cannabis resin to a lot of people and as I said I used to score off him but had stopped by the time he was busted. He did put the finger on me but as I knew I was clean I was happy to do the drugs test and along with Cy. We were cleared by the railway occupational health and so we continued to work. Some of our mates weren't as lucky as us and were given their P45's.

I know Carl had financial problems and the social group at the house regrouped at church and became a bit more cosmopolitan.

Carl was only allowed to carry on, on the understanding it was our duty to support him in rehabilitation but everyone else shunned him because of his treacherous nature. Outside the church group he was on his own. He was allowed still to travel with us on the minibus. I think the last one was the trip down Kent, which was just a fantastic outing. I think apart from the cloud that was over him, that was as good as it got.

Just for the record, nobody wanted him dead. The general feeling was he had overstepped the mark and nobody would ever trust him again. Then he needed to kick his habit and repay the money he stole from the house."

Pat leant over towards him, "Is there anything else we need to know?"

"Well, no not really, unless there is something specific you wish to know. I can only really talk in generalities, about stuff that is in the public domain.

Carl was a big lad. He was over six foot five and twenty-two stone. He didn't do shy and retiring at work or church. He was going in his own direction and no one was going to stop him. At least when he died, he was square with the world moneywise and there was enough for a small funeral. Even Judas Iscariot was forgiven by God despite, the fact he hung himself, at least the money was used to procure a field to bury foreigners in by the priests. I think it is called the Field of blood and is still there. Carl still had a long way to go but that is no longer important. He didn't do anything that none of us in the same situation would have been tempted to do or many other people in life when caught by the law; to escape the gallows they would turn Queen's evidence. He just betrayed everyone he knew."

Jane picked up on one remark he made, "Daz you said square with the world! What do you mean?"

"I am not 100% sure at all but I think it was something to with the sale of his house he was able to pay his bills that is all. I mean he still continued to work with the railways. Our paths only crossed once at work as I had to get some paperwork from the stores and also at church. Although we saw each other there was always a vast distance between us. He still had a drug smell about him, so despite our best efforts he was still using. How he passed the drugs tests at work we are not sure, but then that was powers above our pay grade."

"What do you know about his death?" Jane queried.

"Only what you guys told us, he was staggering back from the pub and stepped in front of car. He was full of drugs and over the limit for drink drive which was in his drinking nature although he was never an alcoholic. The car was never found and Carl died of multiple fractures and choked on his own vomit, not a very nice way to go. We agreed to forgive him his sins and pay our respects as he had paid in full for any errors. That was er 2018, I think after the time Joyce vanished."

"Is there anything else you think we should know Daz?"

"No, I don't think so."

"If you do think of something, then please contact us."

Pat stood up, shook his hand and along with Jane they left the room and walked to the station car park. The drive to the police station was only a minute in the car, Pat stopping outside the front door, Jane got out of the Beetle and walked over to her car to go home.

CHAPTER 3

*I*n the morning, the two detectives teamed up over a bacon butty and coffee breakfast in the canteen at the police station. Eventually the conversation turned from personal talk to the job in hand.

"What do we know about Cameron, Jane?" Pat asked, signalling the change in tone of the conversation.

"What we do know is that he started off on the railways as a conductor, he moved over to the Ambulance Service and has worked there for nine years without incident. Then during the last month, he was subjected to a series of incidents that led to his dismissal and he committed suicide by hanging himself in the stairwell."

"Ok, let's hear what revelation the Ambulance management can offer us."

The two finished their drinks and walked over to the office. Jane phoned the Ambulance Service and arranged for the meeting between the two services for ten o'clock. This gave them time to check their work and to drive out to the office block not far from the A1M Tyne crossing. They arrived at the appointed time and the receptionist showed them into a large room that clearly had been used for teaching, as it was decorated with posters of resuscitation algorithms and anatomical models of body parts. There was a large table and blue cloth padded chairs. The detectives were invited to take a seat.

Shortly afterwards a tall thin gentleman entered dressed in green overalls and a green jacket with pips on his shoulders. "Hello, my name is Gary Wight, I was Cameron's station officer how can I help you?"

Gary was a time served officer and not one of the degree entrants. He had elected to remain as a technician mainly because there were less problems with the drugs and protocols in place following strict management rules. He was still capable and competent for frontline duties but had progressed down the management route.

"Hi, I'm DI Pat Nottage and this is my sergeant, DS Jane Richardson. We are just reviewing the circumstances which led to him taking his own life, can you tell us what was Cameron like as a medic please?"

"Cameron was an enthusiastic technician and he really was passionate about his work, even describing it as almost a religion for him. He had a knack of doing just the right thing and coming up trumps. I believe he had an army background, he joined us after the first Gulf war. He was also involved in a voluntary first aid organisation and was also doing private ambulance work, he really couldn't get enough of it. When he joined us, he was a shining star although average when it came to other skills. He was above average when it came to patient care and his experience showed. We knew he was also very religious and enjoyed the history part of it. He would talk about being a Christian and if he was going to some villa or cathedral then we all knew."

"You said technician not paramedic why?" quizzed Pat.

"He was happy doing what he was doing but then he applied a number of times to be a paramedic and was turned down. The management didn't think he would cope with the studies as he could barely read and write. His written reports were atrocious and often he would need someone to help him."

"If that is the case, why did he die by his own hand?"

"It was his lifestyle back in early 2019, it was chaotic, it started when his uncle died at the start of the summer. As I understand his dad was demolishing an outhouse in his pub and his uncle was a roofer who went up to start the job but fell through, knocking himself into a coma and died two weeks later on the intensive care ward.

Cameron came to me asking for compassionate leave but it was declined, so he took annual leave to attend his funeral. His work fell into decline and then his motorbike was stolen. This made him dependant on public transport and opened him up to more disciplinaries for time keeping and performance. I think it was around this time management started dumping all their complaints on him. He even got a complaint that he got a patient to the hospital on time. But his biggy was leaving a patient at home stuck in the hallway. He fessed up to that when I interviewed him. I was forced to give him a written warning and suspended him for a day without pay. It got even worse when Karan, a nurse he was dating dumped him. Not surprisingly he started to spiral out of control. He claimed he was being stalked by some unknown stranger which was sheer fantasy.

Then, the last day he worked with us he reported a lad to Ambulance Control, who told him there was another complaint in the pipeline. This was out of order and the operator was disciplined for his indiscretion. According to his crew partner for the day, he turned white and left the job taking a taxi home. When we realised what had happened, we sent a paramedic round to his house for a safe and well check but sadly she was too late, it took her time to get over it as well. He had a strong social group at church so we decided under the circumstances to keep a low profile and the Ambulance Service didn't attend."

"What was the time between Cameron's departure and the safe and well check?"

"About an hour and a half."

"Why the delay? Why not straight away?"

"It took time to realise what was going on and nobody expected to find what they found, nobody realised that for him things had gone so far."

"Were there any reports made of his behaviour or of him being followed up?"

"No, we didn't think it was important and beside his behaviour in the last couple of weeks was so bizarre it was impossible to know what he was about."

"And you didn't suspect that he was a suicide risk?"

"No."

"Ok, thank you Gary, we appreciate your time." Pat got up and along with Jane, left the Ambulance headquarters and returned to Police headquarters. They had been out of the office for a couple of hours, so they went to the canteen for a cheese toasty and cup of coffee.

"Pat, sorry to say but are we wasting our time here?" Jane said thoughtfully.

"Jane, I can't answer that, but if these are coincidences then it still isn't a waste of time. We are ensuring that the people we are entrusted to protect and defend have those rights in death as well as in life, but I hear what you are saying.

I think the Reverend sent a message that he has a list of the events the group attended, then I think we need to draw a timeline to see how everything fits into place. I also want to see if there is an at-risk group on the list, maybe then we can put this to bed."

They took the drive to Cramlington and once again they were in the vestry talking to the Vicar.

"Here you are Detectives, a list of the places we visited."

Pat looked at the list. The Reverend continued, "It starts with one cancelled out of respect for Joyce and finally next year in 2020 we are planning to walk Hadrian's Wall in honour to our loss."

"Reverend, what can you tell me about Cameron and his involvement with the church please?"

"Well mainly it was passive. He was friends with Cy, Carl and Daz from the railways but then he left for the ambulance service but remained in the congregation. It is fair to say that he wasn't as active as some of the group but he did come up with idea to visit Stonehenge, Woodhenge and Avebury henge and stone circles, taking in some of the fourteen white horses and the Roman Baths at Bath. He also came up with the idea to go to the Southern Cathedrals festival."

"Sorry, what is that?" Jane chipped in.

"It is now, depending on the organiser, three to five days long comprising of concerts, a choral masterclass, an organ recital and evensongs sung separately by each choir. The Fringe is a distraction which is penned and implemented by the accommodating cathedral. It also involves solos crooned by lay clerks and comedy acts, it has been going on for over a hundred years. Admittedly, it has morphed over the years but it is like a cross between the Edinburgh Fringe and Glastonbury for the Christian world, all rolled into one. It rotates, being shared by the three major Cathedrals in the area, Chichester, Winchester and Salisbury. It was a fantastic experience for the group and they all came back energised. They are still talking about it today with a wish to return with a larger group."

"What about the last time he was with the group, how did that go?"

"He had turned from a practical joker of the group to one with a permanent cloud over his head. His first girlfriend Karan left him after being tormented by a work colleague at a night club. This left him devastated, and along with a death in the family, I think he was close to a breakdown. Then we heard he had problems at work which was understandable with what was going on in his private life. I think he was in freefall and suddenly took his own life, very unchristian so we had to pray for his soul."

"So he was quite disturbed before he died?" Jane asked.

"Yes, I would say past redemption."

"Did he say anything about being followed or stalked?" Jane retorted.

"No, not in as many words, he was suspicious that something odd was happening but we just dismissed it as part of his mania."

"So no-one took that remark seriously then?"

"No, I don't think so," replied the vicar.

"Why not?"

"Cameron, loved life. He had many setbacks but then he would always bounce back and that was, we thought, what was going to happen. In many ways he was like a rubber ball, although it would have been tough for him at Christmas 2018. But please the Church doesn't consider suicide a sin and started to change in 1880. Assisted suicide is something different. But we are still allowed to endorse or not a full Christian burial if a person perished in this way. The outmoded attitude towards the burial of suicides mirrored the belief that all suicide were a solemn sin. Public attitudes have changed noticeably as understandings of mental health have developed and now we are allowed to offer a standard service to our flock."

Pat thanked him and the DI and DS took their leave. Once in the car Jane turned to Pat, "So we have a chap here who either was barking mad or has had his life destroyed by a sinister figure, at this moment I wouldn't want to guess which."

"Jane, I agree with you. There is something odd about the whole affair. To look at the facts there is absolutely nothing suspicious, a sad case maybe but nothing that's murder. But then my spider sense is screaming at me saying this is all wrong from Joyce to Carl, an invisible third party in the background," Pat paused, "a small community should have such a high mortality rate. Joyce Grey disappeared or died, then three months later Carl died with no-one caring and another five months later still, Cameron died, committing a sin doesn't seem right for a Christian."

"Oh my, what if, in the great scheme of life, Joyce was an innocent victim caught in the cross hairs of an attempt on Cameron?" Jane exclaimed.

"Thank you Jane for making the job ten times more of a fucking headache!"

"No probs boss, that is why you're the boss with the extra pay grade."

"How is Shelly, Jane?"

"She is fine, enjoying the sun. She wants a barbeque, you game?"

"Yes, to bloody right." Pat pulled into the police car park and dropped off her friend. So that she could drive home.

The following day she saw an email from SOCO, so she went round to the office. "Yes sir, you beckoned."

"Ah, Pat good of you to come around."

"Carl Mills, what do have for me sir?"

"Not much, strictly small time druggy, he was getting bit a cheeky on the railways and was starting to move up the food chain to be a target. Transport were hearing rumours and getting snippets of information, which you knew anyway. He was moving in circles from Blyth, was getting known in the wrong places and was believed to be shifting quarter of a kilo sometimes a week but mainly a fortnight depending on demand. He was quickly becoming the railway supplier and also turning up to work stoned. He turned on his mates.

Of course, we have our eyes on Blyth. He kept his nose clean with the Carter syndicate, his suppliers, not crossing them and paying promptly. There was a bit of pressure to diversify and expand his product range to E's, spice and LSD. Then it went south on them and they had to calm down while the heat was on. We are not too sure if Carl stopped altogether or was keeping a low drug profile but six months later, he is killed by a hit and run, the night before his next drug's test. It looks like he hadn't learnt his lesson. According to the post mortem blood test results he would have failed the test at work and instantly got the sack from the railways. The results were known to management. It is possible that someone was pissed off with him for fucking up and if that is the case, then unless someone grasses, we won't find anything out properly for years to come."

"Thanks sir. So we are still in the unknown to knowing whether his death is an accident or a drug related hit?"

"Yes, sorry we are not much help for you but still we wish you good luck."

With that Pat got up and returned to her office, a bit dejected but then her mobile phone rang. It was Brian and after a short bit of chat he asked if she would like to go out with him for a long weekend on the weekend coming up. He was going to take a trip around the Midlands for a change of scenery. She agreed as it would be nice to relax away from policing and not risk bumping into her criminal associates.

Jane turned up. "I have just been talking to PC Gareth Price, he was the uniform who dealt with Carl's accident."

"Anything interesting?" Pat turned giving Jane her full attention.

"No. It was in a CCTV blind-spot but forensics collected evidence from the car and Carl and here is the report." She handed over the report to Pat, who began to read with interest.

So, the make of the car is a Peugeot, a white car van, glass fragments were retrieved. The impact speed was approximately forty to fifty miles per hour in a thirty zone, with the likelihood the car was accelerating. There were no skid marks at the scene. However, there were mud tracks suggesting the vehicle did stop and backed up, indicated by the two angles of the tyre tracks. The tyres were of a Pirelli design and medium wear.

We have the clothing Carl was wearing also with blood stains from two blood groups, AB positive and A negative. Carl was AB positive and we have two sets of DNA.

Both samples are blood, which suggest the Driver was injured at the time of impact and came in contact with the victim. There were no footprints on the pavement and no record of a 999 call or hospital admission at the local hospital with no unaccounted incidents at the time.

There was no Match for the second DNA on police records which suggest the driver was without a criminal record.

"Jane, this was eighteen months ago, get Forensics to run a match again. There might have been an update. On the whole PC Price did quite a competent investigation."

Jane set about organising another trace. She reported back it would be ready by the following morning, instead of the normal five to ten days from the UK's National DNA database. They would only be tracing the two profiles which were already documented and if the hit is positive then that would already be on file.

It had quite a busy morning for the two, so they went to the canteen.

"Brian rang me Jane and wants to take me out for the weekend, so I said yes."

"Oh darling that is brill, did he say where?"

"No but he hinted at the Midlands, so it looks like fun if the weather holds out."

"Sounds cool hun and it is great things are on track for you to have someone to cuddle up to."

"Thank you, it means a lot that I have your blessing as I consider you my sister as well as a friend and a work colleague. I wouldn't have it any other way."

"Well, you will have to bring him round to mine but don't forget the following weekend for the promised barbeque at your daughter's and then he will have to earn my seal of approval."

"I wouldn't have it any other way, just as long as he is pre-approved." With that they both laughed.

That afternoon they drove back to Durham Rail station and met back up with Andy, the station master in his office, he then asked what he could do for them.

Pat took the lead, "We're looking into another friend of yours, Cameron. What can you tell us? How did you meet?"

"Blimey, that goes back to the early nineties when we were all just qualified as kids on the railway. We were conductors, or if you like guards, based at Newcastle. Me and Carl were Pink Floyd fans and so was Cameron. We needed somewhere to live and so we merged our funds to buy the house that was to become the epicentre of our group. We didn't really get it; it was really a front for Carl and his drug dealing. Cameron was a biker as well and he and I bought a CG 125 together. We had a lot of fun on it taking it in turns to ride. Neither of us had passed our bike test. Cameron had a car licence so he was good to go but I had to take the CBT first. We had done some pretty dumb stuff but for the first year we were very tight as a group even a gang. Cameron was first to break away, that is, his heart wasn't in the railways, he wanted to join the Ambulance Service. As soon as he got the chance, he went for it. We were also into the church. When we got the chance, we would all go together depending of course on work and other social events. As I told you the other day, history kicked in with the church and me and Cameron would often duel with tracking history, it was quite stimulating. It has to be said Cameron would often win and we would try to visit the places that we had found out about. Although Cameron wasn't a leader, he was a huge power cell knowing a mountain of facts and history."

"How did he get on with you lot once he left?"

"To be honest, nothing really changed, he lived with us still and socialised with us. As soon as he past his bike test and brought himself a 200cc Honda, he just didn't do much with the trains. We were proud that he was doing God's work from a real hands-on point of view."

"Did he have any enemies who hated him enough to kill him?"

"Sorry, I thought he took his own life?"

"He did but we still have to ask the question."

"Ok, Cameron was a sort of marmite person, you either loved him or hated him, in part he was liked by the majority of people and had a subtle sense of humour. He would see a situation and love to turn it on its head and walk away leaving you to pick up the pieces of his remark but he tried never to be offensive but there were moments when he couldn't help himself."

"So no one really wanted to harm him then?"

"no."

"Did he report being followed in his last months to you?"

"Yes, but he wasn't sure what was going on. Things were moved in the house or disappeared and reappeared. He thought he was going mad as he was going through a really bad time in life where everything was going wrong.

He never said who he thought was following him. He said he had seen the same person hanging around various places but again wasn't sure. he was getting manic at the time and saw his dream of working on the ambulances slowly disappearing as well as everything else. He had lost his girlfriend and his motorbike and his uncle all in a month. He knew things were out of control and couldn't deal with it."

"But he offered nothing to substantiate his thoughts?"

"No he didn't"

"Ok then thank you for your time." The two detectives got up and left the station.

"Well Jane, let's see if your DNA search renders any information as and when it appears in the future"

"We will see Pat, but the way things are at the moment we have a tragic accident and a hit and run with the latter being the only dodgy thing out of all of them. Also, a half mad suicide case who may or may not recognise a random stranger, not a great conspiracy really."

"I agree with you Jane. We are not dealing with much here, come on let's go home."

The following morning Jane was greeted with an email that made her sit up and smile. She went and got two Latte's and when Pat arrived, she was grinning from ear to ear. "Ok babes who is he?"

"Who?"

"The guy?"

"Well, you're right, it is a guy called Jonathan Swindell, who lives down in Margate and has previous for five years for robbery in 1989, which is why he never showed up on the United Kingdom's National DNA Database, which was set up in 1995. Three months ago he was arrested for drink driving. He didn't get time again but he was sentenced to Community Service plus a driving ban."

"Right, let's speak to Kent police, have him arrested and brought up here for interview, to see what he has to say. I will go and speak to our boss."

Pat returned to her office. Jane documented her report.

"Right, we have issued a warrant for his arrest and I have organised his transfer up here. Never mind."

"Why?"

"I could have called into the old homestead in Marsden and met up with the folks."

"Ah, never mind eh, perhaps you can screw another trip out of the company doing some research."

"Clever girl, now what is on the itinerary for today?"

"I don't know boss, but it is a six-hour drive or ride by train, three hours flying from London; with airport time and getting to London means it will still be six hours and that also depends on what time they arrest Mr Swindell. So, whatever happens, it is going to be a tough Friday or Monday."

"Oh my, remember that is going to complicate things. We have up to 24 hours before we have to charge him with a crime, which shouldn't be a problem with the DNA evidence or release him. We can go for the 36 or 96 hours. That will be the weekend sorted as we are talking at the very least death by dangerous driving and leaving the scene and anything else that may manifest itself."

"So Boss, that means we'd better be prepared otherwise you ain't going to the Midlands for your weekend of snogging er sorry did I say that, I meant sightseeing."

"Very funny, remember I sign for your overtime, but yes let's get stuck into Mr Swindell."

An hour later the phone rang and the Kent Police confirmed that their suspect was arrested for dangerous driving and leaving the scene of the incident and would be in Newcastle by the end of the day.

Jonathan Swindell became the product of a broken home when his alcoholic father was killed at a level crossing by an Intercity train, his mother dying from the shock. He was taken into care and then misbehaviour led to borstal and him becoming a small-time criminal.

It was January 1989 when small-time villain Jonathan Swindell from south London had made his move on the post office. He had gone in armed with a bat and started to smash the place apart before threatening the post master. Although he never actually hit him just being there scared the living daylights out of the post master. He got £321. A member of public recognised him running out of the post office and immediately dialled 999 from a nearby public phone box. Within the hour he was picked up drunk in the pub, having drunk away fifteen pounds of the stolen money. He pleaded guilty straight away and, due to the circumstances, he got five years.

While he was inside, he learnt to read and write and also the trade of baker. It was his plan to open his own shop; because of his good behaviour and progress in rehabilitation he was released early from the Scrubs. He started work at a local bakery playing a part in producing the whole range of baking products. He has been there for twenty-five years without incident.

Then three months ago he was arrested for drink driving. He crashed his wife's car into his garage, a stupid mistake, but it was witnessed by a police officer who was casually driving passed. Again, he pleaded guilty. The police have his DNA because of that conviction. It didn't affect his 'criminal licence' as it was seen there was no criminal intent, or injury or harm. It would have destroyed his job and the good work of his rehabilitation. He was given the customary driving ban and fined.

Pat said to herself, "So why did he come here to commit a crime for which he could be caught and risk the key being thrown away and never being with his family? I don't get it. If it was a hit, then it was extremely amateurish, even an ex-con knows better than to stand over his victim with an injury and make a gift of DNA."

Pat decided that because of the speed of Jonathan's arrest and transport they would interview him in the morning, giving him the chance to recover from the journey. Meanwhile they gathered more evidence to the crime. That afternoon the shift was approaching finishing time when the police car from Kent arrived. Pat made a point of witnessing his arrival.

She saw a medium sized middle-age chap with a moustache. Otherwise, he was clean shaven and despite the circumstances was smart in appearance. He was handcuffed but stood upright and smelt of Brut.

He approached the desk sergeant who asked him to confirm his details. He went through the booking in process but when asked if he understood why he had been arrested, he said no. He was searched for anything that could be used as a weapon and also for drugs.

In the morning, Pat and Jane arrived at the station and went straight to the desk sergeant to organise the interview with their suspect. The duty solicitor had also arrived.

At nine o'clock, the three of them and Swindell arrived in the interview room. Once all were seated Pat opened with, "Good morning, this interview is being both videoed and recorded. For the tape I am DI Pat Nottage, also present is," Jane announced herself, "I am DS Jane Richardson," and the solicitor, "I am Norman Pointier, acting as council for the accused," and the prisoner, "I am Jonathan Swindell." Pat the read the caution out from the card.

"You have been brought here as I have evidence that you were involved in a motor vehicle incident that resulted in the death of Carl Mills on the date of 12th May 2018?"

"12th May 2018, not possible," came the response almost instantly.

Pat was taken aback, she expected a denial but not such a strong response, "Please explain."

"I was in Spain, specifically Barcelona and if you return my mobile phone, I will show the pictures and access my e mail and bank account to prove it and just to be sure you can contact HR at work."

Pat was stunned and looked at Jane. "Can you explain how we have DNA evidence linking you with the crime in the form of blood, how do you respond to that."

"Other than you have planted it I have no response but reunite me with my mobile and I will prove where I was."

"For the tape I am suspending this interview. My sergeant and I are leaving to retrieve the suspect's mobile phone." With that the two got up and left the room.

The moment they left and were out of earshot, Pat turned to Jane, "How did we get it so wrong, what did we miss?"

"Pat, we have a convicted armed robber with a drink driving offence and DNA at the scene, we didn't get it wrong, but to be sure let us see the phone. We need to know how that blood sample got on the clothing of the victim."

Pat returned to the interview with Jane and the mobile phone.

"For the tape, DI Nottage and DS Richardson have returned with the suspect's mobile phone."

Pat handed over the phone to her suspect. He switched it on and scrolled through the photographs. "Here we are," he announced and handed over the phone for the detectives to look at.

Sure enough, there where selfies on the beach with the location and date in the metadata, restaurants and meals eaten and also the hotel. Pat took notes on them and also the phone number. The bank account confirmed the card usage in Barcelona, even the HR at his bakery confirmed he was on booked leave at the time.

Then the solicitor spoke. "My client has given me permission to offer the phone up for forensic examination. You can see that there are pictures with metadata confirming the location. He can also provide detailed bank transactions carried out while at the said location via his bank statements, he has the app on his phone. He also has details of his flight and holiday booking via email."

"Thank you, can you do that please?" Responding to the request he pulled up the details on the phone and sure enough Pat saw the banks details for the time in question and noted it came with a bank surcharge for the conversion from Euros to Pounds Sterling.

The solicitor said, "My client has both cooperated and provided you with a cast iron alibi for the time you have stated, and proved without a doubt that he was out of the country. I suggest he is discharged and returned back to Kent at police expense."

"Jonathan Swindell you are to be released from police custody on police bail. I require that you report to the main police station at Margate in a week's time pending a thorough check into your alibi. We thank you for your understanding and help. This interview is now terminated, we are finished with you for the time being. Thank you Mr Pointier. I will be glad to return you and your client to the hands of the desk sergeant who will make the appropriate arrangements for your return home."

Pat and Jane got up and left the room.

"DNA! Blasted DNA I want to discover what is going on and how it got there and what the fuck did we do wrong? An interview should never fall apart after a matter of minutes."

"Boss."

"WHAT?" snapped Pat, then in a softer tone, "Sorry Jane, what?"

"We have two universities in town let's find out what we have missed from them let's speak to the experts at the university."

"Good idea Jane, let's go."

At the university Pat found the School for Biomedical, Nutritional and Sports Science, led by Professor Richard Bassett.

"Hello Professor, I am DI Nottage and this is DS Richardson. We have a problem I hope you can help us with, a problem we have encountered with the lab," enquired Pat.

"I am not a professor yet, but I am Doctor Kevin Morgan in Genetics, please call me Kevin, that would be fine, oh and great I love problems, what's up detectives?" he asked.

"We are dealing with a case that has a verified time of death for a hit and run incident. We know the vehicle stopped and the body was dragged to the pavement before the offender drove off. We have two DNA matches one with the victim, AB positive and one A negative, matching a suspect with known form for violent behaviour and yet at the time of the crime he was overseas on holiday. How is that possible? We know the DNA doesn't lie."

"Detective, DNA doesn't lie but interpreting the results does."

"What do you mean?"

"DNA is only foolproof if you know how to read the language of science. I studied Genetics at Leicester under Professor Jefferies. So I come from a great academic background. Whereas we thought DNA belonged to just one person there are exceptions to the facts. Firstly, you need to rule out poor technique from the source of DNA by the officer collecting the sample and secondly, getting cross sample contamination in the lab.

That might include a medical mix up. You will find the answer there not in the science, but then it could be a Chimera effect."

"Chimera effect, what is that?" Pat was intrigued. "You mean the ancient Greek mythology chimera? Isn't that a mix between a lion, goat and serpent?"

"Ooh, Detective you have an education!" sneered the Doctor.

"Yes Kevin, I have a classical education, that is why I am a detective," countered Pat.

"In our case, or the case of modern day, the term "chimera" has come to describe any mythical or fictional creature with parts taken from various animals, or to describe anything composed of very different parts, or perceived as wildly imaginative, implausible, or dazzling. Hence some rather tedious low budget Hollywood science fiction films, like the Chimera film where a journalist investigates the death of his girlfriend at a fertility clinic, where she worked. It has some bollocks about a plan to create a new type of human, very droll and far from true science, based on mixing the genetics of a man and an ape.

Strangely though, one type of chimera is actually quite common! Anyone who has received an organ or bone marrow transplantation is actually classed as a chimera. When someone goes through either of these procedures, they are receiving cells with DNA from another person. The goal is for the donor cells to permanently live in the recipient. So, the recipient will have two sets of DNA: their own and the donor's in the donated organ. So if you've ever had a blood transfusion or organ transplant, you might be a man-made chimera! For example, a blood marrow recipient will have different DNA in their blood from the rest of their body. If we ever needed to look at their DNA directly, we may need to look for other tissue types instead of blood.

We also have Microchimerism from pregnancy but I doubt that would be the case for you. It turns out that most mothers are a tiny bit chimeric. During pregnancy, some cells are exchanged between a woman and foetus. Most of these cells die off, but occasionally a few may stick around. If so, the woman essentially has a few cells that have her baby's DNA Fusion chimerism.

Another type of chimerism can be more dramatic. If a woman is pregnant with twins and one embryo dies in the womb, the surviving foetus may absorb some of the cells of the deceased twin. If this happens, the surviving foetus has two sets of DNA: its own DNA, and DNA from its twin. This type of chimerism can be seen in what is known as the "vanishing twin" phenomenon. We now know that among twin embryos, up to 30% will end up as single embryo pregnancies."

The Scientist paused to give the detectives a moment to absorb the information.

"Sorry detectives, but that is why it is important to ask if the DNA sample from the victim and or suspect has been subjected to or involved in a blood transfusion, as the normal longevity of the blood cells is a hundred and twenty days before dying. Then it is processed in the liver back to its basic components for reuse or excretion. That process would have been stopped at the time of the victim's death.

Now if the victim has had a recent blood transfusion, up to three months, then you will need to check your DNA samples from non-blood products. There have been experiments like face transplants. Remember the first partial face transplant was carried out in France in

2005 and in 2010 Spain saw the first full face transplant. Then there are limb transplants. In September 1998, again in France, they performed a successful hand-forearm transplant.

So an individual's DNA profile in the future is going to make your job interesting for cold case profiling as both blood and body parts of the deceased perpetrator or donated blood could be used to convict an innocent person on DNA, frightening thought, a Frankenstein monster and something that will hit the courts with the impact of a meteorite. There have already been a few cases but nothing in the main stream."

Pat and Jane were stunned at what they were hearing but it made sense to them, they just hadn't thought about it.

"Hence detectives, that is why we are better developing stem cell growth with 3D printing. It is one way to reduce the Chimera pollution and more importantly reduce transplant rejection but at the moment one high profile miscarriage of justice with a Chimera will undermine DNA evidence for ever and if it is involved in capital punishment it will be end game for the entire science."

"Thank you."

Pat and Jane returned to the car completely stunned by what they had just learnt. Jane turned to Pat and asked what the story was behind the Chimera.

"A Greek, accidentality killed his brother, so he fled from Corinth to be with King Proetus. The queen fell in love with him but he rejected her. So in a fit of rage she asked her husband, the King, to guarantee he didn't return alive. At the time, his country was being ravaged by the Chimera."

"A mythical monster that was a mix between a lion, goat, and serpent?" quipped Jane.

"Yes, the Chimera's parents were Typhoon and his mate Echidna. They were the progenitors of many infamous monsters in Greek mythology. Echidna was a monster, half-woman and half-snake, who lived alone in a cave and was the mother of many of the most famous monsters of Greek myth.

To aid his task, he was lent Pegasus, the winged horse, by the Goddess Athena. He was then able to pounce on the Chimera and kill it. So he was put into the army but hadn't read the plan to die and defeated all the armies in front of him including an assassination squad.

As always happens in this type of stories, he upset Zeus, King of the gods, when he tried to fly to Heaven on Pegasus. Zeus sent a thunderbolt and knocked him off of Pegasus. Thus spurned by the gods he wandered the land blind."

"You're just mine of information Pat, and a pretty hot chick as well, babe."

The two walked into the station from the car and saw Mr Swindell sat in the waiting room.

Pat walked over to Mr Swindell, "Do you have transport?"

"Yes I do."

"Sorry we thought the DNA identified you…."

"So you tried to fit me up when you saw my record." Jonathan interrupted.

"No…"

"Yes but now I'm out a day's pay and I have never missed work before this."

"Mr Swindell.."

"What?"

"Have you ever donated blood?"

"Yes, the company I work for have started a new scheme, it means a paid break and they give us an extra days holiday, so we all signed up to it and the company looks good in the media, that is assuming that I have a job to go to thanks to you."

"Sorry sir but it looks like the victim or another person unknown received your blood."

"I know you know my past, but you jumped to conclusions for a quick and easy result but here is thing. I am straight. I learnt a trade and how to read and write and on a whim you were going to destroy that on the basis that in the dock with my past they would throw away the key, thank God we don't have hanging anymore otherwise I would have been lynched by your lot and any free loading politicians."

"I am sorry about that sir, goodbye." With that the two officers went to their office.

"That was awkward," Jane muttered to Pat.

"But he was right. I had him bang to rights, doing life and I would have pinned the other two on him given the chance and he was innocent. I'd better go to see the Super and explain myself."

"Pat I was as bad!"

"Love, I get paid to be the boss and the boo's come with the cheers."

Pat disappeared through the door and rounded the corner. The Superintendents door was open, so she knocked and went in.

"Boss I need to update you."

"Ok Pat what is happening?"

"Sir I was following leads on Joyce Grey and the suspicious group of events, at a small Church group. We had a DNA match for one of the victims, links to an ex-con for armed robbery. Confident we could start a case for multiple murder, I had him brought up from Kent, but it turns out that the chap had a cast iron alibi for the day. He was in Spain and able prove it with photos and bank statements. I have since found out the DNA match happened because the company he works for invited the Blood Transfusion Service in, he gets an extra days holiday for making a donation of blood which is why he gave blood. I still need to check but I bet the victim had a blood transfusion not long before he died.

Apparently, the scientist even had a name for it, the bloody Chimera effect."

"First things first. Pat thank you for coming to see me, I really am pleased with your honesty, despite the inconvenience to the alleged suspect. There isn't a miscarriage of justice and that is the most important thing. Secondly, learn from this and don't dwell on it. I am aware of the Chimera effect with DNA science and strangely enough we discussed it at the Police Chief's conference last year. Look Pat if after the weekend you want to carry on or drop the case that will be ok with me. You go away this weekend, think about what you want to do. Then if you are sure that you are dealing with multiple murders then tell me, if not I have a stack of cases here waiting to be sorted. In the mean-time chase up the passage of the blood and see if there is a third party involved. You have the source and the destination; all you need to know now is the recipient. Is it the victim or that of a third party? In which case you might have someone else in the frame, which will just be as cast iron."

"Thank you boss." Pat got up and walked out. She was still worried about getting stick from her colleagues, once the word was out.

It was getting late and it had been a long day for both detectives. Jane was in the office working on the computer. "Well it wasn't the day I was expecting Gal pal."

"I know, er Gal pal but what has the big chief Hiawatha said?"

"He has thrown it back into my court again."

"Pat, when you get to wherever you are going tonight get drunk and if you sober up get drunk again and make sure you find out if Brian has a mole on his bum or more importantly, he sees the one on your bum!"

"You can't say that to me, I am your boss."

"Yes I can."

"And why is that?"

"I am the only one with your mum on speed dial." That remark made them both laugh.

"Come on then, let's go home. By the way, I want your input on this so you'd better come up with some thoughts on it." And with that they both left for the car park so they could go home.

CHAPTER 4

Once home Pat managed to have a soak in the bath, after which she dressed in jeans, tee shirt and a fleece. Her bag was ready having been packed the night before. She had a cup of tea in her hand and looked out the window, waiting for Brian to turn up.

She saw the white motorhome glide around the corner in its not so majestic state. It wasn't scruffy but it lacked the new gleam that some of the posh homes have. It was the size of normal van with a Fiat Ducati front and a box sleeping compartment with Le wish written on it. Pat thought what an earth had she let herself in for. Brian pulled over to where she was waiting outside her Westerhope home and disappearing from the cab, emerged out of the side door. He walked over to her and gave a slight kiss on the cheek.

"As promised, meet Katy," he whispered as he picked up her overnight bag and put it on the bed in the back of the saloon.

"Wwww what? Katy, why Katy?" a puzzled Pat enquired.

"I love the film *Ice Cold in Alex,*" he replied quickly, "and Katy was the name of the Army Ambulance that took them across the desert."

"You haven't told me where you're taking me," she said with some hesitancy.

"With your permission we are going to a place called Ironbridge in the Midlands."

"That sounds interesting, what's there?"

"The world's first iron bridge, the area is really beautiful, so I thought I might take you there to avoid distractions from work."

"Brian how far is it from here?"

"About four hours, on a good drive but worth it."

"Okay then, let's go." Pat climbed into the saloon, squeezed between the two seats in the front, sitting down in the passenger seat. Brian looked at her and with a smile he softly said, "Wow, sorry but I think you are really gorgeous."

"Why thank you, kind sir and I think you look pretty smart yourself."

Brian released the handbrake with his right hand and pulled away. Within minutes they were on the A1 Road travelling south.

"Christ, I have done some miles on this road," Pat muttered.

"Yer me too, but then, that is my job and this is the main artery through to London."

"I had to go to Derby with work as well, as part of a case which I was working on," Pat recalled.

"Well, we will be travelling past Derby and down the A38 to the A5 which is the Roman road, Watling Street. We should be there in time and it shouldn't take too long to set up the motorhome for the evening. It is already booked in as I was planning this for myself. We even have time to stop for tea on the way down."

Pat thought for a moment, "I don't mind where we eat but I don't think I want any attention from the yokels in Derby, as I sent one of their popular nurses to prison for murder. Well, I say popular, she was a nasty piece of work who destroyed a man's reputation and life because she felt he was a know it all. So I don't think it will be a good place to eat. I heard the officers who brought Dr Shipton to justice had death threats and abuse hurled at them."

Brian glanced at her and then said reassuringly, "Ok Derby is to be missed, but I had planned to take you to dinner at the Meadowhall

Shopping Centre near Sheffield. As we hardly know what each other likes to eat, I thought that gave us plenty of options." Pat signalled her approval as she switched on the radio. The drive was uneventful and the traffic was heavy, as always on Friday evening, due to the weekend migration of people. After two hours the massive dome of Meadowhall, the cathedral of all shopping centres, came into sight. Parking the motorhome wasn't easy as it was more about the space than occupying a marked parking bay. Brian and Pat decided to go for pasta, Brian going for a seafood special, whereas Pat chose the Pullo. After a break, Brian signalled it was time to move on. The two would-be lovers returned to the vehicle to continue their journey.

The hard chore of the journey had been done as a single leap. The next part was to be broken up into smaller sections, the first being the A38 and as predicted the Derby section was the worst due to heavy traffic.

The traffic flowed throughout the journey from the M1 down to where the would-be adventurers joined the A5. Cross country traffic was clearing up by now. They made good time and soon crossed the M6 which merged onto the M54. The conversation inside the motorhome had dried up to passing comments on local features and eventually, to their relief, they saw the ring-road for Telford. The conversational silence was now broken up with Brian saying, "Not long to go now Pat." They were now following the signs to Ironbridge and Broseley B4373 indicating the journeys closure.

As they drove into Ironbridge town the River Severn came into view through the trees and buildings. Pat felt the excitement grow inside her and the tedious journey was quickly becoming forgotten. The beauty of the small town and valley was offset by the four cooling towers belonging to the power station dominating the valley. These were a marker for Brian. They came to a T-junction turning left the road crossed the river at a bridging point which was unremarkable and modern. They had just past it when Brian exclaimed, "Lakeside View, that's it, that is the camp site we are booked in." The road they turned into took them alongside the river and railway. The four towers from the power station were now really dominating the scene. They arrived at the camp site, Brian booked them in. It only took a few minutes, he emerged from the office smiling.

"What?" queried Pat as Brian climbed into the motorhome.

"We have a hook up by the lake itself which is cool don't you think?" Pat nodded in agreement. In less than a minute they were parked up and Brian turned the two seats inwards.

"Cuppa?" Brian suggested.

Pat nodded, "Yes please Brian."

He stepped out and turned the gas bottle on and returned to the saloon. Using the tap he filled the kettle and placed it on the gas ring. He got the electric coupling cable, connected it to the electric hook up and changed the setting on the fridge to mains electric from battery. He had done his prep and the cupboards where fully stocked with fresh food and drink - wine and beer.

He went outside again, pulled out a tent and had set it up in minutes with a sleeping bag and other bedding by which time the kettle was blowing its whistle. After the hot coffee he then bade goodnight to Pat and left her in the motorhome until the morning.

Pat awoke in the morning thoroughly refreshed. When she looked at her mobile phone it was approaching nine o'clock. She got up and went to the bathroom corner. There wasn't much room, the small cubical had little standing room but the water was hot. Brian had shown her the night before how to use it and also reminded her that Katy only produced nine litres of hot water at any one time. So after a brief but satisfying shower, enveloped in a towel she emerged and dressed in a black tee shirt, a pair of black leather jeans and a lightweight waistcoat. By now she was hungry and ready for breakfast. She opened the door expecting to let Brian in to do the cooking but got a shock when she saw fresh bread and butter and bacon on the neatly laid table with a coffee ready to hand for her. Brian had a table laid out with chairs and an outside cooker already set up and had collapsed the tent.

"Madame, would you like to dine a la petit déjeuner? That's a posh brekky to you Pat."

Pat was ready for a bit of fun replying in perfect French, "Pourquoi merci gentil monsieur mais avez-vous des tomates fraîchement grilles?" Brian had a dumbfounded look about him. "I was asking for tomatoes," Pat told him. So he put ketchup on the table, they both laughed.

When breakfast was finished, Brian stowed the outdoor kitchen and said, "Right you beautiful young lady, let's get a closer look at this bridge, jump in." They climbed into the motorhome and Brian drove Pat the short distance into town. Once they had parked up, he took her to the Iron Bridge. The bridge itself had just been restored and was now open only to pedestrian traffic. Despite being pre-Victorian, Pat thought it reminded her of one the crazy and over-elaborate Victorian constructions seen on the crazy comedy films from the sixties. It was essentially a semi-circular arch over the river, topped by a flattened upside down 'V' but she certainly agreed that it was beautiful.

Then Brian piped up after reading a sign, "Oh, I thought it was by Thomas Telford but it says here that the designer was a chap called Thomas Farnolls Pritchard and Abraham Darby had built it." The couple wandered around the bridge for an hour.

Brian turned to Pat and offered to take her for a coffee. They found a coffee shop and while they were having their hot drink Brian asked, "Pat, do you like Roman stuff?"

Pat looked a little surprised. "Well I would normally have said no, but as a result of my last case, I am reading the book based on the letters of Cicero after I had heard an interesting story on Radio Four."

"Well just down the road is Wroxeter roman fort and I would like to see it, would you?"

"Lead on," Pat encouraged. They returned to the motorhome and drove the seven miles to Wroxeter roman town. When they arrived, they saw a field to their right with lines of rubble and a building that looked like an old cricket pavilion. The car park only had a couple of cars in it so parking was easy. It was English Heritage, Brian was a member, he paid the few pounds for Pat.

They crossed into the area and saw a massive wall with orange streaks across it. "That is the largest freestanding wall in Roman Britain."

"What was it?" enquired Pat.

"It's a basilica, a kind of public building were the courts and other administration offices were housed." They toured the rest of the area reading the provided information boards using it as a pallet for discussion.

"Oh, and the baths were built on the orders of Emperor Hadrian in AD 120, so there is a connection to the north east. Do you know Pat there is a chap who believes that the historical King Arthur lived here?"

She looked shocked, "So what? This is Camelot? I thought that was in Cornwall?"

"Well, no as Camelot is just a theme park and nothing to do with Arthur. Even English Heritage freely state that Tintagel Castle isn't Camelot."

"So that is just a medieval theme park, is that all?"

"Sadly yes." Brian produced a paperback book out of his pocket.

Pat pounced, "You planned to be here anyway?"

"Sort of, had you said no I would have respected your decision and taken you elsewhere." He showed her the book by Graham Phillips and his take on this work.

"How do you know this sort of shit Brian?"

"Oh I watch this shit on daytime telly when I wake up from nights," came the short reply.

After spending some time looking around, Pat found the claim that it was, at its height, the same size of town as Pompeii a bit hard to understand as she had once been to Pompeii. She took a few minutes to look around the shop and brought a bottle of overpriced fruit flavoured wine. Reembarking in Katy, Brian took Pat for a drive.

About ten minutes later he pulled up by an open field and beckoned Pat to come out, "What are you showing me now Brian?"

"It's a surprise, come with me."

He opened the door, held Pat's hand as she emerged and they both crossed the field.

"See that bridge? Believe it or not that is an aqueduct. I promised you a Thomas Telford cast iron bridge, well there you are, that is all that is left of the Shrewsbury canal and it's a grade one listed building, so it is just stuck there." After looking at it they jumped back into the van and continued to drive back along the country roads to Ironbridge. By now it was a Saturday summer's evening and still warm, so Brian suggested to Pat that it was time for some dinner. She agreed. Brian pulled over into the first pub serving dinner. The waitress greeted them, Brian replying, "A table for two please." They followed her to a table where they were seated and presented with a menu before leaving them for a few minutes. She returned to take the orders. "I would like the Hunters chicken with pommes frites and a large orange juice please," Pat ordered, turning to Brian he announced, "Can I have the Lamb shank and roast potatoes, with a large cola please." All that was to do was to wait for the waitress to present the chef's masterpiece.

"Well Brian you are full of surprises, three different histories in the one day, how do you do it?"

"I had a private education that failed to recognise I was dyslexic and so failed at everything. I believed that I was stupid but then after a newspaper article on Dyslexia was published, a friend suggested I was a match to the list, so I was able to get myself tested and found out that I was positive. I had lost my study skills but then I was so interested in history programmes on the telly that I would target those areas for a start and I would look at what is around and what interested me. The other thing being a lorry driver I do get to drive around the countryside, with the advantage of height I get to see stuff that you wouldn't normally see from a car. Like I said, I also like to watch documentaries so when I see something I mark it out just so I can come back to it at a later date, with a bit of self-education going on.

Pat, look you are a DI, trained to be inquisitive and not be stupid, look for the hidden pattern and find and exploit the criminal's mistakes; and so a quick drink and kebab and fumble down the back alley – I don't think so."

"Why thank you kind and noble sir, that is very nice of you."

Just then the waitress arrived looking at them both for direction, "Hunters chicken with pommes frites and lamb shank and roast potatoes." They both confessed their preference and Pat sipped at her orange juice and they started eating their dinner.

"So Brian, why did you become a lorry driver?"

He finished his mouthful and continued his story, "You have to remember that dictator Thatcher had started her reign of terror and to exert pressure through her lies and Scargill's obstinacy, that broke both the miners and industry's back. I couldn't find work with the knock-on effect. I was put on a YTS, do you remember the Youth Training Scheme? Pat nodded. "Training to work in the warehouse was fine as I had no idea what I wanted to do. So armed with a fork lift licence I got a warehouse job. Then I joined the Army and was able to get my motorbike, car and HGV licences. I have been working as such ever since, just different bosses.

So Pat your turn, why did you end up working for Northumberland's finest, because clearly you aren't local to the north east?"

With a twinkle she started, "Well I was walking the streets of London as a prostitute and I needed to hide from my pimp as I stole a kilo of coke from him. Then with the proceeds I bought a forged birth certificate and education certificates change. With my new name I came up north to hide and decided that I needed to make amends. At a jobs fare I joined up mainly to team up with a handsome copper."

Brian's jaw hit the floor. Seeing Brian's reaction she burst out laughing. After a few a minutes Brian realised the joke was on him and recovering from the shock answer, joined in the laughter.

The waitress approached the table, "Excuse me sir, madam is everything alright?" The two in unison nodded and agreed it was and Pat resumed her story, this time offering a more realistic brief summary. "I started off as an ambulance person. Then the bastard Tories described us as only overvalued taxi drivers, that shattered the morale at my depot and I began looking for a way out.

I was also a TA medic based in London and was deployed during the first Gulf war to Colchester Glasshouse. The main medic had been posted to Riyadh so I was tasked with running the medical centre for soldiers under sentence, that was where I got my interest in joining the Police service. The Metropolitan Police were not taking on new recruits as they were fully staffed at the time. I had just split up with my boyfriend so I decided to relocate to the north east as it was fresh ground and they had jobs for women detectives. I moved up and bought a large house with my half of the money from the house sale and settled in Westerhope.

I got my best friend to come up as she was a journalist and she retrained as a detective as well. We worked the cases, passed our exams for promotion and here we are. I am so lucky that my sidekick was my besti before we joined up.

It wasn't long before I met my husband and had my gorgeous daughter. When my husband died, he was such a wonderful man, I found it difficult for anyone to match up to him, so I just looked after my family and concentrated on my job. I have been on a few dates but nothing serious. Just my family and the job and now you. Now it's your turn."

Brian blushed a little, "I have been married and divorced, been in the forces, and then I had numerous relationships that didn't stand up to the passage of time; ladies who seemed to last a year, a Kath, a Kathy, a Karina, a Katy and a Karoline, it was getting a bit spooky. Then I met Wendy, she was special and not only because she broke the 'K' curse but she lasted two years. Then, a lady call Linda, that lasted two years but she died a couple of years ago. We didn't have any kids so we were just thankful for each other's company. Frankly, I wasn't looking and the nature of the job with nights out and tramping all over the country, it has been a bit of a barrier to meeting someone. It didn't really bother me. So when I saw you at the club I couldn't help but come over to speak to you even though I couldn't stay. I am just glad you agreed to spend time with me away from the maddening crowd of the clubhouse."

"Brian, I get it, what did Linda die of or is that indiscreet?"

"No but the answer might be, Cancer of the, well let's just say Cancer and just leave it that." Pat nodded as they both reflected on the sadness of deaths of their partners.

By now they had finished their dinner. Brian went to the bar and paid the bill, turning to Pat he said, "Come on, let's go." They returned to the motorhome, climbed into Katy and headed back to the camp site.

"Pat, I started with an old Triumph Bonneville which was named after the salt flats in the USA. It's a decent bike. I have owned a number of bikes through time and then I traded the last in for the Triumph Rocket.

I don't ride with the crowd, don't get me wrong, I enjoy their company and go for ride outs. I don't ride with any particular club as I don't like the biker politics of MC or MCC, I think the clubs respect me for that and whereas I like the scene and the people, I also like my solitude as well. That doesn't mean I am not open to change or company, it means I don't like, as I said, the biker politics, but if anyone needs help and I can, I will and I would like to think that same would be returned if I needed help with something."

It wasn't long before the journey back to the camp site was coming to its end, announced by the satnav. Once again, they drove down the country lane and alongside the railway line into the camp site. Brian drove to the pitch and parked next to his tent. It was still a warm early summer evening and Brian brought out a couple of deckchairs, a small table facing the lake with the power station to their back. Once again Brian set the motorhome up for the night.

"This is the life Pat, nice summer evening and a great peaceful view, what could be better. Would you like a drink, hot or cold?"

"What do you have in cold?"

"We have coke or orange or you can have a bitter or a lager assuming the battery connection to the fridge is intact, it might even be able to throw in some ice."

"A lager, no ice, will be fine please Brian." So he pulled the ring on the can and poured it into a glass for her, placing it on the table. He then poured himself a bitter, joking to Pat, "Well I hope we don't need to move the home as I don't want to be stopped by the police for drink driving." They both smiled.

"Brian, what do you transport in your wagon?"

"I work for a national haulier, so basically anything and to anywhere, occasionally I go to France and Italy and you?"

"Oh I have just been to Italy on my holidays which was just as well as work is getting a little heavy. It is our job to speak for the dead and provide answers for their families and in the role, emotions can be really heavy."

"That's ok, it's not really important. I firmly believe we aren't here to live for work, but if we are here and make our way through life, then I won't be bound to another for handouts but rather get paid a decent wage so I can live my life in an honest fashion and not beholden to anyone, cheers," as he raised his glass to the thought and Pat raised hers.

"So you're a free spirit then?"

"No Pat not a free spirit, but I left school with nothing and no prospects. I earned every penny I have, through honest work and not being enslaved in a factory. When I go home my time is just that my time and so long as I have money to buy what I want then I am happy."

"Well no man can ask for more, me, I like to solve puzzles. I can see the patterns in life and work things out. It was what I liked about being on the Ambulances and when I worked at Colchester military nick, I saw changes. There were two groups of soldiers, those awaiting discharge to a civvy prison and those who needed retraining within the army and given a second chance to change their ways and do something positive. It was that notion and the fact the military staff really cared about those under their charge, but you wouldn't find anyone openly admitting it."

"I'll bet," Brian chipped in.

By now the evening had closed in and the sun was setting. "What delights have you planned for tomorrow?" Pat queried.

"Not much Pat, it's a four-hour drive back home, so a lazy short walk and brunch and home is that ok with you?"

"Oh yes." Pat got up and continued, "It's late. Thank you Brian, I have had a fabulous time, I am turning in." As Pat stood up she stretched her legs and opened the door but her legs buckled a little. Brian was stood behind her as she rested back on him. He remained motionless while he felt the warmth of her back as he opened the door. She stood up, turned around and kissed Brian as he wrapped his arms around her. "If I was at home I would invite you in for a coffee but the kettle is outside."

With that Pat shut the door behind her and Brian returned to his seat to finish his drink.

"Brian quick, there is something in here." Quick as flash he was in Katy and was confronted with Pat dressed in a white night dress. "Shut the door and come here." She demanded softly and they were very quickly interlocked and kissing. She pulled his shirt off and as he dropped his trousers, she swung him around onto the bed.

In the morning Pat woke on her own. Once she had completed the ritual of getting ready for the day, she eventually emerged to find Brian wasn't about. She walked down to the lake and there she saw him fishing.

"Good morning Brian have you caught anything?"

He returned the compliment. "Good morning Pat, there a few tiddlers which are in the keep net. He emptied the net back into the lake.

"You been up long Bri?"

He replied, "Since six o'clock, give me a minute and I will pack up. I will make us breakfast as I was just waiting for you to wake."

He continued packing the rod, stool, weights and floats. It took only a few minutes as it wasn't a fishing trip but just a way to pass the time until Pat awoke. They carried the equipment back together which was only a few yards. Brian put his gear in the compartment under the bed and then went to the outdoor kitchen he had set up putting water into the jet boil.

"How does beans on toast for breakfast grab you Pat?"

"Fine if you can throw in a fried egg."

"Yip, no problem, one or two?" Pat signalled one would be enough to Brian.

"Brian don't think I am easy but I really needed that last night."

He looked at her and replied, "Yes, I did as well. Much as I want nothing else as much as to see more of you, I didn't want it to happen in the back of a van, well not the first time anyway. Which was why I slept outside the first night, even lorry drivers have a bit of class, trust me Pat,

I am really into being with you but I don't want a quickie in the back of a van."

"Well kind and noble sir, you have my favour and I appreciate your gallant action." She went to him and beckoning him to stand, he complied. She kissed him firmly not letting him move away, not that he was in much of a hurry to but they were disturbed by the water boiling in the Jetboil.

"Looks like it is getting a little steamy here Pat." He noticed Pat smiling at his remark. "Pat, I don't have family but you do, what are you going to tell them about us."

"Well Brian first of all, there isn't any us, but don't fret I hope there will be and trust me unless the family are on board you won't be, but keep going tiger you're doing ok and the family will be on board." He smiled, handed over her coffee, checked the beans and rearranged the toast to cook evenly.

"So Pat you aren't worried about not being something of a highflyers and I am just an ordinary bloke."

"Brian stop over thinking and enjoy the morning before we both overthink what is going on and make the wrong choices. Okay?"

For the first time Brian was a little unnerved and was suffering a crisis in confidence, still he managed to smile. He had left the week a long-term singleton and happy but now he was leaving the weekend with a girlfriend; one, who despite her years, was still gorgeous beyond belief. He pulled out two plates and buttered the toast, poured on the beans and placed the egg on top.

"Madame, breakfast is served." It was well timed.

"Well thank you sir," and with that they tucked in. Afterwards Brian collected the dishes and put them in the motorhome to be cleaned later. He to the seated Pat, extended his hand and pulled her by her hand straight into his arms for a kiss. Again, Pat wouldn't let go for quite a while. With his confidence returning he ask Pat to walk with him. The two were now fifteen and not fifty. He led her by his hand to a large pylon near the power station and woodland only to find a dirt track with a wooden arrow pointing the way to Ironbridge.

Once they got behind the wood line, Brian pulled her in tight kissing her in the process. Things for them both were getting strange as they both seemed unable to walk more than a hundred yards before they found one or the other pulling the other in tight and kissing each other. They finally arrived at the river where they sat down together watching the river and eddies swirling around. They even saw some trout chasing the insects in the shallows. They cuddled up to each other absorbing every minute frightened that, in the innocence of the moment, it might be corrupted forever by some intrusion. Pat finally broke the silence and said, "Brian I get you drive around and you're into history but how did you find this place?"

"I have been here before." This thought sent Pat cold; Brian sensed this as she sat up with a cold look. "No I don't bring every girl here. You are the first, the last time I was here, I was fifteen, it was a family holiday, the last time we were a family before my parents got divorced. I remember fishing with my dad and being so excited. I couldn't sleep in the tent, mainly due to my dad's snoring, and then when he stopped the bloody klaxon from that power station over there went off for an hour. I also remember mother throwing a tantrum over our friend's bread because they used unsliced bread and it created a doorstep sandwich, which we had never seen before and so were excited about it. Pat this is the first time I camped here since then, honest."

Pat warmed back up. "I deal with the scum of the earth, liars and thieves. Trust is a valuable commodity as far as I am concerned. I am not a precious snowflake but I am not a link in a sausage factory and don't want to be! One warning, don't treat me like such and we will have the time of our lives together, fail then hell hath no fury, said the man."

Brian stood up and pulled Pat close. "Pat, you have my word that nothing of the sort will happen." Their journey back to the camp site was just more of the same as the two found they were increasingly unable to walk without kissing or embracing.

Soon they got back to the motorhome. Brian packed the rest of his gear back into the van while Pat watched on wondering what the hell she was doing with this new person but she couldn't help herself, she was caught up in the moment.

"Time to go," announced Brian and the lovebirds climbed into the motorhome. Brian switched on the radio and caught the Elaine Page show on Radio two. "*…..and then this song echoed the blossoming relationship between Kate played by Hazel O'Conner and Danny played by Phil Daniels: From the sound track Breaking Glass and written by Hazel O'Conner, Will You.*" The two looked at each other as the radio burst into life.

"Blimey, is that last night or what?" interrupted Pat, "The song is about the eagerness and hope of the first night, yes wondering if it is safe to cross a line or stay safe, well I hope you got the message Brian?"

"Oh I have babes, I really have and although I have no regrets of caution, I can't help it if I was brought up as a gentleman but then I guess we have found our song before we have got home."

The traffic was light, it was about half past five when Brian dropped Pat off, and of course, she invited him in and this time he followed her in.

"As much as I want to stay Pat, I can't as I have to ready myself for work tomorrow and clean Katy." Pat agreed that she had to do the same so they kissed one time and Brian left to go home.

Just as he left the house a car pulled up outside. He paid it no attention and drove off. Pat heard someone at the door and thinking it was Brian, rushed to the door. "Brian ……….. oh it's you Michelle, come in."

"So was that Brian, you sly old dog?"

"Oi, less of the old and anyway what are you doing here?"

"Mum, I was just coming round to see why you weren't answering your mobile." Pat looked at her phone, it was still on silent from when she had wanted some quiet time with Brian. She saw Michelle had wrung a number of times. "Sorry babes, I had it on silent. I am here now, what do you want?"

"Oh no, you ain't getting away that easy. Who is the man in the motorhome I saw coming out of our home and kissing you at the door?"

"Oh you saw that did you?" her daughter noticed Pat blushing.

"Oh my god, you have finally found a bloke, it's written all over your face. Mum what have you been doing?" answering her own first question.

"Michelle calm down, calm down, you're not angry or upset, are you? I haven't forgotten dad you know."

"Mum! Hell no, not if you're happy and he is right for you, it is about time."

"Well, ok yes, I am happy but as for the latter only time will tell."

"You have got to tell me the details." She was more interested in the gossip element but was still all ears and genuinely shocked.

"Well, I first met him last year on a case I was working on but that was only briefly as I was undercover at the biker's club with a work colleague. Once the case was closed the colleague's wife dragged me out a few times and then she decided to act as a go between when he approached her for a better introduction to me. Last week he suggested we go away for the weekend. I thought about it and when he promised a lockable room to myself and no moves, I thought it might viable. I didn't say anything because I didn't know what was going to happen.

So on Friday we travelled down to Ironbridge and he kept his word and made no moves. He took me to the iron bridge and the place where king Arthur was believed to have lived. Afterwards we went to an aqueduct built by Thomas Telford and then for a pub lunch. By this time I had taken a fancy to him already, I thought he was really nice, so we kissed!

I had slept in the motorhome called Katy; he slept in a tent. Well the first night anyway I left it unlocked. The second night, he was a bit slow so I tricked him into breaking his promise. In the morning we were like two teenagers, I would really like for us to take it to the next step but I told him not at your expense, so how do you feel about it?"

"Mum! That's not fair putting it on me, BUT, he isn't dad, end of. Look Mum, if he is making you feel happy, then who am I to say no. Just have fun, stay safe and bring him to our barbecue next weekend. Let the family meet him and give him the third degree. Oh and see if Jane and her family are coming over, let me know won't you?"

"Ok Mitch, I will ask him, let's see how it goes. He is a widower himself and a biker and, like dad, he is a lorry driver."

"Mum it is time you enjoyed yourself, honest, but what is your friend aunty Jane going to say about it?"

"Well I will find that one out tomorrow. She is with her family at the Wetlands today but she isn't the one I was concerned about."

"Mum, I will be fine,"

"I know, it has been a long time now, I hope it isn't seen as a betrayal of your dad's memory. You know babes, I still miss him. Brian isn't a replacement, but he is something."

"Mum, nothing could replace dad, even he would want you to live more than just the job again. Speak to Brian and bring him round next weekend, tell him 'NO' isn't an option."

"Okay Mitch, you win, er, isn't it time for you to pick up my granddaughter?"

"No, her dad is doing that, I am just here to torment you and get more gossip."

"Well I am glad I you have me to talk about, I will see you all next weekend, now I have some laundry to do, so do you want something or can I give you lift home."

"Mum it's a ten-minute drive to Hazlerigg, so chill but I can take a hint now you have a boyfriend, you don't have time for your family. Is that how it's going to be?" she teased.

"Yes, now go, I love you, go."

Pat unpacked her clothes and started the washing. All these years she had been the mother on her own but a switch had been activated and now she was transformed into a teenager wondering what was going to happen next.

She knew that there was now a decision to be made, should she close her major case? If she did, that would be going back to deal with small time felons, then she could relax at work for a moment.

She opened the fridge, selected a carton of fresh orange juice and poured herself a drink. Her phone rang, "Brian, hello stranger how many minutes has it been?"

"Not more than fifty-six, babes," he replied.

"We have been seen together."

Brian was a little taken back, "how?"

"My daughter saw us on the doorstep kissing."

"Well I knew it was never going to be a secret but .. ah well, so was the jury out?"

"Well let's put it this way, the trial is Saturday and the court room is my daughter's garden, I am your only witness. The family are the jury and the prosecution for the case against you, my daughter supported no doubt by my granddaughter and the execution is poisoning by barbecue."

"Sounds formidable, but I am up for the challenge," Brian laughed.

"Don't get cocky sonny, I wouldn't want to face them."

"Ok babes I get it, but I would love to escort you to your family even if it's to my execution, it will fun."

"Would you free to come over tomorrow night?"

"Sorry I am on nightshift through to Wednesday taking a load down to Hams Hall, Coventry, I did warn you. But I can see you Friday, if that is ok?"

"You bet; you have got me wound up now."

"Pat, ring me any time day or night, if I can come round I will, but my job means I drive all over the country. I will be doing my best to win you over because you are fantastic and beautiful and I will work every day with you so you know that lowering your standards for me is really worth it."

"Smoothie, but keep it up and just don't let me down or it will be over."

"Trust me Pat, I will never let you down. I had such a great weekend with you. I wish it could be the start of the weekend again so much."

"Well are you working tonight?" Pat enquired.

"No I am not," came the reply.

"Well how long would it take you to come around, if you want to, that is?"

Just then the doorbell rang. Pat went over to answer it saying, "Bri give me a mo, there is someone at the door."

But when she opened the door, he simply said, "Is that quick enough for you?" They both disconnected their phones and kissed each other in a hot embrace. Pat dragged him in and locking the door she led him upstairs.

"Let's keep the nosey neighbours out of this."

In the morning Pat was the early riser. She prepared some toast, orange juice, and the kettle was on the boil when finally Brian emerged.

"Here I am darling," he said as he sat down at the kitchen table. Pat presented him with some toast and an orange juice.

"Tea or coffee?"

"Tea please, white no sugar."

After the weekend he couldn't help admiring Pat's figure and she caught him staring at her. So she loosened her satin dressing gown and with the back light from the kitchen window shining through allowed the light to penetrate and show off Pat's figure. Brian instinctively stood up and wrapped his arms around her. "Good morning to you." He kissed her.

"Sorry babes, I have got to go to work, but thank you for a fantastic weekend. It is going to take some beating but not so much of a chance next weekend as you are going to meet the family, so don't let me down."

"I won't Pat, that's a promise."

They both left together, Brian returned home and Pat to work. The weekend had really been a good distraction with the added effect of the starting of a new romance had done its job from relieving the emotional trauma of getting the arrest so wrong and Pat was had recharged her batteries.

CHAPTER 5

$\mathcal{M}$onday morning came around all too quickly and at the Police station canteen Jane was grilling Pat over the weekend over a latte. Jane's journalism instinct kicked in. "You know there are weird types who have full-blown anxiety attacks at the very thought of seeing a decent looking woman. Isn't the word for such a fear or phobia, Venustraphobia or sometimes called Caligynephobia, you know something like that? Don't they feel that every good-looking woman would be threatening, even though that is not the case. Has he been jilted or poorly treated by a beautiful woman? If so, that could have developed into such a phobia. Maybe that is what is up with new lover?"

"It is possible Jane."

"Pat, we know that men are bewitched by women like me and you of course."

"Of course," mused Pat, "I think he had a bad split at the hands of someone, which would account for how he is. A song came on the radio, it was Man of the World by Fleetwood Mac, he sang along with it and knew all the words. Afterwards he said that if ever a song expressed his life, this was it."

"Interesting ..... oh the boss wants you!" Jane broke off, pointing to the superintendent beckoning her.

"Yes boss I was coming, meet you at your work station," Pat responded. The two walked to the office. He offered Pat a seat, she glided neatly onto it.

"Pat where are we with the case now, any further on?"

"No boss, I thought there was something there, and I still do, but at the moment there is nothing but a hit and run with no ID, a suicide and what looks like a misadventure. I can't help thinking they are all connected but I have no idea how or why. It's just a higher-than-average attrition rate from a young population in a church group and my spider sense is saying there is something wrong."

"Okay Pat, put it on the back burner and get on with the other cases. If any of the group meet with an unconventional end, we will pull it out and investigate fully. I will keep an eye out on any deaths in that area and review in six months. Ok inspector?"

"Yes boss". Pat replied submissively.

"Good, well-done detective, don't be a stranger."

On her return to her desk she saw Jane receiving a load of files signalling their work load for the week.

"Ok let's see what delights we have preprepared for us, eh Jane."

Pat picked up the file and started reading through the notes, whereas Jane had turned and was entering her notes on the report she had just completed from the previous case.

"Jane, it looks like a neighbour's dispute with an ex-con."

"Ouch! That's a bit of a drop from a murder enquiry."

"Never mind babes, let's go to the flats on the Wall and see what is going on." With that the two walked to the carpark with the topic still being Pat's weekend.

The journey to the Wall didn't take too long. The two ladies emerged from the silver Beetle and looked for the address given.

"1169, here we are Jane." Jane knocked on the door and they waited for the answer.

"Mr Glynn Stout?" The gentleman was only five foot five but stocky in appearance and dressed in blue jeans and blue denim waistcoat. He had short red curly hair and a freckly face. Glynn sometimes worked but mainly he was dependant on State Benefits for a living, playing on a tentative diagnosis of fibromyalgia and exploiting it to the full.

"Aye that is me, just call me Glynn," came the reply in a thick Geordie accent.

"Ok Mr Stout, I am Detective Inspector Nottage and this is Sergeant Richardson. We are here as you have made a complaint against one of your neighbours and we have been asked to investigate, can we come in please?" He showed them through the passage way into the living room.

"Excuse the mess but we have been robbed!"

"Robbed sir? What was taken?" Pat looked around she noted there didn't appear to be anything awry in the room. It looked like it was indeed in a cluttered mess, but then she noted there wasn't the devastation that she would expect from a robbery, usually where the place had been violated and areas had been selected for mass disturbance. Despite the mess it was random. Pat gave Jane a cursive glance, which she picked up.

"And you reported it, when?"

"Last night.'"

"What was taken?"

"My Giro was taken yesterday by those thieving scum bags living two flats down."

"And was anything else taken sir?"

"Yes my Nikon camera and a collection of coins."

"Sir have you disturbed the scene from the time of the event until now?" enquired Jane.

"No." he replied

"Ok sir, can you give me the time the alleged burglary took place?"

"Two in the afternoon, er I went to the supermarket for bread."

"How long were you out for and how can you be sure of the timing?"

Pat then took a turn, "You mention 'scum' sir, who are you referring to?"

"The flat down the end. 1180. it is a safe house for those probation scum bags, we told the council we didn't want them here but they didn't listen and now we have to put up with them and their fucking criminal ways."

"Ok sir, please watch your language while speaking to us and er sir, I think you need to come down to the station to make a full statement and bring a full list of missing items, may I suggest later today, while we have a chance to investigate your claims?"

"Claims! They're not claims, those thieving bastards have stolen my money."

"Right sir, I am not prepared to put up with this language. May I suggest that when you have calmed down, you will have to come down to the station and we take down your details and make it formal. In the meantime, we are leaving due to your language."

With that the two ladies left, Glynn still reciting his well-rehearsed rhetoric.

"That is not the way to go, to get our help," murmured Jane. They walked along the walkway through the doors to the next row of flats including 1180. After knocking, a skinny man in his mid-thirties opened the door. He was about five foot ten tall, with a bit of dark stubble on his chin.

"Hello, how can I help?" he enquired.

"Good morning sir, I am Detective Inspector Nottage and this is Sergeant Richardson. We are here as there has a been a complaint made against you from one of your neighbours and we have been asked to investigate, can we come in please?"

"Sure, what has old Stouty been claiming now?"

"Oh, why do you say that sir and who are you?"

"I am John Faith and Stouty has said something about us every day for the past year, ever since I have been here."

"Why is that sir?" This time it was Jane that spoke.

"This is a halfway house, I am on licence for robbery and he knows it, so any trouble, we are always first on his list for blame, in fact we are the only ones he accuses."

"Ok sir we have open minds but what were you doing and where were you doing it, yesterday afternoon?"

"Easy, I was at work at twelve and nipped home, er here to get changed from my work clothes. I work as a car mechanic as part of my licence. I finished early as I needed to see Mr Manfred, my probation officer. I was there from two to three, I had to walk there and walk back as I can't quite afford a car yet. Why?"

"Did you have any witnesses to that?"

"Well Mr Manfred, my probation officer, his secretary and I suppose old Stouty could, as he saw me go in the flat when I got back from work but other than that no one, what is going on?"

"Mr Stout saw you come home? Pat looked at Jane, "It is him who has raised a complaint against you. He alleges that yesterday afternoon you saw him leave and then removed several items from his flat. Do you have Mr Manfred's address or telephone number to confirm your account?"

John handed over a business card. Jane photographed it with her phone while Pat continued with John.

Jane left the room to telephone the probation officer and returned a few minutes later confirming John's story. She also was able to confirm that there had been a long history of complaints against all the occupants of the flats used by the probation service in that area, all with the same single source of complaints. John had also discussed specific details with him over more aggressive complaints.

John was concerned that his licence could be revoked at any time and he would have to return to prison. She added the probation officer had said John had showed a strong desire to return to normal life and change his ways with an honest trade.

They thanked John for his time and details he supplied to them. They went and interviewed his boss at the garage, who also confirmed that they had receive threats from a single source to remove John from the work place. Despite that, John had shown a single determination to bring his prison course in mechanics into a workable skill and being a trusted employee and was shortly to be taken on the fulltime books.

"Sir, do you know or are you aware of anyone who might want to rob Mr Stout?"

With an intense stare John replied, "I want nothing to do with him, I don't care for him and his shit attitude but I have heard nothing and want nothing to do with that bigot. He will twist anything to turn himself into a victim and he's good at it, but no I have not heard a thing and I don't walk in those circles anymore, so wouldn't."

"Ok sir." with that Pat and Jane left his flat.

"What do you think, Jane?"

Jane thought for a short time and once she was seated in Pat's car she turned to Pat. "It does not add up. The crime scene is chaotic in the sense that it appears to be only half a robbery, quick sale items are still there, the bling on the window ledge and the victim has a clear stated objective, which is to remove someone he disapproves of. Let's speak to the council who run the place and see what has been going on."

They walked past the big Guano covered bronze statue outside the council building and were directed to the head of Housing.

The door was open to the open plan office so they walked in and asked to speak to the head, who they found was a Mrs Brown. They identified themselves and why they were there.

The enquiry was quite illuminating as they found out that Mr Stout had led a group of people who would target individuals they disapproved of and would literally bully people out of the flats including many vulnerable people.

"The trouble is, he stays within a gnat's breath of the law. He always has witnesses proving he was elsewhere or witnesses against him withdraw their complaint in strange circumstances, leaving us with no complaint to prosecute. Moving him has just been as problematic as he plays the system making life very difficult for his neighbours and us," said an exasperated Mrs Brown.

"So he is a paper bag king then?"

She replied, "Very much so, is there anything else detectives?" and as she got up she said in a release of breath, "For the sake of everyone please, he needs to be taken down."

Pat smiled but didn't acknowledge the remark. "Come Jane, let's go back to the office."

Back at the station the two were at the desk drinking coffee when the desk sergeant rang and told them that a Mrs Stephanie Stout was in the lobby wishing to speak to them. They went and greeted her and escorted her to an available interview room.

She was shabby in appearance appearing to be about forty with long drab black hair, about five feet tall and looked down, lacking in confidence. They sat down with a hot drink and Pat took the lead.

"Hello, how can we help you Mrs Stout?"

"Well er it's about the robbery, my husband demanded I come in and make a statement to say that we were robbed by the cons from down the way."

"And?"

"Well, we weren't robbed, he couldn't get a loan from the Independent Living Allowance so he invented this story to get something and those poor chaps that have just come out of prison were easy targets."

"Stephanie, we have to ask, why are you telling us this?"

"My children won't have anything to do with us because of his attitude and it just wouldn't be right if those lovely lads have to go back to jail for something they didn't do. He has pushed all our real friends away when he lost his job and turned on everyone who didn't agree with his views. Finally he had an argument with Sean and Dean as they refused to lie for him, I have never seen them since." At this point she broke down crying. They handed over a tissue and gave her a chance to compose herself.

"Why do you stay with him?"

"Where would I go and who would have me? Besides I still love him warts and all but I just miss my boys."

Jane returned with a printed statement and asked Stephanie to read through and sign it. Which she did. "Thank you I know it was difficult for you." They gave her a few minutes to compose herself and Jane arranged for her to have transport home in a squad car.

One hour later Mr Stout made an appearance in the lobby and demanded to see the officers. Pat sent the message that she was interviewing and would be down shortly, meanwhile they went into the canteen and had a coffee.

"Ok Jane get him up to room three. I am going to sort him out."

Dutifully Jane went down to the lobby and saw Mr Stout pacing up and down, clearly getting agitated. She made contact and he followed her up to the interview room, there sat Pat.

"Hello Mr Stout please sit down and for the purposes of the tape I am DI Pat Nottage"

"And I am DS Jane Richardson," Jane stated.

Pat continued, "And the witness.. please state your name.."

"Mister Glynn Stout," came the short reply.

Pat smile to herself. Glynn was used to getting his own way but he wasn't in charge, Pat was and he didn't like it.

"You are here to make a statement alleging a robbery and identification of a suspect. For the tape, in order, please state the time and place, the items taken, the people you suspect and why with any evidence available."

"It was at my home address, while I was out from two 'til three. I had my money, £175 cash, and a Nikon camera value nine hundred pounds stolen."

"Where did you go?"

"To the Byker supermarket."

"Any witnesses see you there?"

"No."

"What did you buy?"

"Bread and milk."

"But sir where did the money come from? Did you not just allege all your money had been stolen?"

"No. I said my giro was stolen not my winning from the turf account."

"You gamble your giro?"

"No, I invest it on a sure thing only as I hear whispers."

"Is that how you could afford a camera worth £900?"

"Yes."

"And you suspect whom?"

"Having a bunch of convicts on your doorstep doesn't leave much to the imagination, now does it?"

"What if I said they were at work?"

"Impossible, I saw one of them come to his flat."

"So you assume it is him do you? For the tape please."

"Yes I bet he saw me leave and thought he would have a go."

"Did you lock your door?"

"No, I shouldn't need too around 'ere as everyone one looks after each other."

"But sir you believe that there are known thieves on your doorstep?"

"Yes well I shouldn't have to lock my door, an English man's castle and all that."

The interview continued, Jane taking down his statement. She left the room and returned with a printed statement, handing it to Pat.

"Please read this carefully and, if you agree, sign it."

Glynn offered a few corrections then signed it.

"Thank you sir"

Glynn got up to leave but Jane, who was standing by the door, stopped him. "Sir, can you remain seated please."

"Why?"

Pat produced several pieces of paper and started to read from them.

"Sir, this is a statement from Mr Faith's employer stating he was working all morning; and this is Mr Faith's statement confirming you saw each other at 12:30. This is a statement from his probation officer that says he had a two o'clock appointment with him and was with him for an hour."

Pat looked at Glynn. His facial expression had changed from being cocky to looking slightly more troubled.

"Well it must have been his mate."

"These statements are irrelevant as we also have a statement from your wife Sue, stating you coerced her into making a false statement confirming your story. The alleged robbery was in fact a staged event for insurance money and you are trying to exert your power over her."

Glynn started to turn white as he realised he was being outsmarted.

"Mr Glynn Stout you are charged with making a false statement with the intent of causing distress and or harm and the unlawful suspension of an innocent man's parole, so that he would be returned to prison for a crime that wasn't committed. You will also be charged with wasting police time. Have you anything to say about these charges?"

This time he knew he was cornered. He didn't like it so he just shook his head.

"The sentence for these is one to two years in prison and a heavy fine so, sir, you might just get to understand what these chaps have to endure on their return to post prison life. However, that isn't my choice. First it is the Crown Prosecution Service and then the courts to decide your fate if guilty. So, I suggest we don't hear from you and you forget today's events for your sake."

"Er ok you mean that you will only give me a police caution?"

"No sir. You were willing to send an innocent person to prison and make a financial gain at the same time, I cannot overlook that. Personally, I hope they lock you up and throw away the key but that isn't my call thank God. As I have already said, the CPS and the court's will make the decisions about your fate. For your own sake stay out of our way and those on licence as you WILL join them if convicted. You are released on police bail until such time the CPS decides what to do with you, now get out."

Jane ushered a downcast Glynn out of the room and down to the desk sergeant to begin the admin process. When she returned, she was surprised to see John Faith sitting in the chair opposite Pat.

Pat told John that despite his past, as long as he stays within the law he has nothing to fear from us, despite any natural misgivings in this case, the law protected him as it should protect all our citizens.

"John, you should watch your back as Mr Stout isn't finished yet despite their warning. I fear he may retaliate via a third person, once he regains his confidence. Thank you for your help and good luck in your new career."

With that he stood up and left. Jane took him out of the building via a different exit, she didn't want the two to meet as Glynn was still being processed by the desk sergeant.

"Well that's one down, how many more to go before the weekend starts?"

"Don't think about it Jane, it's too many but it is good for the soul and ego, I am told."

"I know Pat but it is usually told by those crapping on everyone else."

They shared a smile and Jane produced a couple of coffees.

"Tell what you Jane, take your time typing up the report but make sure it is done, then we are finished for the day. I ain't starting anything new today." It didn't take long for the reports to be completed and the two ladies were out of the office and winging their way home.

For most of the week it was much of the same sort of police and detective work, ranging from petty squabbles through to random acts of vandalism. On the Friday morning, Jane arrived in the office early to complete her report on the previous day, when their boss approached her and told her to send Pat to him once she arrived.

This sounded strange but before she could pass the message onto Pat, she had appeared, she waved at her and walked straight in the boss's office.

After half an hour she came back out, Jane had a latte waiting for her. "What's up boss?"

"There has been a development with the church group of cases. With all the hoo-ha, the lab failed to complete a full admin investigation and only recorded the victims and one other DNA; because there wasn't a match with the unknown and the profile of the known, the data was overlooked in a technical error.

So, our guy in Kent was really innocent. Now we know there is a third person unknown or persons unknown, this opens up the case again. We start with a full recap and then brainstorm where we go. We need a plan and that starts with me having a coffee."

Jane handed over Pat's drink with a wry smile. A lot of the morning was going through the statements and notes, discussing them from a cold case point of view and what evidence had been revealed.

In the end they were no further forward and couldn't actually say whether or not it was just coincidence, bad luck or foul play. Pat turned to Jane and signed "lunch time." Jane nodded her approval and smiled. "There is a cheesy Jacket Potato with my name on it, come on then boss."

Pat just had a coffee as she was in deep thought which had burnt her appetite. Finally, Jane turned to her and asked what is eating her up.

She turned to face Jane and breaking her trace like stare said, "Sorry Jane, it is just my thinking about the future and is coming back in circles. I was asked to recommend DCI Roger Possessor's replacement. All the teams have been asked to recommend someone if they think they meet the challenges. It means promotion and heading up a team so when they asked me, I put your name forward without hesitation. So you have some thinking to do, if you want to go for it. It will mean prepping for the interview, which is not an issue, you can have the all the time you want as you have earned it thrice fold plus I think you will make a great team leader."

Jane was stunned as she hadn't chosen the promotion route but at the time concentrated on her family and was comfortable with that decision.

"Pat, you want to break us up?"

"No Jane, but I am not standing in the way of promotion."

"Ma'am with respect, fuck off!"

"Jane!" came the shocked reply. Shocked because she had used the term Ma'am.

"Pat I only came to this shitty part of the world because of our friendship. Ok, it meant marrying a local – bonus and my family being brought up here. I only joined the police because of the crap I was being offered as a journalist and it meant I could still keep doing investigation work which I enjoyed."

"Jane, you're a better investigator than me, I have been propped by you forever and we both know it. No, it is time you got a pay rise, the boss will call you into the office tomorrow morning, don't give an answer now, give it to the boss after a night's sleep on it, and a chat with your hubby, if you want to, but the answer must come from you and be without regret."

"Thanks Pat, I will give it some thought but I really can't be bothered with all the crap that comes with it. Besides, I enjoy heckling you. Here is a thought: we should pay a visit to the church, just to see if anything is amiss since we last met up with them."

Pat nodded with agreement and decided to let the matter of promotion drop.

The two detectives drove to the church at Cramlington in Pat's silver Beetle. On arrival, they were greeted by the Reverend Sam Hunt who was in the process of posting the order of service for the weekend. He asked if he could help and this time Jane took the lead and asked if they could go indoors to talk as there was a mild wind that was causing a bit of a chill.

He obliged and took them into the church where they sat in the pews.

"Reverend," opened Jane, "the reason we are here is because we have a few questions to ask prior to closing down our enquiry. If you wouldn't mind, can you get us a list of those involved in these trips with the usual who, when and organiser and those who missed out. Is that possible?"

"I will try but if you remember these trips were mainly self-help events and not church funded, but anything is possible, give me a couple of days and I will see what I can do."

"Please treat it as a matter of urgency sir, as we require it to move on and we can't until it has been received."

As they left the church Pat looked at Jane, she just shrugged her shoulders and smiled. Once they sat in the car Pat looked at her again.

"Look, I just want to see if there is a pattern in these deaths. He is holding back and I don't know why. I just wanted to see what his reactions would be like. He might be right in the sense that there was no official church involvement but that doesn't mean he wasn't active in the role, besides I don't want some geek pointing fingers later on saying I didn't do my job right."

"You really have got the bit between your teeth today Jane, I hope we are ok."

"Why shouldn't I be," came the blunt reply.

"Jane if you really don't want the promotion don't take it and stay with me but don't say I held you back. You had still better be coming round to my daughter's barbecue, but remember this, I am grateful to have you in my life as my Besti and we work well together babes."

Jane looked at Pat and calmly said, "there'd better be plenty of beer."

Pat smiled, "Enough, but not enough to get you pissed, you drunkard."

With the point at the church made, they drove back to the station and Pat signalled knock off time.

The following morning the two detectives arrived for work bright and early to start properly on the newly reopened case.

Jane was deep in thought when Pat asked a penny for them. Jane had been thinking about the case and she looked at Pat in a distant way.

"We have three incidents that on their own they are meaningless but throw in the fact that they go to the same church may be a coincidence or may constitute a common interest!"

"Yes, we know that Jane so what is the next step?"

"They all attended the same events, so perhaps they could have also shared the same event where something may have occurred that put a mark on them to put them in jeopardy". She paused for thought, "Three of them are confirmed dead, perhaps there may be more at risk. If the assailant has been patient and intelligent enough, over a period of time, to create an illusion of misadventure with these three confirmed kills, then we are dealing with something a little more sophisticated than a straight forward stabbing or shooting in a single moment."

"Jane, you know what you are suggesting."

"First we need to know what happened that was out of the ordinary."

"Yes, we are not dealing with an amateur, or a lunatic turned serial killer but a professional with a mission."

"Oh my God, you are right. As a thought, retribution, punishment or being able to identify the assailant once they become enlightened to this event!" Pat was following Jane's train of thought.

"The Boss is going to love us for this – not!" Pat crumbled as she thought how the hell she was going to sell this to the bosses. "Jane you're going to have to come with me on this, come on let's meet the boss." The two ladies walked up to the office to make their report.

John was busy with the roster when the two detectives appeared at the door. "How may I help you two ladies?" he asked as he beckoned them to sit down on the chairs opposite him.

Pat smiled and launched into her theory, with muted enthusiasm for a much-flawed idea which she could readily dispute.

"The Grey case sir, it is highly flawed and grey in nature either to prove or disprove, I can't put it to bed either way. My sergeant, Jane, has made some compelling observations which I feel I must support."

"Go on Pat," he encouraged, "tell me what you are thinking and where you want to go with it."

"Boss, firstly we have three incidents that on their own are meaningless, but throw in the fact that they go to the same church may be a coincidence or may constitute a common interest. Strangely that is what is bothering me, both conspiracy or coincidence, they all attended the same events, so perhaps something might have occurred that put the sword of Damocles on them, excuse the religious connotation but then sir, if the assailant has been patient and intelligent enough, over a period of time, to create an illusion of misadventure with these three confirmed deaths, then we are dealing with something a little more sophisticated than a street robbery."

John sat back in his chair and gave it some thought. "What is your gut instinct Detective Inspector?"

"My gut says something doesn't add up, but don't ask me what, maybe there is a specialist at work."

"Ok thank you ladies, I will speak to upstairs, er yes and Jane can you stay for a moment please."

Pat got up stood next to Jane and put her hand on her shoulders, "Be brave my little poppet." With that she gave a sniff.

"Ok, thank you, enough of that DI Nottage." as she winked to her friend.

"Jane, there is a promotion course available to promising candidates of sergeant grade and you're the strongest, so we would like you to put yourself forward."

"Sorry sir, I am currently considering a position with the daily local, as you know my training was originally in journalism, my biggest story was the Clapham rail disaster in December 1988, which was my springboard for becoming a good investigator."

This was a complete shock to the chief and not the normal reaction he got.

"But Jane, this is a great opportunity for you, what is the problem?"

"Sir, mainly I haven't considered it. I had a family to keep and I kind of enjoy working with Pat as we go way back before we joined the force. She has a couple of years on me but we work well together and it will be folly to split us up."

"Jane, nobody is talking about splitting you up, you can still be part of her team, do the course, get the grade, then it is under your belt if and when you need it and you can decide if you want it, you have options."

Jane was still apprehensive but in the end she agreed to allow her submission to go forward as the course dates were six months away and she had to sort things with her family.

With the final words from John being to forget the journalism angle and stay where she could make a difference. He also respected the fact she was reluctant to make the move as all too often people sort power positions for the wrong reason and that was something he wasn't going to tolerate.

On Jane's return to her office she saw Pat and once again gave her a scowling look.

"Whatcha!" Pat defended herself instantly.

"You know bloody well, you stitched me up you cow," Jane smirked, "I told you I wasn't interested. Now the chief has still pushed it onto me and it appears I am on a promotion course in the autumn, so we had better have a result by then."

"That's Cow-BOSS or Cow-Ma'am to you detective sergeant!" Jane paused for a moment and with that the two ladies laughed."

"Ok what's the plan Pat?"

"Fucked if I know," came the reply but then after a brief pause Pat spoke up, "brew and then chase the names we asked for from the reverend; but we can do that on Monday morning because we have some R&R and you are buying the drinks tomorrow night, so bring wine and the family to the barbecue. Oh and Jane, thank you."

"For what?" Jane look puzzled.

"Being my friend, being there and being a total bitch when I need it."

The two giggled as they walked down to the car park

CHAPTER 6

*I*t was late that Friday evening when Brian called round. He explained that he had finished his delivery and there was a new warehouse assistant who didn't yet know the routine and he was running late.

Pat had joked that he lost his bottle to which he laughed. The two had decided that they would have the night together and watch a film on the tv with a pizza, as the following day was going to be a big day for them both at the family gathering at Michelle's place. To be fair, the film they selected only proved to be background noise to them making love on the sofa, they were so intense on each other that it could have been considered at waste of electricity.

This continued in the bedroom far into the night. So it wasn't till the midmorning that the two lovebirds were awakened by the birds fighting with the neighbour's cat. Brian woke first and went down stairs only wearing some shorts. He started making a cup of tea for himself when he heard Pat almost fall out of bed, so he quickly made her coffee as well.

"Ooh did we really do that all night?" she murmured.

"Yes my darling, we did several times I seem to remember."

"Come here big boy and give me a squeeze." Brian stepped forward and gave her the cuddle she wished for. "Oh I see you are ready for round two as well." She gleefully let her dressing gown fall open revealing her naked body. Brian soaked up every inch of her golden skin and pulled her close to him by her hand and kissed her. As he slid his hands around her back she directed them down to her buttocks which he enveloped in his hands and gently caressed.

By now they were on the sofa once again and as they moved around on the sofa Pat found herself staring at a familiar pair of horrified eyes looking through the window. "Stop!" she screamed making Brian jump and fall to the floor somewhat bewildered.

It was Michelle looking equally as horrified at her mum making out on the sofa.

"Mummm!" Pat hurriedly covered herself up from Brian's gentle caressing and ushered him up the stairs with her hands before recovering her composure to answer the door to her daughter.

"Note to self, remember the to close the fucking curtains." she muttered.

"Mum, I can't unsee that you know," protested her daughter.

"Shouldn't peek though people's windows then should you, what do you want anyway?"

"Well I was checking up to make sure you were on track for four o'clock but it looks like you might be too tired for a barbecue with your new fella."

"Me and his name is Brian and yes, he is the first chap since dad passed. So if you don't mind I have some unfinished business with him and……."

"Stop please mum, spare me, I already have one unforgettable image sadly and I don't need two today. See you later for tea ok, I will say goodbye mum and I love you."

"Love you too Mitch, see you later." Pat ushered her daughter to the door and the second it was shut, Pat turned around and ran up the stairs to find Brain lying on the bed, she dived onto him. "Kids eh, better than contraception," she muttered as she kissed her new playmate.

It was later that day when the two lovebirds emerged ready for the world and this time their focus was on the family gathering in the garden. Brian was quite apprehensive and nerves were getting the better of him as he felt he was about to be put on trial. He handed Pat a coffee. As he sipped his tea, she noticed he was being a bit quiet. "What's up love?" she enquired, "looking forward to the family meeting but dreading being a celebrity or worse a defendant. Don't worry babes you'll do fine." Pat tried to reassured him.

It wasn't long before the two arrived at Pat's daughter's address. The two got out and were mobbed by Michelle and her family. Tom shook Brian's hand saying, "Hi, nice to meet you, I've heard quite a bit about you, come on both of you to the garden."

They went round the back to a large garden with a vegetable patch at the far end and flower borders for the two edges. There were various garden toys littering the garden, including a small trampoline, towards the house was a small patio. For the barbecue, there were two large tables in the centre with chairs sited around it, with plates, cutlery and a few different sauces; the second table was offset and divided into the different components of salad and other cold foods and different styles of bread. On the other side were a few assorted cakes and a cheese board. The barbecue itself was a full-size oil drum that had been cut in half and was clearly designed for cooking food in large amounts. The fire on the barrel was going through the flame stage as the wood was burning having just been lit and encouraging the charcoal to burn off the carbon ready for cooking.

Tom had prepared pork, beef and lamb by cubing the meat with different marinades and left them to soak in the flavours overnight, to be impaled onto steel rods in the morning. The chicken was cut into strips with herbs, then the fish was cubed and all speared with king prawns.

There were two bins filled with ice and water, one white which was stocked with soft drinks and the black bin with alcoholic drinks, mainly beer.

Tom had a big enough drum to be able to control the temperature, using three zones of heat from burning hot to warm. This meant he could move the food around to change the cooking speed. He preferred this as he was sick of going to these sort of events where all that was on offer was burnt sausages that were raw on the inside. He also disliked the gas burners as they didn't offer much to the experience. The daftest thing he saw was a gas-powered cooker that had sawdust sprinkled on it for the flavours, which he found bonkers. So he only used wood and wood-based charcoal as this would add to the flavour something that was unlike the coal-based charcoal.

Pat and Brian sat on the bench, then Jane and her husband Michael turned up with her daughter, Shelly. Pat jumped up to greet her friend and family, leaving Brian to give a polite 'Hello'

He had just met Jane so was unfazed with the greeting. Brian shook hands with Michael, "So this is the chap who chiselled through Pat's heart of stone and melted it to something squishy."

"Hey that's me you're on about," protested Pat and Jane just thumped him, "and my besti."

Just then the doorbell announced the arrival of two more guests, it was Andy and Sophia Norman with her normal delicate tornado vibe. It seemed she was able to change the atmosphere just by showing up and brought the sun out with a new intensity.

"Hi my lovelies," she announced, "so glad we made it in time for food, how long chef?" He looked up and smiled, "A few more minutes darling, don't worry, we have a few more turning up as well."

It was now that Michelle put some music on from her iPod linked to her speaker. The music was on a film score theme, the tune playing was the theme to the sci-fi film, Blade Runner. This prompted a conversation about films and a debate to which was the best. It was during this that Andy spoke, "My favourite was the theme to Silent Running by Joan Baez." Everyone looked as if to say, what are you on about? They were all expecting some of the big sci-fi films. He went on to explain that it was a quirky space film about a guy, played by Bruce Dern, who tried to save some of the earth's forests in big bio domes with three robots called Huey, Duey and Lewy. He also explained the song was a folky type of song that matched the story and was beautifully sung by Joan. Her most famous song being, 'The night they drove old dixie down' and although it wasn't on the play list Michelle found it on the net and played it. This brought about a bit of quiet as the song played through, having done so she returned to the playlist.

Sophia turned to Andy, "You sly old dog, keeping that away from me." Sophia gave him an extra cuddle.

He whispered into her ear, "I also love Jodie Mitchell."

"Oh babes who doesn't but for you that makes a change from Deep Purple or ACDC."

So the conversation morphed to favourite artists and tracks but then was silenced with the Star Wars theme and then the Storm Trooper march.

Michelle had in the interim been bringing the salads and extras, the majority of which had been red peppers filled with mixed rice and mushrooms that had been kept warm after being grilled on the barbecue. The obligatory homemade potato salad made an appearance along with the salsa and the bottled sauces.

It wasn't long before the food was being greedily devoured by all. Brian had to endure the grilling from all the family members and just about survived with his dignity intact. Then the conversation turned to the motorbike association. Tom asked if he was in the Local MC bike gang.

Brian remained composed and corrected him, "Sorry Tom, I don't understand, yes, I am biker and like the type of music being played but no the Local MC isn't a gang. It is a committed bike club that deals solely with the promotion of motorcycling and raising money for charities through bike runs and such, but I regardless, am not in any club. It is just me, myself and gorgeous Pat here. Now, I am a person who knows people from the forces and a lot of independent traders and can get things done. So, if people need support like transport or food stalls and even gift stalls, I can get people connected. I have even declined an honorary membership to the club as I feel it would compromise my independence, but hey, I also get invited to some great parties," and with that he raised his glass in salute. This brought about a general giggle from everyone."

"Yes but aren't they violent?"

"Seriously Tom, when was the last time you heard of biker related violence. It has been twenty years and the before that you would have to go back to the Mods and Rockers fighting it out on Brighton beach. If you go to a biker pub you can relax as you know nobody is stupid enough to cause trouble. But now, when was the last time a kid was stabbed by another kid who couldn't handle their beer in town on a Friday or Saturday night? I bet you won't go past last weekend and when did you last see that group of people taking toys to kids who have none!"

"True," Tom conceded the point.

"In turn I have helped hundreds of small businesses earn a living by being the middleman and taking nothing for it. I help connect people and yet I go anywhere without being charged such is their gratitude. Because I help a national bike club, I know if should I break down anywhere in the country, I can get better help than the AA with just a phone call."

"Yes but wasn't there a case not so long ago where some bikers beat up a kid in a car for no apparent reason."

"Tom, I read about that and if you believe that toilet paper then of course you will be miss informed, as the story goes that so called kid drove dangerously into a crowd of bikes on the Queen's highway and nearly knock one of them of his bike. I think his lesson was fare and well learnt, don't you?"

Tom gave a nervous laugh and nodded.

"Then Tom just look at your mum in law, Pat. She investigated the death of a biker; the club was cleared and it was two nurses who had planned the murder and were found guilty. Makes you think doesn't it."

Sophia then broke the tension that was building up by shouting "Game, set and match and what's for pudding."

Tom smiled and turning to her replied, "I made some lovely cakes and ice cream and a trifle but the jelly is strictly for adults as it was made with vodka."

Pat turned to Brian, "You're driving, so I am going to have some jelly and ice cream," he smiled and asked for some of the small cakes he had been eyeing up.

The conversation morphed from the grilling of Brian back to music and family. Soon the evening began to draw to a close. Pat signalled time to leave and this seemed the point when a few others chose to leave. This made departure a slow laborious procedure with all the goodbyes and promises of a further rendezvous.

Once sat in the car Brian breathed a sigh of relief, "Ok darling, yours or mine?"

"Yours babes, just in case the family check up on us."

"I thought Tom was getting a bit intense but then he backed off."

"Don't worry about him and besides, I think this evening went very well. I was a bit stressed but not now, we have done the deed and they can accept it or bugger off." This made Brian laugh.

The following day was a bit of chillout day which they both needed. That evening after a light meal Brian took Pat home so she could prepare for work on the Monday.

Monday arrived to quickly, and Jane arrived to the sight of Pat typing away on the reports that her boss had requested from her. She had enjoyed the weekend and this of course dominated the morning conversation over a couple of coffees. Pat was struggling to find any way forward at present. She knew the three deaths were in some way connected but she was unable to join the dots and felt there was still something not quite right about them. What was it? She had worked hard on building up her reputation as people would often judge her by her good looks. For a while nobody took her seriously but she managed to break that stereotype with some really good pieces of deduction. This led not just to her first murder conviction but a double murder conviction. All of a sudden she was the star of the department. The chief inspector had let her carry on with the investigation despite her own and his misgivings.

"Brew and then chase the names we asked for from the good reverend, ok Jane? That is the plan, let's hope they reveal something." The following day the two detectives carried on with their brain storming.

"So Jane, we have a quiet church going girl possibly drowned;

we have an ambulance technician committed suicide but claimed he was being stalked; and a railwayman involved in drug dealing starting to move into the bigtime, caught out and killed by a hit and run driver."

Pat paused for a think so Jane spoke, "So if these weren't accidents and Joyce was drowned by someone; Cameron, who claimed he was being stalked, was onto something; and Carl was hanging out with a high-risk group, disappointed them and paid the price in a drug punishment of sorts but we are led to believe that it was an ordinary RTC, we have a serial killer by definition, if the same person is involved. But we don't yet have a motive and until we can establish one, we are in trouble.

"So if the killer has a target and reason then that could be the same reason for all three; then there is a good chance that there was a joint reason that brought the target onto them and by definition there may be more at risk and ….. those in the group and attended or witnessed the same event could be at risk despite the lull."

"Yes Jane," this was quite a sobering thought. After a moment's thought Pat continued, "I wonder if Carl had spoken about his fears to Andy the station master, I think I will give him a ring." Pat picked up the grey office telephone and punched out the numbers. There was a ringtone which burst into life and then after a few rings was answered by the secretary.

"Hi, I am Detective Inspector Nottage from Northumberland police, can I speak to Andy Reid the station master ……. ok."

She put the phone down and turned to Jane, "That's weird, she has referred me to the Transport Police!"

Pat dialled the Transport Police who in turn insisted they visit the detectives at the station. It just happened that someone was on his way to the station for another issue and would come up to speak to them. This left Pat and Jane puzzled but were starting to think something was wrong.

It wasn't long before the detective from the Transport Police arrived and was directed to the two ladies. They recognised him.

"Hello again remember me? Detective Superintendent John Oyelowo from the Transport Police," he continued, "I believe you are making enquiries into Andy Reid the station master I directed you to?"

Pat nodded and beckoned him to sit down, which he did. "Hi how did Andy die?" Pat pre-empted his speech.

He was a little taken aback and looked puzzled. "How did you guess?" he mused.

"Just that, a guess, but there is a pattern developing and it isn't good, but please er John."

"Well, I was going to say that there was an incident last week with some rail works going on and Andy was required to block and chock…."

"Block and chock?" Jane interrupted.

"Sorry er?"

"DS Jane Richards, but I am good with Jane."

"Block and chock is a rail term meaning if there is a points failure, someone has to manually put wood blocks in the points to stop them from moving while a train passes over them. This is done under the direct instruction of the signalman. It is a dangerous place as by the nature of the task the person is exposed to the trains in not a good way. There are normally two, as someone acts as lookout while the other puts the blocks in. It appears that for some reason, Andy walked along the track for a pee and then disappeared. He was found unconscious but then died of asphyxia as he lay on is back. He had only been gone a couple of minutes and was only found as the result of the lookout going to investigate why he hadn't returned as quickly as expected. The premise was that he tripped either on the ballast or the rails. We don't have a third rail DC current up here, as it is overhead AC wires, so touching the track isn't as dangerous as it is elsewhere and rules out electric shock."

"What is your thinking?" Pat asked.

"Well right up to now, the thoughts of the investigation are that he just tripped, a tragic accident but then judging by your reaction I am going to have to rethink what is going on, so what have you got that can help me?"

"Well, frankly we don't have anything really, it's just a hunch. Three bodies all died from different causes but they all belong to the same church group and now the number has just risen to four."

The Transport detective gave out a mild groan as what he had imagined to be a simple industrial accident had just exploded in front of him.

"So, we have four combined deaths in mildly suspicious circumstances. It looks like we are both going to have to speak to our chain of commands to sort a way of information exchange to get the right outcome."

"I agree," confirmed Pat, "we needed Andy as a witness to one or all the deceased as a group member and as a close friend to one of them. There were reports from one of the deceased that he was being stalked, so can you bear that in mind during your investigations please. Also, his friend Carl Mills was a railway worker known to you and Cameron Wood was a former railway worker now turned ambulanceman, a possible suicide."

"Oh God, thank you, we should factor it into our investigation, I will let you know our findings." They got up exchanged pleasant goodbyes and left.

"Phew, that was a weird morning," Pat smiled, "er Jane, I had better speak to the chief inspector and give him the heads up, my spidery sense is in overdrive."

With that Pat walked round to see the chief inspector. She briefed him on the visit with the Transport Police and her concerns and theory about the four deaths. He agreed and still keeping the investigation low key he was happy to extend the time allowed for the two to carry on.

On her return to their desks, she updated Jane and warned her that time had been extended before they were to be moved on to different investigations.

"Of course, we will wait to see what our friends in the Transport Police have to offer, but my guess is we need to be more proactive with the church group and find out what was the catalyst for this groups early demise; and if they are being targeted, then why and who else might on the shortlist? I also want to know why there was a two-year gap in whoever's offending and what prompted their return. Jane, you asked the reverend for a list! Have you got it yet?" Jane shook her head.

"Ok we have a pretext for a visit, I still want to treat him gently but a bit of tough love might be the order of the day, I want that list of names."

With that, the two detectives got up together, made their way to Pat's silver Beetle and drove the half hour drive to the church. They found the reverend inside the church in the vestry. He was at the desk undertaking his paperwork.

"Hello detectives, how may I help you."

Jane took the lead, "Reverend, do you remember I asked you for a list of the events that your group have attended and who attended them?"

"Yes I do, I haven't compiled it yet but the information is here in this book."

"I thought you said they were organised independent from you?"

"That is correct detective sergeant I did, but they also rented the minibus; that requires insurance and I also needed a list of names so I knew who was in the vehicle, in case something went wrong."

He handed the detective a large book that was full of events. Jane took her mobile phone out and asked, "May I?" He nodded his approval and she photographed all the pages of information.

While Jane was photographing the book, Pat continued the discussion with the vicar. "Are you aware of Andy Reid passing away?"

"Sadly, er yes detective. The church tom-toms were rumbling away all day last Monday and the family have provisionally approached us for his send off, though nothing has been discussed, it is just they have given the nod to us."

"How do you feel about Andy's passing?"

"Tragic for his family and a great loss to the church, he will be missed greatly because of his wit and knowledge."

"How does the congregation feel about it?"

"Obviously those I have been in contact with are distraught. As I said he will be missed because of his wit and knowledge; they are talking about the group being jinxed."

"What do you mean jinxed?"

"People have noticed the holiday group is getting smaller by the month and are wondering what the hell is going on."

"What have you told them?"

"Despite the bad luck, they are all tragic accidents and nothing to do with the club."

"When was the last time Andy was seen."

"A few weeks ago, as I think he still has to work the occasional weekends."

"When was the last time you saw him?"

"As I said, a few weeks ago."

"Ok Reverend let us know when the funeral is, we would like to attend." The two detectives returned to the car Pat had a troubled look about her.

"What's up Pat?" enquired Jane.

"No nothing, it just seems a little weird that the good reverend has kept a record of trips he doesn't attend or get involved with, but then lets the parishioners use his minibus for the sake of the community. I don't understand.

It just seems a little too cosy for me. He is the only one to have access to where and when the visits took place and those who went on them. I think he is up to no good and his victims have stumbled across clues and paid the price with their lives.

Jane when you get back to the office do a full check on this guy, see if he has a record or contact with the police either here or elsewhere. See if he has any known criminal associations."

They pulled up in the car park of the main police station and returned to their desks to start their search. While the two were sat together writing up their notes there was a disturbance at the door of the office. In came John, the chief inspector, with him was a middle-aged man who stood just short of six foot tall. He was medium build wearing a very smart dark blue suit and looked like he could disappear easily in a crowd of businessmen. They approached the two detectives; John stopped and introduced his companion to the ladies.

"Hello DI Pat Nottage and DS Jane Richards, ladies this the Police and Crime Commissioner, Liam Staveley."

"Ladies," he spoke in a soft velvet voice as he shook both their hands in turn.

John continued with the introduction, "These two ladies are currently our stars of the month as they solved a high profile and complex case. They are now involved in a cold case review that we conduct every so often."

"Why is that chief inspector?"

"Yes sir, why is that sir?" Jane chipped in cheekily. John cast her a stern glance and Jane winced as Pat kicked her under the table.

"Every few years we review unsolved crimes and see if there is new evidence or new crime detecting techniques that may or may not yield fresh information for a conviction."

"Awesome, Chief," Liam sounded his approval, "am I allowed to ask what you ladies are working on?"

Pat replied diplomatically, "Sir you may ask the question but sadly I am not free to answer due to the Data Protection Act and the Caldicot principles."

"Very good, detective glad to see you're on the ball." With that the men turned and walked away.

As soon as they were out of earshot, Pat muttered, "Fucking politicians, I hate the money grabbing bastards, come on Jane let's get out of here, the place stinks." As they left the office Pat turned to Jane, "Let the diary show we were observing the reverend, ok?"

"Yes boss, see you tomorrow."

CHAPTER 7

The following day Pat was on the internet looking up the Police and Crime Commissioner (PCC).

Liam Staveley was forty years of age, not the average person having been born into a vast fortune, the last quote being over a 100 million pounds sterling. He inherited ten million pounds from his father, who worked for a stockbroker and had taught Liam how to play on the stock market from his early childhood. He had gone to Graham Hill Prep School and then to another boarding school in Kent. He went onto Oxford University where he studied and majored in English politics. While being active in politics from the days of the Student Union; then the young Conservatives before he was finally elected as a member of parliament in Essex. He was being groomed for high office, while still increasing his fortune on the stock market, but was caught up in with the "Pestminster" national scandal in 2017 when a large number of politicians were reported for inappropriate behaviour and were referred to Parliament's Independent Complaints and Grievance Scheme.

He was suspended from the party for two weeks. The Independent Expert Panel ruled he had abused his position by making unwanted advances towards a female member of staff which resulted in the whip being removed from him. He was allowed to keep his seat as the woman concerned did want to take it any further than a mere formal apology.

He lost his seat, being a toxic brand in Essex, moved up to the north east to escape the embarrassment and rebuild his marriage to the beautiful Eleanor, a former model, and to stand for PCC.

He won his position with a promise to clean up the drug gangs from the more deprived areas and reduce burglaries. He had been more vocal about supporting the stop and search tactics and wanted to use his contacts in the Home Office to pilot a few new programs to prevent crimes. He was a formidable debater and was a ruthless politician. It was said he would have sold his mother's soul for a Cabinet post and was slowly making it to a junior member in the government. This was his second term as PCC and he was going to use it as a meal ticket to get back into the only game that really concerned him, the big league of Parliament. He still had his eye on the top job and was wanting to show he was competent and regain the whip with the Conservative Party on a crime prevention and punishment ticket. He knew that after a few years in the political wilderness he could stage his comeback targeting the Home Office.

It was rumoured he built up a formidable team behind him, a model that he had styled himself, as Churchill had done after he resigned from the Gallipoli disaster. It had served Churchill well as he infiltrated the National Socialist party in Germany and in doing so, he was warning of Hitler long before he came to the international stage.

Staveley knew what was happening on the streets with a separate source of information from the police. He was astute enough to understand what was trending in the criminal world and direct counter measures against it; and had introduced polices that had reversed the number of burglaries.

Since Brexit he was also keeping a close eye on the ports on the rivers Tyne and Wear and was ready to exploit any opportunity that may arise.

Domestically he had kept his family home in Essex, ready for when he could return to the big game; but for the moment he had brought a working organic farm near Stanley and had already turned a tiny profit on it by installing a manager and farming sheep. It didn't need to be said that he saw the sheep out of the bedroom window and that was the extent of his involvement in farming, even the management of the farm was confined to just living there.

He kept the field outside the back yard empty so the noise from the sheep didn't disturb him too much. Making use of this space fell to his wife Eleanor.

She had been a firm Tory supporter and a fashion model. She had a degree in art and design and was elegant, so while she was studying, she was persuaded to model for a London fashion house and received a tremendous amount of media attention which she enjoyed. Taking a sabbatical from university before completing the final year.

She had met Liam at a fundraising event for the anti-fur lobby and started dating him straight away. She found the power he had at the time as a junior minister intoxicating.

They had been together for fifteen years with one ten-year-old daughter, currently at private school. This gave her time to work on her own fashion brand and spend time with her horse which was stabled at the farm and made use of the field. The household was basic with a housekeeper called Meg, and part time chef James. This was all the domestic staff employed at the farmhouse plus Bob the farm manager. All three lived away from the farm but had rooms in the large building reserved for staff so when they needed to be on hand for their duties they had somewhere to stay.

Liam really couldn't be bothered with all that farming stuff but it looked good on the CV and he could milk the country vote for all its worth, even appear environmentally friendly because of the organics.

Pat continued to read his biography on the website just so she knew a little bit about him. It wasn't long before the chief inspector walked past Pat, "Sir!"

"Yes Pat," came the reply.

"How come the PCC has just happened to be passing by and why haven't we heard from him before?"

"Well, actually DI he is here on a regular basis, it is just that you haven't been around when he is here, trust me that is a good thing."

"Oh, so he isn't nosing into my case then?"

"Good God Pat! He never asked about you or the case or any other case come to that, only what he asked you so let it drop, and for your information only, he is just here about the strategic planning meeting with the Chief, ok?"

"Yes sir." Pat returned to her office and to discussing the good reverend with Jane.

"The Reverend Sam Hunt obtained his theology degree at Manchester University. He had been involved in his local church since Sunday school days in the eighties. He married his university girlfriend, Katherine and after qualifying they took up missionary work in Kenya together for two years. They returned to the UK with glowing reports. He began training to be a vicar with the Anglican church which led to him settling down in the parish of Cramlington, where they brought up their son, who is now at university studying microbiology.

He has not been in contact with the police in any of the areas he lived and police checks have denoted a clear history, not even a speeding fine!"

"Ok Jane, thanks for that, I'm still not happy, I think he is involved to some level but without evidence or a confession I don't think we are going to find much on this bloke unless there is a big change in available information."

"Pat didn't he say that they booked accommodation?"

"Go on," Pat encouraged.

"We know they went all over the country attending events and places of religious interest."

"And so," Pat smiled.

"When we go on holiday, don't we have to fill in a register? Well, there has to be a register or something even if it is classed as a short term let and they booked on line."

"Ok Jane, if we can find the account holder, then look at who attended what and where and build up a picture as it is a group event ………"

"Oh my God …. there may be more victims in the wings," Jane acknowledged as the realisation dawned, the two look at each in horror as the real possibility of going from a body check to a serial killer on the rampage.

"Jane, we need to get something solid to take to the boss, and rightly so as at the moment we only have a half-baked theory."

"Yes boss, but then we are going from a theoretical leisurely exercise to a murder hunt to a full-scale chase to prevent further murders."

"When we have something to go on." Pat was distracted by Chief Inspector John Haydon approaching them.

"Ladies."

"Sir, have you come for an update?" Pat took the lead.

"Partly, as I was going to reassign you," John replied.

"Sir that would be unwise."

"Why is that?" the Chief enquired.

"We believe this should be upgraded from a cold case review to a murder enquiry and er …"

She paused to look at Jane, who in return nodded.

"Despite the lack of evidence, I am now in the belief there are potentially more victims or soon will be."

"Okay, explain."

"We have a mountain of evidence of a small group of church-goers slowly dying in apparently normal circumstances but at a rate that shouldn't happen."

"And? Give something a bit more than that."

"If it was straightforward murder, vengeance or any other traditional reason, then why not use a gun, knife or lead piping. So, it means if murder isn't intended, the perpetrator doesn't want to draw attention to what is going on and allay suspicion; therefore, murder isn't the objective, just a result of a search for something. The deaths are covering their tracks and we know they still haven't found what they are looking for, hence the ongoing search as the recent fourth death shows."

"So what is the plan?"

"We need to go into the group find out what is going on, what was point zero and identify as well who, if any, are at risk."

"Ok, I approve your plan, make some progress on it will you please." The chief turned and walked out of their office.

"Wow! Where did that assumption come from boss?" an open-mouthed Jane whispered.

"Pressure babes, when you do your course you will understand."

"If I do the course, I might have the Norovirus."

"You bloody well dare."

Jane downloaded the photographs, printed two copies so the two could read the notes independently, and got a pad of foolscap paper making four columns; Year, Event, Personnel and finally Accommodation.

She read the listings out, "So, according to this, the first trips were local 2014 and 2015. The places they visited could be easily done as day trips, Durham and York Cathedrals, Holy Island and even a walk along Hadrian's Wall. Then they must have got more adventurous as they went down and stayed in London. This must have been a trial event to see how they got on visiting Westminster and St Paul's Cathedral, travelling down by train and staying at the Tower Hotel.

In 2016 they took the minibus down to Kent where they visited Canterbury Cathedral and Lullington Villa."

Pat looked it up and brought Jane an up-to-date map.

"Yeah, it's a Roman Villa that saw the conversion from Roman paganism to early Christian religion and an early church."

Pat informed Jane, "Ah Ok, that will probably explain why they went to Richborough fort, the Roman connection."

Jane continued, "2017 they visited Stonehenge, Wood Henge and Avebury Circle, the Vale of the White Horse and Winchester cathedral.

2018 they visited Lincoln Cathedral to see one of the copies of the Magna Carta, St Peter's Church at Bradwell, Duxford Air Museum, St Mary's Church in Saffron Walden.

2019 and 2020 were cancelled due to Covid.

2021 was High Force and Malham Cove done as day trips

Finally, 2022 just hasn't happened yet."

"And accommodation?"

"It appears they were all booked via homesforbedand breakfastonline. com."

"And personnel?"

"No-one has done all the visits but in total there seems to be eight who undertook these trips, some have had their plus ones with them. We have our four deceased and four survivors, Darren (who we have already spoken to) and three others."

"Ok. We will need to speak to them, I think that needs to include Darren, also Superintendent John Oyelowo from the Transport Police and let him know what is going on, he might be able to help with some resources."

"I'll get onto it."

Jane rang the office number John had left them with. It was only a five-minute walk from the police station to the railway station and Pat was glad of the air. It wasn't long before the two found themselves face to face with him on the platform waiting for them. He guided them up to his office and with a smile asked a colleague to bring in hot beverages for himself and the ladies.

To the right was a sofa and an easy chair so he directed them to them and opened up the conversation. "So, ladies how can I help you?"

"We would like to work together with you John. We have three misadventure deaths on our turf and one on yours, as you know from the last time we spoke. We are now working on the basis that these have been contrived by a person or persons unknown. We are now working on the suspicion that another member of your staff may be at risk, so we need to work out a plan with that staff member for his safety."

"This is?" he enquired.

"A guard by the name of Darren Hilton, an ex-serviceman we are led to believe." This struck a chord with the superintendent being a veteran himself.

"Apparently three of the lads were conductors on the railways, as well as devout Christians, and lived in the same area of Cramlington," Pat began, continuing,

"The two who died in 2018, one was a large chap called Carl Mills, the other was a Cameron Wood. Cameron strung a wire around a pole and hung himself in the stairwell after drinking a bottle of whisky. Carl died, when he was knocked over crossing a road, stoned on dope and six times over the drink drive limit had he been driving.

They both died after the disappearance of a young lady and before her body was found.

The other two were Andy Reid, you told us about him, and Darren Hilton who we have spoken to you about. So, you can understand that we are getting concerned as the body count is now four and we don't want it to be five. There are four others but not associated with the railways, if you need the names, we will email them over but we are wondering if we can make him safe while at work?"

"Well, let's find out where he is at the moment first shall we."

After typing the information into the computer, he dialled a number and asked to speak to the guard inspector. There was a brief discussion, closing with a thank you.

"Well, we have a week to work out what to do with Darren as he is in Tunisia at the moment on his annual leave."

Jane was by now looking a little puzzled. Pat saw this, "What's up Jane?"

"John, if Andy's death was an accident, it would have been difficult to plan wouldn't it. But assuming it was preplanned how could it be so?"

"Well, firstly to target anyone on the railway you need to know their shift pattern, secondly you need to know how to get the points to fail on time and thirdly, that your victim was the one to be drawn out."

"Can you check to see if that was the case please?"

"Sure, the Health and Safety investigation is under way. Basically, they will be looking into the points being tampered with. I'll ask them to check for some kind of control system to prepare and trigger the points at the right time. IT will do a forensic audit on Andy's computer. Those guys are awesome when it comes to computer wizardry, there should be some kind of audit trail."

"What sort of time span are we looking at for getting the information?"

"Mmm tricky, the initial hands-on investigate may well be over. The time frame for analysis of the information is a technical question I am not qualified to answer. I'll get the information to you asap. What has the coroner indicated?"

The ladies looked at each other dumbfounded. Detecting this John smiled, "Ladies please, let's call it my jurisdiction, I will chase it up and forward it to you asap for your consideration."

"Thank you John," came the reply.

The two detectives stood up and shook his hand. As a parting shot, Pat stopped by the door, turned and spoke, "Mr Hilton needs to be made aware of our thoughts, we would like to be present when he is updated as a for continuity for us, as we seem to be working together. Another point John is, we need to keep this on a need-to-know basis, will you be assigning a detective or handling it yourself?"

"That is a good question. We are a private company, modelled on the civilian police. I will take the case on and enlist one detective to assist me, please go through me. As for cooperation, it will happen but my focus must be on our staff, that is my mandate but if that means looking at a bigger picture then I am game and I can justify that."

"Brilliant, thanks John, come on Jane," and the ladies took the five-minute walk back to the police station. As they passed the museum Jane mocked Pat over the strand of DNA on display by reminding her of the blood sample with two DNA samples in it.

Back at the office Pat and Jane did a bit of brainstorming over how the investigation was stalled and then suddenly blew up in their faces.

Pat called into see the chief, briefing him on the new developments. He made it clear he wasn't happy when he heard the level of involvement of the Transport Police but in the end, he acknowledged that the extra resources without an impact on his budget would be appreciated.

When Pat returned to the PCC he shut the conversation down immediately. "Pat he is a profession politician, he is ruthless and will destroy anything that gets in his path. He doesn't need the money to live off, he wants the power. While he is waiting to return to parliament, which is all he wants, he is out to build a law-and-order image. So while is working for Northumbria Police he is an omnipotent ally, it is important to keep him on side. Remember Pat he isn't a copper he is a politician slippery and dangerous if crossed."

"Okay boss, understood, I will forget about him, besides I have too much to do now."

Pat returned to Jane, who had been working on the lists of who went on the trips.

"So Darren 2016 Kent, 2017 Wessex and missed the 2018 trip; James 2016 Kent, 2017 Wessex and Essex in 2018; Steve missed 2016 but attended 2017 Wessex and Essex in 2018; and finally Sophie 2016 Kent, 2017 Wessex and missed Essex in 2018."

She had also written down the addresses for the stays in 2016 Kent 2017 and 2018 Essex.

"They seemed to have chosen farm houses, no doubt to accommodate the numbers staying near Maidstone, and Toothill near Swindon, and also Rayleigh in Essex."

"Boss are we going to get to travel to these properties?"

"No, we are not Jane so don't get excited," Pat scolded.

"Ah, party pooper," Jane teased.

"No, I think the victims witnessed something on their travels although I don't think we can rule anything out. Let's hear what the rest of the group have to say and see if there is anything out of the ordinary, you know the usual, absence of the normal and presence of the abnormal," Pat paused for a second, "did we get the address as well as the names Jane?"

Jane looked through the printed sheets she had prepared and shook her head.

"Okay gal we are going to have to take a trip to Cramlington again."

Half an hour later they pulled up outside the church and once again walked in.

"Good morning reverend how are you today?" Pat enquired.

"Good morning detectives, are you relocating here?" he posed sarcastically.

"No, but we do need some addresses of a few of your parishioners that went on these trips, as now it is time we started looking at what is going on."

"Don't you need a warrant for that kind of information?"

"Yes, but we were hoping that being a charitable God-fearing man you might want to help us out of the goodness of your heart."

"Here." He handed over another note book to Jane, she looked at the relevant pages and took photos of them with her phone.

"Thank you reverend we really do appreciate that."

He smiled a said, "May God be with you and your good work." The two women left the church. When they were sat in the car Pat directed Jane to go to the first on the list.

"Sophie Hall, she lives near in the Southgate estate. She went to Kent in 2016 and Wessex in 2017 but didn't go to Essex in 2018."

They were minutes away so it didn't take too long for them to get there. They pulled up to the house with a standard white plastic door and knocked. Sophie was married, in her late thirties with long light brown hair to the left of her nose. She wore John Lennon style glasses and worked part time in the local charity shop. It was something for her to do as her husband worked out on the oil rigs as a computer technician. It meant he was away for three weeks, but then home for three weeks and the money was good so they didn't have to worry about much.

After introducing themselves, Sophia invited them in.

Pat took the lead. "Good afternoon, Sophie, first of all don't worry you are not in trouble in any way, have you heard about Andrew Reid also known to the church group as Cy?"

"Yes," she replied.

"We are following up on Andy Reid's accident as a matter of routine and we would like to know how much you knew about him?"

"We didn't socialise much but I like to think that he was always pleasant with a bit of a sense of humour, we have been away for a few weekends with the church group…"

Jane interrupted, "Can you tell how things were on these weekends?"

"Yes sure, um pretty ok, we went around various locations and tourist stuff of a religious nature and we would give a little talk on the site or event. On the trip to Canterbury Cathedral one of us talked about the murder and martyrdom of St Thomas Beckett and then someone else gave a talk on the building through the ages, that kind of stuff."

"Was there anything unusual happened on these trips?"

Sophie looked puzzled and thought for a moment. "Er sorry I don't think so, I'm not sure what you mean."

"Any strange events, happenings, people being stalked accidents, that kind of thing."

"I don't remember anything like that, nobody mentioned anything but it was such a long time ago"

"Can you remember where you stayed?"

"Christ, they are all blurred into one, these were all before the pandemic and a different age."

"Ok Sophie, thank you for your help. If anything comes to mind that you may think is out of the ordinary let us know. May I suggest that with the time delay you look at any photos of that time and see if it does trigger any odd memories, please it is important."

"Why should I?" Sophie was rather indignant at this.

"Sophie, a friend of yours, Andy died last week, now it may be an accident but then there might be something else. To be honest we don't know but we have been asked to look into it. There have been reports of somebody stalking him and we have reason to believe his associates are being targeted as well……"

"And he is targeting those from the church group who went on these trips?" Sophie interrupted.

"We are not sure," Pat was trying to be diplomatic, "but please be on the alert for anything strange, certainly there have been reports of Andy being stalked which is why we are talking to you."

"Oh, do we know why?" Sophie was looking concerned and deflated.

"No, but as I said we aren't sure." Pat tried to reassure her.

"Boss are we done here?"

Pat replied, "Yes Jane, I think it is time for us to go."

Pat turned to Sophie, "Ok Mrs Hall, we will see ourselves out, you have a lot to think about, but please keep it in context, it may not be anything at all."

With that the detectives stood up and left the house. Both of them were silent and deep in thought as they got into the Beetle.

Jane eventually broke the silence. "We having chops and chips for tea, what are you having babes?"

Pat just looked at her. "What?"

"Well, I wasn't going to ask, you were thinking and I didn't like the silence to I thought I'd just say I am having chops and chips for tea."

Pat replied, "Sorry darling, I was just thinking we might get the same response from the others, then what do we do?"

"Fucked if I know! Have chops and chips for tea." They both burst out laughing.

CHAPTER 8

The following day at the Police station the DI and the DS were planning their itinerary.

Jane had already made a number of calls from the list she had been given so she was able to give Pat an idea what they were doing.

"We have two visits today and will just leave the one on holiday to talk to, our Mr Hilton."

"Coffee first, can't face the world without a canteen latte, whose first and what do we know about him."

"Steve Benczak, in 2016 he missed out but then went on the 2017 Wessex trip and Essex in 2018."

"Probably thinking he was missing out on something good. Okay Jane, are there set times or just loose timing?"

"Just loose timing."

The two finished their drinks and went down to the car park. "Benczak, is that Polish or something? do we need an interpreter?"

"Certainly, European, I think it might be Austrian but no, we don't need an interpreter he was born in Jarrow."

"Now he lives and works in Blyth as a Store man at the Capri clothing company." The traffic was heavy but the journey went quickly while the two ladies chatted about the previous barbecue.

They turned onto the industrial estate, parked up at the main reception. The young lady receptionist immediately telephoned and summoned Benczak from his work.

He was in his mid-thirties, small gentleman in stature but large in frame. He was wearing a blue boiler suit and safety shoes. "Hi, I am James Benczak you are?" Jane stepped forward.

"I am Detective Sergeant Jane Richards and this is my boss, Detective Inspector Pat Nottage. I spoke to you on the phone, is there somewhere private where we can talk, please?"

"Er, yes there is a reception room for visitors to wait just here."

He looked at the receptionist and she nodded. The three made their way into the room and sat down. The young girl instinctively came into the room and offered them a hot drink but they declined explaining they were coffee'd out.

"Mr Benczak, have you heard about Andy 'Cy' Reid?" He nodded. "We are looking into his situation at the request of the British Transport Police, just to collect a little information on his case." Pat continued, "How well did you know him?"

"Not well, well I say not well, I only know him through church, we don't not get on but we don't socialise with him, it is just we move in different circles. I mean although it wasn't a tight clique that wouldn't talk to others, they were openly friendly. There was an unofficial railway branch of those who went on these trips. We get on, in the church and we have been on a few trips together, so there has been a bit of bonding going on but only for the church, nothing against Andy but that is just the way it is."

"Ok Mr Benczak."

"Please Steve is fine."

"Ok Steve, there have been some reports that are concerning us, so what we would like to know is, has there been anything odd going on, did you notice anything strange, was there any talk?"

"No pet, I wasn't able to gan at that time as I was at work and couldnae get the time off to go, I were a bit jealous, so I made sure that I didn't miss out the next time."

"Why?" Jane interjected, "why was it important to you?"

"Well pet because we visit religious or Christian sites that help build on our knowledge. I am a storeman I have a good basic intelligence but I left school and started work here and remained here ever since and I will retire here I hope. I didn't know a lot of this stuff existed and I look forward to when these trips restart. Seeing all this history attached to the veneration of our Lord brings it all together for me."

"So there was nothing on these trips that was unusual?"

"No pet, I seem to remember that we went to see the pagan Stonehenge and a drive through the Vale of the White Horse and an afternoon at pre-Christian Avebury Circle and the Hyde Abbey at Winchester and the Christian king, Alfred the great. We also had a quick trip to the hill fort at Battlesbury Camp it was spectacular. We all had a brilliant time with no arguments and that was the same for the following year on the Essex trip. We all got on, having a wonderful time and it brought us closer to Christ by looking at some of his wonderful works."

"And since you have come back, either before or after lockdown, have there been any strange events?" Jane pushed the question.

"No pet," Steve shook his head.

"Ok thank you for your time, and if you remember anything please let us know."

The Detectives got up and were shown out of the factory reception. Very quietly Jane muttered under her breath, "No worry lines on him me thinks."

"Sssh," as Pat tried very hard to suppress her sniggering.

"Well boss, let's hope the next one is a bit more fruitful, there is nothing so worrying as being in company of someone who is a friend with the Lord."

"So who is next, the second person we need to interview?"

Jane looked at her notebook, "We have a Mr James Waldron. He works on the Cramlington taxi service, he works nights or at least until four or five o'clock in the morning, probably picking trade from the late nightclubs and early flights from the airport. So he has asked us to wait till after 2pm before calling on him, to give him a chance to wake up and get himself sorted. He went to all of the sites, both the day trips and the three stay away trips."

"Well if he has been on all the trips and being a taxi driver means that he's a nosey bugger, so if anyone is going to know, he is!"

"Ok Pat, does that mean we get lunch first?"

"Yes it does, er, do you fancy chips?"

"Yer if you are buying and throw in a sausage, I am game."

"Yes, I am game."

Pat turned off the road and drove to the sea front car park, where they called into the chip shop. Pat brought the dinner and a hot drink each. They chatted about the weekend of the barbecue.

After a second coffee and a bit of a rest Pat looked at her watch. "Ok Jane, it is time to go." They returned to the Beetle and drove to the Cramlington address of the next witness.

He was waiting for them at the front door and invited them in.

"Mr James Waldron?" He nodded in response. He was an overweight forty-year-old with thin wispy hair, a small tash and goatee beard. Jane's favourite joke was the three 'f's, fat, forty and follically challenged. He was dressed smartly wearing a light blue denim shirt and jeans

He had had a number of different jobs the last being a bus driver. Then after an argument he had a bit of cash and decided to invest it in himself and with both the car and himself badged for a hackney carriage. He left the buses and became self-employed. The three went into the living room and sat down for the chat.

Pat took the lead. "Mr Waldron we are detectives from Northumbria Police. We are looking to the recent death of one of your friends in the church. We don't think it suspicious but we are asking the question to all of your group who went on these trips, which is, did anything unusual happen involving any of you on any of these trips?"

"Well, I did the driving for all the trips and apart from contact with a few lunatics on the road cutting us up, the day trips were pretty straight forward. I mean there was to intrigue to be concerned about, I think there was one of the lads, Carl, was rumoured to be having an affair with one of the girls from the choir, but that was all really."

"What about the 'stay aways' did the rumours carry on?"

"Well, in 2016 he was supposed to have secretly met up with Barbara Henshall at Canterbury Cathedral. He had disappeared and missed the minibus back. It caught our attention as she was a bit of a catch, all the blokes wanted to date her, the paradox of religion, thou shalt not commit adultery, but then he turned up in the early hours of the morning. Someone claimed to have seen them together, but they were going to keep it a secret, he was single and she was going through a divorce. We decided that we wouldn't say anything and it was their own business. I think they had split up by the time poor Carl died. She met someone else and so it seemed pointless to rake over old coals. They had a good few years together, assuming they were together, like I said if they were together they kept well away from the church. They never went to any of the events officially together but would often end up talking together. We know she went to Wessex in 2017 again but she stayed away from the group. We spotted them praying together and Carl would disappear, as was his custom, but then this only lasted up to Essex in 2018."

"Can you explain please?" Jane interjected.

"We had got use to him disappearing. Everyone knew they were together but respected the fact that they were keeping it secret, it was a bit of a joke by the end."

"And when was that?" Jane asked.

"The Essex trip. We were at St Mary's Church near Saffron Walden. We had been there because it was the biggest church in the area with a long history dating back to the Norman times. There were a few dignitaries buried there, we visited their grave sites and someone had read up on the personage and would do a graveside presentation, just to make things interesting. It was then when we heard a noise which drew our attention. We heard them arguing round the back. It was a heated argument as there was shouting and both were waving their arms at each other. We think that was when they split up as the following week she stopped coming to our church and a year later we heard that she had remarried, this time to an Australian and emigrated, can't blame her for that."

"Does anyone know what Barbara and Carl were arguing about?"

"No. He was in the railway clan, they were a group of rail workers who hung out together, they might know what it was about but they certainly didn't let anyone know in their group. Then when Carl was caught with the drugs, he went from being on the 'in crowd' to the fringe, that was shortly after his split with Barbara. Carl must have been having a tough time, but they still did the Christian thing of forgiveness as in the Lord's prayer, we respected that. A lot of us think that the break up was the trigger for all his problems, then when he was knocked over and died, well we were of course sad but we felt that it might be mercy or a release from his pain and poor life choices."

"Has anyone been in contact with Barbara since she moved, phone calls and letters, or emails and social media?"

"I don't know, but I haven't."

"And do you know what her married name is now or which part of Australia she emigrated too?"

"Sorry I don't know, as I said it was only what I had heard, but I do know she did disappear from the choir after Essex in the sense that we never really heard from her again. Perhaps the good Reverend might know or he may not remember either, as I said nobody was in contact with her."

"Ok sir, we understand and thank you. er would you be kind enough to make a formal statement at any police station but if isn't Newcastle Central can you please ask it to be forwarded to me at this address on the card, email, fax or snail mail will be fine. It must be everything that you have just told me. If there are any problems ask the police officer taking the statement to ring me and I will brief him. Thank you again you have been a great help and if can think of anything else please let us know."

Pat, flashed a quick look at Jane and in unison they got up, shook James' hand and left the house. As they sat in the car Pat turned to Jane "Finally! We are getting to the truth and now we may have a motive, we can start a murder investigation.

Jane ring our Chief and John the BTP Superintendent, arrange a meeting as soon as possible make sure they understand it is urgent."

Jane complied with her boss's request. On arrival at the central police station the two senior officers were waiting for them.

Pat and Jane were instructed to go straight to the Chief Inspector's office where they both entered and sat down.

"Good afternoon sir and good afternoon Superintendent John Oyelowo. As you are aware I have spent the last five months looking to the group deaths of three, lately four people.

From the start I was suspicious that foul play was at large and deeply suspicious of the coincidences. They were from a small Christian group, there deaths independently appeared to be from an accidental or misadventure cause but as a collective they were not suspicious until an hour ago, I had no evidence or motive.

We knew that Carl was involved in drugs but his death was recorded as an accident or hit and run.

We thought that Joyce Grey was an accidental drowning and Cameron was a simple suicide.

This may still be the case but I have taken a statement from a Mr James Waldron. He witnessed an argument between Carl Mills and Barbara Henshall in Saffron Walden, who were having a secret affair. We don't know what the argument was about but it was strong enough to split them up and for Barbara to leave the country, married to an Australian. We still need to find out the details but we know Carl was a drug dealer, albeit small time but still a dealer.

We know from our friends in the BTP that he was under investigation for escalating a drug involvement on the rail services: two motives either the people he informed on or the people he dealt with were rather ticked off with him and I am guessing that so was his girlfriend.

She emigrated and his friends are also targets if not already targeted. So that kinda narrow things down very quickly.

I suspect that the latest victim Andy Reid will be the same."

Pat looked at the Transport Police superintendent, "Sir you have already started an investigation into Mr Mills while you also look into Mr Reid. If you can consider these connected and suspicious and assist us I will be grateful, and if it is the case then we have to ask ourselves why the others and not a simple shooting or stabbing? Normally drugs and gun crime go together, generally unsophisticated, but these deaths were designed to look like accidents and not punishments, which means the murderers wish to avoid publicity or attract attention.

Why? Probably they wish to recover something they believe Carl may have taken. My guess is either drugs or the proceeds of drugs. The drug dealers must be convinced that whatever they're after, someone still has it and they want it back and to have these resources they must be top of the pile of shit. I suggest they are avoiding a public execution to distract from the real reason.

This is why, some of the victims have reported they were being stalked by person or persons unknown to friends or officials before they died. The innocent are collateral damage and they consider it acceptable."

"Why?" Her chief broke her stride but she continued with her flow of thoughts.

"Sir, any street drug dealer is going to be oblivious, the use of a gun is common, even a knife, but we can assume observation due to the reports of stalking or being followed. Also, the elaborate methods to commit the crimes indicates they were dispatching their victims in a way not to draw attention to themselves, not your regular hit. So, these people have been exposed to something and or an event of some description that they are clearly unaware of but it has been fatal."

"And you suspect more victims?'

"It is very likely as those in the group are clearly being targeted but there is a pay off."

"What's that Pat?"

"Sir, each weird death on its own is nothing but as a collective group it brings more attention from ourselves which is precisely what they are trying to avoid judging by the time frame and research they are going to."

Pat then directed her next part to the BTP Superintendent, "Sir, if you could conduct two investigations into the death of Mr Reid, one high profile looking at misadventure or an accident and a secret investigation linking your investigation with our investigation. May I respectfully request that you keep your number who know the true mission to just one? Public information I leave to you and how you handle your own investigation.

I want to flush out our murderer, stop whatever is going on and if we can make our streets safer from illegal drugs too that would be a bonus."

The Superintendent turned to the Chief Inspector, "I am good with that and you?"

"Yes, it would be good to have interservice cooperation. We welcome your resources as we are stretched to the limit as it is, but first, well done Pat, you have done yourself proud, do you need anything?"

" I need the input from the Drug Squad to see if they have heard anything and sir," turning to the Superintendent, "we know you were investigating Carl for drugs can you let us access that information?"

"Pat for me to investigate these days is unusual, I get the need for secrecy but for that to happen I need the detective who investigated Carl to do the liaising with your Drug Squad, it happens more commonly than you think at every level. I will supply the contacts and instructions to treat it purely a drugs case so there will be nothing unusual about that."

"Ok sir, that will be great."

"Okay Pat, thank you."

The two detectives got up from the easy chairs and returned to their office."

Jane insisted returning via the canteen where they grabbed a Latte.

"Well that was a turn up for the books. We started the day without a case and now we are thrust into the middle of a drugs investigation."

"Yes how weird is that. We have to speak to the Drugs Squad see what they know before we go any further, but in the meantime, we will have to review what we have, do a board for the presentation. A timeline might be good."

"I was thinking along those lines myself. I'll get some pictures from the files, build up a profile of all the victims and put them in a timeline for you."

"For us babe because if I'm in the firing line, you are next to me, soon to be DI."

"Enough of that DI stuff, but as a lifelong friend and the only one who knew you before the job, count me in."

The rest of the afternoon was dedicated to the presentation for the new team.

CHAPTER 9

The morning brought a flurry of activity for the two detectives preparing the Conference Room for the briefing with the Drug Squad and British Transport Police. There was only going to be a small number but the room was chosen for its seclusion from their offices to avoid being disturbed by others.

One of the canteen ladies brought a flask of boiling water, a tray of sachets and a jug of milk to allow various brews to be concocted. Jane arranged the photos of the deceased in the order of the deaths, a list of the survivors and pictures of the churches in Saffron Walden and Cramlington.

She also booted up the computer so they could use the electron whiteboard and record any notes made during the brainstorming session.

Soon two men both dressed in jeans and polo shirts and a smartly dressed woman arrived.

They asked for DI Nottage. Jane beckoned them in, invited them to help themselves to a hot drink and to sit down as she would be through the door shortly. This they did, one commented that they had the posh biscuits. Just then Pat came through the door with Chief Inspector John Haddon and they sat on the stools Jane had left for them. "I am DI Pat Nottage and with me is my DS Jane Richards. We have a complex case but we need your help and expertise, so please can you introduce yourselves."

"I am Chief Inspector John Haddon, Pat's boss."

One of the men stood up "I am DI Jamie 'Iggy' Ingólfsdóttir, British born but Icelandic descent before you ask, with the Regional Drug Squad and this is my DS Alma Doyle."

The second Gentleman stood up in turn. "I am DS Mark Monroe from the British Transport Police Drugs Investigation Unit."

"Thank you, gentlemen and lady, you have been brought together for your expertise and knowledge, I don't mind admitting we have strayed out of our depth and we need help. But for reasons that will become clear I must ask that everything must be classed as confidential and highly secret, your attendance here is confirmation that your bosses have agreed to this."

She paused to wait for a reaction but noted they now looked interested.

"Six months ago the body of a female was found at High Force that had been immersed in freezing water. She was far to decomposed, as one would expect but DNA and dental records revealed she was Joyce Grey who had gone missing two years earlier.

She was in a church-going group that seemed to have a high mortality rate but she wasn't the first death in the group. We believe the keystone of the group, Carl Mills, was the first fatality. He was 40 years of age, six foot three, twenty-one stone, bald and died in a road traffic collision.

He was a train guard but was reduced to a Storeman after being caught with drugs. A small time druggy, he was getting a bit a brash at work selling drugs and was the 'go to' man. He was from Blyth and starting to move up the food chain and a target for Transport Police. He turned on his mates and grassed them all up. His known associates were in the Carter syndicate suspected as being his suppliers. We know he did not cross them and always paid promptly but there was a bit of pressure to diversify and expand his product range to E's, Spice and LSD. Six months later he is killed by a hit and run.

Joyce Grey was forty-five when she disappeared in 2019, now we know she drowned. She trained as a state enrolled nurse. She was deeply religious, a part time Church Warden in her local church. She left for a visit to High Force and was never seen alive again. Joyce was listed as missing and the file left open, she was last seen wearing blues jeans, a plain blue top with a fleece type jacket and trainers.

In May 2022 her remains were discovered, over a weekend, by a group of canoeists a mile down from the falls, remains were far to decomposed to determine a true cause of death, so drowning was assumed.

Then there is Cameron Wood, thirty-nine and five foot eight. He worked in the Ambulance service for nine years without incident. Then during the last month he was subjected to a series of incidents leading to his dismissal.

He was very religious and enjoyed the history part of the church and religion. His motorbike was stolen and a nurse he was dating dumped him. He even claimed he was being stalked by some unknown stranger which was dismissed as fantasy. He hung himself in the stairwell of his home.

Then we have Andy Reid, five foot ten, forty-two and the Durham Station Master. He was married to his wife Liz for twenty years and had one son who is away at university; a church historian and the most recent guy to die. He is subject to a separate investigation as it was at work. It appears he tripped and fell then asphyxiated due to the time it took to find him.

So we have four deaths by accident or misadventure or suicide. In a group of eight people and over four years, including lockdown, which probably acted as a delay, and now thanks to poor Andy Reid, I think that the murders are going to restart.

We have reports from at least two of the victims that they were being stalked or feared they were.

We know that Carl had a secret relationship with a divorcee parishioner. On one of their group trips to a church at Saffron Walden, a witness saw them arguing, we don't know what it was about but was severe enough for her to leave the church and reports indicate that she has remarried, an Australian, and now lives in Australia. It was shortly after that that Carl died in an RTC, the driver or vehicle was never identified.

It is our conclusion that the nature of the victims deaths as opposed to being straight forward violence which we would expect from street crime, are a bit more sophisticated and designed to eliminate the group without drawing attention to the person or persons unknown.

We are thinking at the moment the motive is drugs as Carl was the first to die and something was shared, almost unwittingly, as the surviving members are completely unaware of any drug connection or information and we wouldn't expect them to move in those circles. Please, what do you think? Is it possible?"

At this point DS Mark Monroe from the BTP drugs investigation unit stood up. "Ma'am, I have just received an email from my boss the Superintendent saying there has been a development to share with you. Yes, this afternoon, I am quoting the text of the message, a gentleman from the public brought in video footage that shows the murder of Andy Reid, it is officially a murder enquiry. The video he says shows a third party. It was recorded by a trainspotter flying a drone. There was a delay due to the kid that shot the footage wasn't aware of the what he had filmed as he was interested in the trains and it is shown in the top right quarter. Apparently, it wasn't until his father saw the footage that he realised what had been filmed. Hence the delay. He then brought it in yesterday afternoon. Can I play the footage on your equipment please?"

"Please do," Pat replied.

While he was setting up, the rest of the group helped themselves to a cup of tea. Mark logged into the computer and downloaded the raw footage, pressed play and the five of them watched it. The sound track was mainly from the air with nothing specific but they watch as the drone took off from Aykley Heads Recreation Ground near the Durham railway station. They first they saw the station, then the drone followed the track looking down on two track workers in orange hi-vis vests. As the drone moved on, they saw one of the workers walk down the track, disappear under the foliage and reemerge. Then the horror played out before them as they saw a shadowy figure appear and strike the worker from behind. He turned his victim onto his back and arranged him so his head would be struck by a train. The drone continued down the track to await the next train.

This left the group silent for an agonising couple of seconds as they mentally digested what they had just witnessed.

DI Jamie Ingólfsdóttir stood up and said, "Ok, I think we all agree that was the last thing we were expecting to see, but without question we will do everything in our power to help you, if for no other reason than to find justice for poor Andy Reid."

Pat thanked him, secretly she was expecting to trigger a turf war with the Drug Squad, so she was greatly relieved.

"Please Iggy, will you brief us all?"

"Like you, we require secrecy and must be regarded as highly secret as we have an informer and he will be killed if exposed. We have your guarantees that it won't be discussed out of this room." They all agreed.

The Carter syndicate or family are an extremely violent family that terrorised Blyth when they were young. I say that, they brought a working farm and sawmill, we believe with drug money and now they are using this as a front for all their criminal operations. It also makes searching the place damn near impossible. We believe they have a lot of stuff buried. We are still trying to locate the exact details, which is why we haven't moved in yet.

The leader is the father figure, Bruno Carter, fifty-four years old, six foot tall and a champion bare knuckle fighter. He has served time for GBH and ABH. He would have been charged with murder but the witnesses were too terrified to testify. He is highly violent and so are his two lads, Tyson Carter and Chris Carter.

Chris is the eldest by one year, at thirty-five, six foot one, again a bare-knuckle fighter and has served time for GBH and theft.

Tyson, thirty-four, six foot two and again a bare-knuckle fighter time served for GBH and drugs dealing.

If you upset this family, you don't need to do anything to do that and you want to live, leave the country. They firmly believe that because they want something, regardless of consequences, they can have it with a total disregard for other people and that their rights, as their own rights, will be enforced by violence; which is why we have a major chunk of our resources trying to secure a lengthy prison sentence. Any contact with the police the henchman will violently punish. We know a driver was pulled for speeding and they put him in hospital for six weeks. They are incredibly tight within the syndicate. Highly disciplined and totally ruthless.

As well as being involved in drugs, they have been known to supply firearms and launder money.

This is a largescale drug operation worth around £1 million with a street value three times that, as well as movements of money and weaponry. We suspect they have international felonious connections.

They regard themselves to be untouchable and last year we seized in-value over three thousand kilos of cannabis, coke and heroin that was found inside farming machinery. entering the Port of Tyne. We have also found boxes full of electronic devices, which is more disturbing as we think they are into a lot more than what we can sadly prove, but then if we went up before the beak and said, 'My Lord, they are selling electrical devices,' he is going to laugh at us and put an order in for a calculator.

Then with import of Cannabis over three years estimated to have been worth around £12 million, this family are really major players.

Customs have already received orders on a number of high value items and electricals suggesting a redistribution network, possible even on the major online shops. That it is funded by drugs is leading to wholesale distribution of anything that is high value and makes a quick profit including tobacco, alcohol, prostitution and even a protection scam.

Which is why for the sake of their victims we are in the middle of a major campaign to break them. That is why it is so important we get all the information we can and assist our international colleagues. This goes a lot further than one small time dealer being murdered, despite it being a tragic loss to his friends and family."

Pat was sat there dumbfounded, slowly she gathered her thoughts. "I am used to seeing the worst of human beings in this job, that is normal but this takes evil up to a whole new level. If they are involved with Carl, then we can wait for the big boys to catch up just as long as the big boys don't forget him and the others that were dragged into their evil world. I think to put four possibly more murders on the price tag will help."

"Good, we are the same page." remarked Iggy.

DS Mark Monroe stood up. "We know Carl is involved with this group. We picked up on him by chance. He was getting a bit of a reputation so we were obliged to investigate. We were planning to raid his domicile but then he was reported by a member of the public at a station and our hand was forced. When he took a drugs test and proved positive for cannabis, he made a deal by giving us his network, both suppliers and customers he was taken off the trains and put to work in the stores being very carefully watched and tested. So just when the Carters want him to push more, he had to stop all together," he looked to the Drug Squad, "Please remember guys our remit and budget is to cover the railways and anything that effects its safety not a major investigation into the county, so Carl was obliged to stop his contact and we took no further action bearing in mind a positive drug test meant that he would be sacked and prosecuted. But I believe that any intelligence we received would have been already passed on to you guys."

"Ok were do go from here?" Pat mused.

This time it was Chief inspector John Haddon's time to speak, "In line with the enormity of the operation in progress both at home and internationally, I am happy for the Drug Squad to take the lead into the prosecution of the Carter family with one condition, they assist us in our murder enquiry and ensure a full investigation into Carl's and the church group's connection.

I want to know why and how and who, is that fair DI Iggy?" He agreed.

"It means the investigation will be split three ways. Our colleagues in the Transport Police will handle the murder of Andy Reid and possibly Carl and any others on the railway and the Drug squad will handle the Carter family. Pat they will liaise with you and we will see where this investigation leads us to now." Then he left the room.

Pat stood up and suggested that it would a good time to have a break and mingle. She knew this is where friendships were made and bonds developed. The talk was all work-based, they were interested in finding different angles on their work. They soon dispersed after about half an hour. All with a new aspect to their job.

Pat and Jane cleared up the mess into some sort of order which was acceptable to hand over to the catering team. There wasn't much mess anyway. By now it was dinner time and so the two went to the canteen for a sit down and a coffee.

"Jane am I right about this case or am I just wasting a lot of people's time?"

"What's this Pat, doubts?"

"I don't know Jane we were supposed to just look into the death of poor Joyce and now it has just blown up in my face, I never expected this."

"Don't ask me for sympathy!"

"What?"

"You want to give me the poisoned chalice."

"Jane no, look you're a natural and now is your time. I remember when you were a journalist you were a brilliant investigator even then and you still are, you should have the chief's job by now and as much as I love John, I think you would have been better."

"You made this case Pat. You have taken scraps of information and made a puzzle. All the deaths had been investigated individually with nothing to indicate suspicious deaths. Now we have it confirmed that not only are we dealing with four murders but we are dealing with international drug dealers. That is enormous and they are playing to our or your tune. This will mean you will be in line for promotion."

"Jane, after my husband died I was lost, I looked after my daughter and my job kept me sane. I got ahead because you had my back, the only offers I got were from those in the job and I didn't want that. I now have something different. Brian is a little quiet but he is just what I was looking for. Perhaps he is what I was missing all my life and the job was just a distraction, but now I feel that I don't really care about the job I just want to get through the week to see Brian at the weekend. I never felt like this before, especially about a bloke. I am now treading water until I can retire from the force with full pension. Don't get me wrong Jane, I am determined to find out the truth for Joyce, Carl, Cameron and Andy and if there is any foul play. Justice for them and their families. That is it for me. My Job is not so much to find a replacement for me but to find somebody that is capable, thinking outside the box is easy, solving murders is challenging but doing that and leading a team is fucking stressful. I don't mind us two, we talk together and we have lives in each other's pockets since our days in the Army.

Now we are faced with what could be the biggest crime in our lives and we need to get it right but I can only cope with that because you are here, trust me I could not do it without you."

"That is just it Pat, we have a fantastic life journey together you have a year's service ahead of me which means I have one year to complete without you. We still have a bit of time to serve, if I get promoted they will split us up and I don't really want to confront all the evil we see without you and that is just what we are facing at the moment true evil. A family group that are so wrapped up in extorting money and selling misery they don't care who they kill, just as long as they get what they want and when we are together, I feel safe."

"Ok Jane, but do the promotional course then at least you have options…what….."

Jane's expression had changed causing Pat to stop mid-drift. "Pat, we need to find the woman Carl was having an affair with, what's her name, Barbara. We need to find out why she was arguing and what was said that was so bad they split up."

"Why surely it was drugs?"

"Was it Pat? Perhaps he proposed and it went wrong but regardless we need to know, just for the record."

"We can go to church tomorrow and speak to the reverend. Ok we can do that tomorrow but if the reverend doesn't know?"

"Then we find out what he does know. He will have his own records. Starting with a maiden and married names and date of birth. Then we put a trace out to emigration and/or social media. Social media might be quicker. Remember it will easier with her new married name but doable with her old married name and a date of birth, as they have to be declared for emigration."

The following morning once again found the detectives travelling up to Cramlington to speak to the Reverend Sam Hunt.

"Good morning, Reverend Hunt."

"Good morning, Detectives Nottage and Richards how can I help you on this fine glorious day?"

"Did you have a Barbara Henshall in your church as a chorister?" Pat enquired.

"Yes I did, why?"

"Did you know she was involved with Carl Mills?"

"Yes, I was aware there were rumours about the two for quite a while and then it went quiet, but I think they broke up and she disappeared, I think she met someone and emigrated to Australia."

"Do you know her new married name, it is important?"

"No, I seem to remember she came and said she was leaving the church and didn't want any contact with anyone. She was upset and that is all I know. I only found out that she married an Australian and left the country and that wasn't from her but it was from rumours from the parishioners, so I am sorry I can't confirm any details."

"Do you have any records with her maiden name and date of birth?"

"Yes I do." He walked over to a cabinet opened a book and once again Jane took out her phone and photographed the page."

"Thank you." Jane mumbled.

"Thank you Reverend Hunt," Pat echoed and the two detectives returned to Newcastle Central Police Station.

Once back at the office Jane emailed the new information to the Australian embassy with a formal police request for emigration details of Barbara Henshall and her contact details. She received a confirmation receipt e mail which confirmed the request had been received and also saying it would take up to forty-eight hours to process the information.

Meanwhile, Pat emailed the video clip to one of the forensic computer analysts with a request to examine the clip for clues to the identity of the assailant.

"Crikey Pat, all we need to do now is to sit back and wait for the information to come, thick and fast."

"I wish Jane, it was as simple as that, but we both know it isn't."

"I know what we could do, boss."

"What's that Jane?"

"Remember that con we saw in the Byker Wall, you know the one who was fitted up by that nasty little fellow?"

"Go on, I think I know where you are going with this but say it."

"Well, a favour for a favour and it isn't unethical either as he was dealt with fairly, and with a reward perhaps he might be able to source some information for us."

"Yes Jane, I like your thinking on that. Come on, let's go."

And so the two jumped into Pat's silver Beetle and drove the short distance to the Byker Wall.

When they arrived at the Wall, they climbed the stairs to 1180 and knocked on the door.

"Mr John Faith?" This time it was Jane who spoke first.

"Yes, oh it is you, I remember you detectives how can I help?"

"Are you having problems with the neighbours?"

"No there seems to be a moment of calm, would you like to come in?"

"Yes please." The two entered the flat and sat down in the chair.

"Now why I am entertaining two officers of the law?"

"John please bear with us; we are not judging and we are not interested in you. We are on the hunt for information and we were hoping you might be able to help us save some lives."

"You mean grass? No way."

"No! We are not asking you grass on anyone but have you seen the news about that chap killed on the railways, he was a family man just doing his job, he never signed up to any unwritten code of villainy. We believe that there might be more families being targeted.

If you do hear of anything please could you make us aware in a way that would not infringe on your no grass rule. We are not interested in anything but stopping people from dying, that is all. We will act on any anonymous tipoff. If the person identifies himself as Blue Boy we will know who sent it and no one else will. We only want information to identify the person, you will not be required to provide evidence. Honestly, we just want to know where to look, I think that isn't unfair do you?"

"Totally anonymous?"

"Totally!"

"And if I don't find anything?"

"I'll let you decide on that,"

"This is a one off?"

"One off, if you want, I will even throw in a good word to your probation officer."

"I will show you out detectives."

The two detectives returned to the office to contemplate what John Faith had said.

CHAPTER 10

*T*he following day at the start of the shift there was a message in Jane's email box which started today's direction.

It was the from High Commission, Australia House. The email confirmed the emigration of Barbara. Jane read it out to Pat.

"*She had emigrated under the married name of Meagher to a chap called Raymond. He had shares in an opal mine in the area of Coober Pedy, located in central South Australia which is where he registered as living. If further information was required not to hesitate to contact them.*"

"Jane, contact the High Commission and ask them if they can facilitate an urgent meeting."

Jane noted the contact number and dialled it. She explained her needs to the operator who in turned passed her on to one of the staff. She explained she was from the police and was concerned for the safety of one of their citizens and needed a confidential meeting as soon as possible. The Australian staff agreed to meet them at fourteen hundred hours. Jane gave Pat the thumbs up. Pat completed booking with first class return tickets and signalled to Jane the time was up by tapping her watch.

"Come on Jane, the train is just before ten, we have half an hour to catch it." Pat checked in with the chief to let him know they were going on the train to London to speak to the Australians and couldn't stop to chat as they were up against the clock.

The two got to Newcastle station with twenty minutes to spare. Pat went to the vending machine for the tickets, printed them off and went over to platform three for London.

They boarded the train sitting in the first-class coach on the side with the single seats facing each over. The hostess came over to them and took their orders for breakfast and a hot drink.

Jane plugged in her computer and the wi-fi, going on the social media accounts to see if she could find their quarry but to no avail. "Boss, Barbara or her husband Raymond don't show up on any social accounts under their known names, which might be a good thing if you want to stay out of touch and don't want to be found but a bitch for us."

"Ok Jane but remember, don't access the PNC while we are on public wi-fi."

"No probs boss, not that I was going to."

The two were soon lost to time with writing up reports and off line collating information. Pat was getting her head around the hastily convened meeting. They were occasionally interrupted with orders of snacks and hot beverages.

They caught the Northern Line to Holborn and then walked down the Strand, taking note of the coffee shops for when they emerged from Australia House.

It was only a few minutes walk down the big crescent to the majestic building where Pat knocked on the door.

They entered asking for the Second Secretary, Sean McGrath, with whom they had the appointment. The receptionist, a forty-year-old Australian with a thick accent. She asked them first to show their warrant cards which they did, then beckoned them to sit in a small anteroom. Shortly after a tall, dark-haired gentleman entered the room. "G'day I am Lionel Collingwood the Second Secretary, how can I help you two ladies?"

Pat and Jane stood up, shook hands with him as they introduced themselves and then returned to their seats.

Lionel Collingwood was in his mid-forties and had grown up in Melbourne in the state of Victoria. He had a middle-class background and gone to the university of Melbourne, which was local to him. He studied Civil Regulatory Litigation at the Parkville College. Once he qualified, he had applied for a temporary job in the Australian Civil Service and promotion came relatively quickly. The temporary job became permanent and morphed into the Diplomatic Service.

This was his first posting in a senior post, he had looked forward to visiting London and his family ancestry.

Pat took the lead and explained they were desperate to be in contact with a British national called Barbara Meagher, possibly renationalised after she married a Raymond Meagher. He had shares in an opal mine in the area of Coober Pedy, located in central South Australia. She was a possible witness and although she may not know it, she could have valuable information to solve four murders, with possible links to major international crime. She and or husband were in extreme danger.

"Ok Detectives you have our attention, how can the Australian High Commission help you protect some of our citizens?"

"We have tried and failed to find her on social media and by conventional channels. If the worst-case scenario plays out and she is murdered then the death toll will increase and the people responsible will get away with it. It was purely by chance that a kid, a trainspotter, recorded the murder on his drone. We know we are dealing with murder, before then we were treating the deaths as coincidence as we believe the murders were staged to look like accidents.

We know her former partner was involved in one of the worst nightmare criminal gangs in the north east, although she was totally innocent. in fact, we have reason to believe that her finding out about her partner's drug involvement was the cause for them to split up. So Sir, we need to know what she knows and to know it in a secure manner, as contact via normal channels could put her life in jeopardy. We also need to interview her in a secure way and ensure her and her husband are then protected until the arrests are made. Sir, in effect, we need your help."

"Wow, I have a meeting with the ambassador this afternoon, I think I will need to speak him first and see where we go. By the way are we talking about an internet conference call or a personal visit?"

"To be honest sir, events are travelling so fast, we haven't had a chance to think about it, but with that in mind an internet conference call would be the most practical but then a trip on the tax payer to the Australian outback would be the most desirable. If you could assist in a secure connection we really should plan on the call."

"Thank you, now I know what I am planning for, I think the best call would be via the Australian Federal Police and not the local force, mainly due their international drug experience."

"Sir, can we respectfully request extreme sensitivity with maximum security at all levels. May I remind you we are dealing with an international criminal organisation who are highly sophisticated, have no compunction in killing anyone they see as a threat and are good at making it look like an accident."

"Thank you. I will be careful, er just in case we need to be sure who we are talking to can we agree on a code word please?"

"Caesar, sir."

"Ok, Caesar it is, we shall speak later."

As if by magic the receptionist appeared and showed the two ladies out.

Pat and Jane left the Commission, walked back up to Holborn, taking the Northern Line to King's Cross. They were in time for the Four O'clock train back to Newcastle. They flopped down in the first-class seats.

Jane sighed, "Great, we will be home for seven, may even beat the rat race and more important we are in time for tea."

Once the train was on the move the Hostess came around taking the food and drink orders, Jane opted for the salmon and Pat had the chicken dinner.

"Pat, you do realize that since we classified this investigation top secret we have two other agencies and a country on the other side of the world involved, at what point does it become secret?. Do you think we should have just called it Confidential and post it in the paper?"

Pat laughed, "You have a point babes but then we are where we are."

"Are we off the clock now Pat?"

"Yes babes, why?"

"What you got planned for the weekend you tart?"

Pat laughed and the two friends chatted all the way back to Newcastle.

On arrival in Newcastle, they said their goodbyes and returned home.

The following morning the two detectives were discussing the previous day. They were amazed at what they had set into motion. Jane was lost in thought. Pat noticed and quizzed her, "Penny for your ....."

Jane returned to the room. "So we have the criminal gang element, the Oz contact and Andy being looked into. Kind of feel a little redundant at the moment."

"Yes that sums it up a bit but what is on your mind Jane?"

"Well, I don't want to doubt our friends in the Transport Police but it would be wrong if we looked into the timeline for Andy's death from the drone footage? Maybe we could find a direction or a CCTV image may have picked up a vehicle or even someone in the area."

"Ok Jane let's have a look see if the killer reveals an exit point."

They pulled out a road map of the area and looked at the station on an internet mapping service.

"We need to look around 30 minutes from the Durham station."

"And the station because?"

"Jane, think about it. That is Andy's work place and would have been under observation for some time, I think this was a semi planned, but an opportunistic attack. Therefore, we need to look at the regular daily parking, commuters will then need to eliminated and Andy's shift pattern needs to be compared to car parking patterns.

Looking at the map it is fairly clear that the south side it too full of people and CCTV. Although it would easy to mingle, I don't think he will be too careless to show his identity. That means the north side and all the public car parks with CCTV need to checked but I think it is going to be difficult.

We know that triggering a speed camera will bring on a punishment. You can bet vehicles will appear 100% legal and not reported stolen so they won't trigger any Automatic Number Plate Recognition cameras. No doubt the address will be legal but no one lives there.

The long stay car park and recreation ground CCTV need to be checked, as does the farm house and the domestic housing estate on the opposite side of the railway.

I think this is significant as we know the Carters will punish any unwanted police attention, he would have surveyed the area for options. So, he would know when the time was right to strike unobserved by us and the CCTV. No one could plan a points failure or could they?"

"Pat, is this really the work of a drugs gang hell bent on thuggery or is there something else at work that we haven't thought of yet?"

"Possible Jane but who else has the resources to plan an unplanned murder. It would have to be a full-time job. Andy was killed in the middle of the day in full sight, but away from everyone. Surveillance would mean travelling from a safe parking point unobserved to a point of contact to carry out the murder once he realised that Andy was accessible to be killed! Chilling thought. I think if the killer is going to be found by CCTV it is not going to be from a public camera, but they still need to checked, more likely it will be from a house or a door bell or even a drone.”

“I guess we are going out to recce the area and take note of what is what.” Pat nodded.

Just then the phone rang, “Hi is that DI Nottage? It is DS Mark Monroe from the British Transport Police Drugs Investigation Unit, we met yesterday.”

“Hi, yes Mark we were just talking about you and looking for CCTV targets.”

“Great. I am just letting you know that the post mortem report has come through, it is what we expected, Andy Reid died from Asphyxia as a result of being knock unconscious, caused by the blunt force trauma to the back of his head.”

“Mark, can you meet us at Durham station please, we can be there in forty minutes?”

“Ok.”

The two detectives left for Durham.

At the station they met up straight away with Mark and he showed them around the CCTV points. He had already retrieved the relevant sequence of film allowing one hour each side of the time of the murder. These were from the car park, the platform and other public areas. He told them that the initial viewing showed nothing unusual, all the traffic matches up with train scheduling, a small build up before the trains and large exodus of those leaving. He had identified regular commuters and staff but so far no one hanging around or acting suspicious.

“Ok thank you for your hard work, we greatly appreciate it. We identified there are three access points, a farm on one side, a nature park on the other and of course the station.”

Jane then added, “The long stay car park for the station and the nature park are covered by CCTV. One thing we know is they are CCTV aware and shy. To avoid any accidental images, they would have accessed the murder site probably from the farm. I don't think they disguised themselves as a member of staff, or at a guess a construction worker because the drone footage showed the assailant wearing black. There is also an additional site to consider as the further along the track there is a housing estate with a locked gate and easy access to the track.

So, we need to check along the two sites, the farm and the houses for privately owned CCTV, because unless we just happen across an eye witness, I think this is the only way we will get evidence. So young sir, let's go fishing, thank you for meeting us. How would you like to investigate the farm and we investigate the housing estate."

"Sure, nice to be involved."

They split up. First they drove slowly along the road and saw no houses with cameras facing out to the road. But then Pat noticed the bus stop. It wasn't outside the gate but it gave her an idea. "Jane let's go to the bus station and see if any of the passing buses caught anything." Pat nodded with a smile.

They drove to the bus station and spoke to the manager in charge, they found out that the buses hadn't used that route for a while and so were unable to help.

On the other hand, Mark texted them to meet back up at the railway station. This they did at the station coffee shop, where two lattes were waiting for them as they walked through the door. They could see that he was grinning from ear to ear. "Ok Mark what have got?"

"There has been a Triumph scrambler motorbike plaguing the farmer for about three weeks prior to Andy's murder and not since."

"What do you mean 'plaguing' the farmer?" Jane looked puzzled, so Mark continued.

"The bike was parked on the route to one of his fields, so he videoed it as he thought the rider might either be after one of his tractors or other bits of farm machinery. Agricultural crime is a nightmare or one of the trail bikers that blight the countryside riding over the fields, frightening the livestock and trashing the crops. It was only there for a few minutes; he only caught a partial registration number. I think we also have a partial description of the rider, but that doesn't help us much as the description is simply all in black, so boots, trousers and jacket and helmet are all in black. Another thing, as soon as the farmer approached him, he sped off. He didn't even say anything or even gesture he just sped off on the black scrambler."

"Finally a lead, can you forward the video footage to us please?"

"Already done ma'am and the farmer will contact me again should the biker reappear in real time."

"Please call me Pat when possible."

"Ok Pat, thanks, that is good thinking as we will need to eliminate him from our enquires if he is innocent."

CHAPTER 11

The following day Jane was hard at work looking into the sale of Triumphs.

"There are nine similar models with two main types of Scrambler, a 900cc in two designs and 1200cc that comes in four colours, red, Matt Khaki and black, and just black. We can narrow it down to two assuming we believe the colour description is correct and doesn't mistake the Matt Khaki for black as it appears in the shadows. We can also discount the red and the Special Edition as that appears in blue, reducing the figure even further.

Now we can identify the difference between the 900cc and the 1200cc, the front shock covering, the exhaust pipe and the type of seat. We can find that out by looking at the video footage.

I suggest we are looking at a black 900cc, the modern Scrambler, it is fifteen years in production. We have already eliminated the newer models on size and colour, so at a guess we are looking at probably about two thousand bikes nationally. We can reduce that number to regionally registered bikes, reducing it even further with the inclusion of characters from the number plate.

We know that the Carter Cartel keep a low police profile with anything that interacts with officialdom; the farm is a front for tax and I guess money laundering. So, we assume the bike is taxed and insured, no doubt to a dead drop address.

As for our chap, I think we are talking about somebody who is observant, knows how to stay in the shadows and obviously isn't afraid to dispatch anyone he's required to, knows how use the surroundings and good at keeping a low profile so blending in. I also suspect use of electronic surveillance to access computers, so they may be expert in hacking into computers in a way to remain undetected. I am guessing the chap might have military training and be able to ride bikes, drive cars, and possibly other vehicle types."

"Jane that is brilliant. Forward it to Iggy will you please. It might help them identify someone who fits that profile. While you do that, I need to update the chief."

With that she got up and took the short walk to the chief's office, the door was open so on the signal she walked in. Pat gave the chief the full brief. He listened intently making a few notes as she spoke.

Pat waited a while then asked the chief if there was a problem.

"Yes there is Pat, a big problem, can you explain this photograph?"

It showed her going into her daughter's house with Brian who was wearing a Local MC cut. Her immediate reaction was one of alarm.

"Sir who took this photograph?"

"I don't know, it was dropped off this morning, in a brown envelope, it is as we speak being examined by forensics."

"Sir it is a fake. Oh my God, my daughter! He knows where my daughter lives. Brian has nothing to with that biker gang and doesn't wear their colours. I would have noticed along with everyone else including Jane if he did. This picture can only have been taken last weekend when we had a barbecue with our friends and family at my daughter's!"

"Calm down Pat, we will get to the bottom of this, but it's fair to say we are running out of time as this is meant as a warning."

"Sir?" Pat looked puzzled.

"Pat think about it, this isn't a good photoshop. The thing to note is, it has been taken outside your daughter's. This means he knows you and knows how to get to you one way or another, in both your professional and family lives. I cannot ignore this and must flag it up to the boss.

There is no question in my mind about you, your competency or even integrity, you have my hundred percent support and confidence. I'm sure I speak for the top brass as well. So, how are we going to deal with this? We see you as the victim and we're going to treat them as Perverting the Course of Justice. In the meantime we are going to secretly keep low level observation on you and at your daughter's home.

I cleared you with Brian and that still stands but please keep an eye out when you out and about. This picture tells me that you are the right road to a successful prosecution. So stay on it and we will stay with you.

Just one thing, I suggest that you get CCTV installed discretely on your house if possible, not forgetting any device can be turned on you and is easily brought onto the internet. Be careful, don't use the internet at home or any devices until the case is done. Remember, he might even be able to use your phone against you so have a secret phase or conversation topic prior agreed on, only known to you and the other person, one for safe and one for danger.

Treat the outside internet as an enemy for the moment. It isn't an order, but just a little bit of advice for your own sake. You had better warn Jane, your fella and your daughter to be careful just for the time being. Ok we will keep you posted on events. Be careful and good luck."

Jane stood and left; this time quite disturbed. Once back at the office she saw her friend and colleague "Jane canteen, coffee now!" She didn't need telling twice as she saw the alarm in her friend's face.

They sat in the corner away from everyone else, Pat briefed her friend in a low voice. It soon dawned on Jane the full horror of the message and the impact it was going to have.

"I don't want to seem altruistic on my own survival but are we in any danger?"

"The boss thinks not, I merely think this is a warning, but whatever it is, our time for messing around is up. We need a result as soon as possible and that means the right person."

"Pat you will have to let Andy and Sophia know what is going on. It could be that everyone who turned up to the barbecue is a potential target, at least if they are for warned they start protecting themselves."

"Agreed, I will go round to speak to Andy. In the meantime can you work on what we have on the Triumph babes and try to find out if we have an owner to speak to."

Pat stopped short and returned back to her boss's office; luckily he was still there. "Sir how did he know we were onto him?"

"What do you mean DI Nottage?"

"Well sir, up until a couple of weeks ago this was just a cold case review of previous incidents, it was only Andy Reid's murder when we went hot! Brian has only been to my daughter's home once and that was two weeks ago. So how did he know to put us on surveillance back then? How does he know we are closing in, we only brought in other agencies this week? Granted the other two just happened to be working on the same case but not together. So as unthinkable as it is, has the Carter family got intelligence on what is going on in this station."

"You do realise what you suggesting don't you DI Nottage?"

"Yes sir, there is an intelligence leak in this department, from someone I would trust without hesitation, to a criminal gang, I don't know who it is or how it has happened but this picture makes me the target."

"Ok, the starting point is the Independent Police Complaints Commission (IPCC). I need you to make a statement now. For your safety discuss it with nobody except the IPCC and follow their direction.

Meanwhile, continue with your investigation and be careful, I don't want to lose you, you're a good detective."

"Thanks boss."

Pat returned to her office. "Jane, I have changed my mind. Let's go."

Once they were sat in the car Pat signalled to Jane to keep quiet. They drove to the police Forensic Pathology department where they went for a walk in the park opposite.

"Pat, what is with this cloak and dagger stuff?"

"We are under surveillance from the Carter family and I think there is somebody playing for the other side. That picture was taken at the barbecue before the case went hot. So we have been spied on from an early stage without knowing it. We need to tread carefully, you are the only one I can trust, I don't know if my home or car is bugged, I have switched off the GPS on my mobile, okay?"

"Yes Pat, I have CCTV on the house so I will check the footage."

In the pathology lab they managed to speak to Andrew to warn him about the surveillance. As he was rushed, he agreed to meet Pat at her home after work. By now it was the end of the shift for the two so they left for home.

Later that evening Sophia and Andrew turned up. Pat offered and gave them a hot drink and asked if they had eaten. They hadn't so she ordered pizza.

"Andy, Sophia thank you for coming round. I need your help but I need to keep it from Brian because I don't want to him in a difficult situation. I will talk to him to tomorrow but only tell him what I want him to know. Can I ask for your confidence?"

They both agreed. First she showed them the photograph. Andy asked if he could take a picture of it. Pat agreed. They were shocked and even Sophia took on a serious look.

"The cold case I was on has turned hot and there is someone on the inside with links to the Carter family." Andy turned white.

"Pat if that is true then we are in serious shit those bastards don't mess around."

"Andy, do you know a security specialist who is discrete?"

"What do you need doing?"

"I need a full sweep for electronic surveillance both car and home and that includes my devices, I need to know if I am being targeted for a hit. As the other victims all reported being followed before they met with an accident. Oh, I also need to find out if a black Triumph 900 scrambler has been nicked or trafficked or for sale on the quiet, as it is known that the assailant was riding one."

"Is there a registration number?"

"Only partial, we can see there is a 'K' and a 'S' in it. We know it will be legit as they don't like to draw attention to themselves, but might be stolen and not reported."

"I will put the word out. There is a biker network that keeps an eye on this kind of thing, but really bikes being stolen can be a fatal activity if the Local MC find out, there is a zero tolerance for that sort of thing. Mind you, they are going to be seriously pissed off when they see the fake picture of Brian wearing a cut in their colours; not with Brian, but the person who produced the picture as they know Brian will never wear or disrespect them like that. Please Pat, for his own sake, warn him and show him the picture as if they speak to him, they will think he is taking the piss and that wouldn't be good for anyone."

The knock on the door was like sounding the dinner gong and soon they were tucking into their pizzas. They carried on talking after they had finished.

As they discussing options, Andrew's phone pinged announcing a new text. He looked at Pat, "Tomorrow night is Friday, is Brian coming round?" She nodded like a guilty school girl. He shook his head to say no he isn't, "Same time tomorrow we will be around with a friend and he will give you what you want, no questions asked, you are a private citizen and no police questions. If he is spooked he will just walk, can you do that?"

"Yes Andy I agree."

"Brian will know the chap and it will be awkward for everyone."

"Yes what about you?"

"We, like Brian are well known and can be trusted, you can't and you also represent everything they want to avoid. It will put Brian in a bad place especially if you two split up later on."

"Ok fair enough Andy and thank you for your help. Please remember I am grateful and will pay the going rate and will need a receipt, NO FAVOURS at a later date to be called upon because that is illegal, I will be flagging this up with my boss. I am desperate and need to know what the hell is going on, no colours to be worn if I am being photographed without my permission. I don't want any photo's sent to my boss like earlier."

Then in tandem both Andy and Sophia got up, Sophia was disturbed by the evening conversation and for once she had lost her glitz and glamour which she normally brought into the room.

In the morning Pat and Jane were summoned to the chief's office where the IPCC officers were waiting to see them. They explained they were aware of Pat's allegations and are looking into it.

Pat and Jane wrote their statements of their actives and the timeline. This took most of the morning.

In the afternoon after the two had come back from the canteen Jane checked her emails and saw there was one from the Australian High Commission.

She opened the email, read it and said to Pat, "The Federal Police have found former Barbara Henshall, now Barbara Meagher and her husband Raymond. They have completed an identity check to ensure they had the correct person.

She confirmed they had a secret relationship together which they were keen to keep away from the church, and the visit to Saffron Walden, where she and Carl had had an argument, later splitting up.

Mainly he wanted to get married but she had just met Raymond. She knew Carl was involved in drugs and was refusing to quit. This came to a head when he was arrested. She decided then to develop her relationship with Raymond.

She was unaware of any contacts.

She also added that Carl had found a large amount of cash, she thinks it was about twenty thousand pounds Sterling, in a tin in a hole in the bedroom wall. There was also a memory stick, some blank passports and birth certificates. They didn't access the memory stick as they didn't own a computer and still doesn't."

Pat listened intently to her friend and replied, "Oh that was disappointingly unexpected, but then at least they weren't fleeing for safety reasons and that's a bonus; but now we need to find out what happened to that memory stick and the documents they found. I guess Carl would have passed them onto the Carter family for their illegal use and we know that he came into money to pay off a huge amount of debt. We need to know he if gave them the stick as well as the blank documents. Just a thought, perhaps he didn't give them the memory stick thinking it wasn't valuable to them.

So that money isn't the Carters, it is the wrong area anyway. It is possible he might have sold them the false documents and kept the memory stick. But the Carters are still in the frame for his murder, because we know he could no longer sell drugs openly and they wouldn't take kindly to that."

"Ok, so we still have a motive and a murder and a suspect. What we still need is evidence, we have a dodgy bit of drone footage but nothing substantial." Jane paused for a thought and then smiled, "Anyone would think it was JFK that was killed and filmed from the Grassy knoll."

"Nicely put Jane but not really helpful. You can forward the email to Iggy with a request to find out if the Carters have the memory stick and if possible the alleged documents. I am pretty sure Carl kept the money as it isn't the Carters and besides there is no trace of it."

"Boss, who can afford to lose twenty grand and not report it missing? And Carl wasn't discrete when he paid of his debts, raising a big red flag drawing attention to himself and his mates."

"Jane you are supposed to be helping, not by shifting our investigation to Essex."

"We need to speak to colleagues down south to see if they are aware of anything. We can get Iggy to do that, I think I need to have a chat with him. Are we any closer to finding that bike?"

"No boss, I am still crunching the numbers. At the moment we are looking at about three hundred and fifty bikes needing to be checked out, that is assuming the offender's bike is registered in the north east. There are currently no bikes reported stolen that fit the criteria."

"Jane, I think I might be able to see if Andrew can help us out on that. I know it is unorthodox, but that is between you and me and no one else including Brian, ok?" Jane nodded, "Okay are we on the same page?"

"Yes boss."

"Let's make it clear for the record, nothing illegal is going here and no deals are being offered or made, other than a little help from the biking community."

"Pat it is me Jane, I trust you with my daughter and my job."

"I just don't want to get Brian involved. It might make things awkward for him later. I don't want anyone thinking I am breaking the law."

Just then, as if by magic, both DI Jamie Ingólfsdóttir and his DS, Alma Doyle arrived in the office.

"Talk of the Devil," Jane muttered.

"We thought we should pop round as there seemed to a lot emails flying about at the moment. Given your circumstances I think thought we should drop in for a chat."

"Please join us, did you see the email from Australia?"

"Yes, it made interesting reading. Certainly from our side, my agent is aware of Carl Mills, but never met him. He confirmed that there was disappointment when Carl pulled out due to the railway issues, they even offered him work as an enforcer. There was no retribution intended towards him or the Christian group, including from Australia when he stopped. Also the presence of blank documents, the passports and birth certificates are still available for use. But there is no talk of a memory stick. Overall, there is a drug involvement from the Carter family and their villainy."

"Great it goes from bad to worse, thank you James and Alma and your agent you have done me a great service of eliminating a possible suspect. The damage to the police and the public would be inconsiderable if we had pursued this avenue and wasted resources plus, the Carter family would consider themselves untouchable. But bugger! That puts us right back to square one."

"Sorry to be the bearer of bad news, really you don't know how bad we feel about it, I would have loved to have pinned it on the Carters, four murders would see them rot in gaol for ever and even been able to take down the whole operation just like Pablo Escobar, the Drugs Barron from Colombia," Alma continued, "At least you still have the lead from the British Transport Police". They bid their goodbyes and left the room.

"Only a victim of crime with no motive and no suspect. Let's hope the motorcycle lead does work for us because that is all we have now."

After they left, Pat called around to see the chief to explain that her case has been completely destroyed, the only lead was now the motorbike. There was the threat against her family and an investigation that was potentially going to destroy morale in the department. Not bad for an afternoon's work.

John knew Pat well and thought deeply into what she had just summed up to him. So, he told her to go home get drunk and to return on the Monday with a fresh idea.

Pat returned to the office. "Thanks Jane an hour ago we had a case now we are clutching at straws, sod it, let's go home our time is done here."

The two detectives, heads held low, took the walk of defeat down to the car park. They felt totally defeated, made worse by the previous high of nearly solving the case.

"So who is it that has us under surveillance then?" Jane asked, finally breaking the silence by the cars.

"Somebody has dealt us into a game and not given us the courtesy of letting us know we are playing.

Jane I honestly don't know but I think we should try and find out as a matter of priority, because they have made us targets and more than that, my family is in the firing line. Jane, go home get drunk and come in tomorrow with ideas. It is me and you and no one else. That is all I trust; I don't even trust the boss at the moment."

"You suspect DCI Haydon as being bent? You know he has a massive crush on you ever since ever…."

"No, no, no, you misunderstand, I believe one hundred percent he is honest and straight. Yes, I know he has a crush on me and if he wasn't married, then who knows flights of fancy. But sadly, the fact is it's his honesty, that's the problem."

"Why is that a problem?"

"He is doing his job correctly, by the book and keeping the high-ups appraised of the situation but somebody upstairs isn't playing fair and I intend to find out who that bastard is. Whoever it was, they put the mark on me and my family and I intend to repay the favour within the law."

"That's my girl, two minutes ago doom and gloom and now she's Henry Cooper."

"See you in the morning Jane."

*　　*　　*　　*　　*

Later that evening Andrew arrived with his colleague and as requested no colours were worn. Pat made them a hot drink before they sat down and chatted.

"This is Charlie Runyon a tech expert."

"Hi Charlie, I am Pat and I need your help, I think I am under surveillance and need to know what is safe."

"Andy told me about you Pat, I have a background in electronics to degree level, ten years in the army and now I work privately but not exclusively for anyone. My fees are £200 for a house and car sweep and £350 for a computer and device search and that doesn't include VAT. That only applies if a receipt is required."

"With a receipt please."

"Okay, no problem it's your money and it is still cash."

He pulled out two laptops from a large rucksack he had brought in and plugged Pat's laptop into one and her phone into the other. "It will take an hour for the program to run through and complete a full forensic examination on the device. This will detect any intrusion from kids messing around to a serious breach. Now, in the meantime, let's sweep for bugs. There are two types active and passive, active are more traditional and last as long as there is a power source." He pulled out an antenna with a handset, switched it on, waved it over the walls and carpets and around the room. Everywhere there were objects they were scanned. Charlie went upstairs and swept the rooms and the stairs and once complete he picked out another handset and this time he asked Pat to read from any book until he had done the second sweep.

Once completed he sat down, looked at the computer and announced it was running through the program.

"Why did you sweep twice and had me read the second time?"

"First time, I was looking for a transmitter and the second time for a Passive cavity resonator. Any kid can make one from a video on the internet, they were invented by the Russians and who gave one to the Americans in the Embassy hidden inside a wood plaque and would listen to the ambassador chatting away. A British officer tuning into a Russian frequency heard his boss over the airwaves, in the US Embassy. It was eventually discovered. When Gary Powers was shot down in his U2 and the Russians were claiming outrage in the UN, they were shut up by showing that their device had been discovered. But as the name suggests, they only work by amplifying the voice into a different frequency, they have no power source and are difficult to detect. The modern ones are the size of a small pea and even find their way into card passes."

"So is my house clean?"

"Yes, but I still need to check your car, can I have your keys please?"

She handed them over and he went out and half an hour later he returned, saying, "Yes your car is clean."

Just then his two computers bleeped into life, Charlie announced, "Your computer is clean but your mobile phone has been turned into a tracker."

"But I switched it off." Pat protested.

"Ok, here are today's locational pings." He showed her.

"My God, you are right."

"That's the bad news but the good news is it was a basic program and easily dealt with. I have a Pac Man program that will turn it against the stalker for an extra £100 and for an extra £200 for video surveillance around your property. How do you feel about that?"

"Done, do it. I will transfer a grand over to your bank account."

Half an hour later he announced that it was set up. He handed over the access code to Pat and promised he would monitor them from home. While this was happening, there was a knock on the door. It was Sophia, her glitz had returned to her and she looked a lot better. "Hi babes," she proclaimed as she came prancing into the house, "just come to pick up my honey husband, hi Charlie how are you?"

He smiled and gave her a kiss and a hug. "Hi there babes, just doing a bit of business nothing more." After the money was transferred over to his account he left.

"Andy, the bike is now the only lead we have, my case came crashing down on me when the drugs family were cleared from involvement, so can you help me please? I am desperate."

"I can ask but can't promise, leave it with me and I will see what I can do, but it might take a while."

"I will take that, thanks."

Then Pat and Sophia sat and chatted, on Sophia's insistence.

CHAPTER 12

The following morning was Saturday, Pat texted Brian as soon as she was awake. 'Please come around asap babes, love you xxx.' She thought she had better put that in just in case he thought she had fallen out with him, which she surely hadn't.

He replied almost immediately to say he was on his way around. It wasn't long before he arrived on his bike. As she heard it pull up outside, Pat went into school girl mode as she rushed to the door to let him in.

By the time Brian had got to the door he had removed his helmet and gloves to find the door flung open and Pat wrapped herself around him. "I take it you are glad to see me then!'

"Oh babes you have no idea, come in, we have lots to talk about."

He did as he was beckoned and the two love birds went into the kitchen. While Pat prepared the first coffee of the day, Brian dropped his bike gear on the floor and took off the jacket and layers he was wearing.

"So what is happening darling?" Brian was desperate to know. She showed him the picture, it took him a few minutes to digest the implications and meaning of the photograph.

"This is a death warrant," he admitted, "for both of us and possibly your daughter." Pat was shocked, she was expecting a reaction but not quite as strong.

"Well I am guessing this will mean you will be sacked at work for associating with a bike club and if the Local MC see someone wearing their colours that are not entitled to do so, they won't take kindly to it."

"Work have been sorted," Pat replied, "they can see it is a poor fake. I managed to get Andy to mediate between us and the Local MC. They have helped ensure a minimal breach of security and surveillance for us and you are in the clear. Last night Charlie Runyon a tech expert came around and checked the house and my tech gear. The only device that was hacked was my phone and Charlie has but a Pac-Man program on it."

"If Charlie is on it, great, he is a good man and will get it sorted, but he is in an MC, how did you get him and why didn't you let me sort it?"

"Andy helped and frankly darling, I wanted to say with a clear conscience that you had nothing to do with it. I even paid full price and got a receipt. I have to be seen to be honest and above board and no chance of misunderstanding of any criminality. I will be declaring this job when I get to work on Monday.

But at the moment I don't trust anyone at work other than Jane and that is only because we go back to before we started this job, friends for life. Mainly, because the gang we had in our sights has been cleared which means someone at work is either following us or is in league with someone. The point is, a lot of the victims on the case are all reporting being followed prior to being murdered, so I needed an independent verification before I went anywhere or spoke to anyone in case I alerted them to my thoughts. Apparently the Pac-Man program Charlie uses turns the efforts of the stalker into the stalked and I get a clue into what is happening."

"Are we good babes?"

"Yes, rock solid babes," Pat reassured him.

"Ok, what about your daughter?"

"She is aware and getting all security cameras set up, don't worry we'll get the bastard and the law will deal with whoever it is."

Pat then dragged Brian back to her bedroom as she had a full night to catch up on.

Later that day they emerged dressed, ready for the world and went out for a ride through the Kielder Forest. It was a good distraction for Pat from work and the warm day made it bearable. That evening they went to the pub and met up with Andy and Sophia. They were all having a pleasant time when a six-foot-tall chap wearing a cut and the badges. On his back were a semicircular patch with the name 'Local MC'. Noticeable was also the badge saying 'Prospect' underneath. He had a serious look about him. The two chaps new that there was trouble and they were going to have to tread carefully.

"Evening gentleman, you're invited to a club meeting." Brain and Andrew both looked at each other, they knew to refuse would be unwise. Sophia got hold of Pat's hand a little out of nerves and little to stop Pat from interfering. The two dutifully rose and followed the Prospect. Sophia whispered into Pat's ear, "Prospects, if given a mission have to succeed in it regardless but let's be on the safe side, keep calm and be ready to leave quickly."

The three bikers walked into the anteroom where the full patch members were all sat around a table.

"Brian, Andy sit." They both did as they were told. The person speaking was six foot and broad in shoulders, covered in tattoos and a deep red beard. On the front of his cut was the title badge 'Sgt at Arms'. He thought the picture of Brian wearing a Local MC cut on to the table.

"Lads, things are going on here that we don't like and I am not happy. Why would we have this picture posted to us?"

"Lads, you have known me well for a long time. I have a healthy respect for the patch and would never disrespect it. You have all asked to sponsor me as a Prospect and I have always insisted that I maintain my independence, you have all had the good grace to respect that. So, you know that I am not a wannabe and you all call on me without hesitation to help the club. This is a very bad photoshop with the aim to cause trouble for me and my old lady. It was posted to her at work with intention of getting her the sack and had they done a better job they might have succeeded. What I know is, there is a murderer posing as an honest biker, that is about as much as I know."

"Andy, what do you know?"

"You know me and you all know where I work and with whom. Brian is right. I know a little bit more because his old lady needed to have a barrier between the club, Brian and her work. She asked for a security sweep which I asked Charlie to do the honours, which he did last night. We can all agree he is one of the best in the area. As you know me, I am independent and trustworthy. We were going to ask the club for help locating the bike a Triumph 900 Sapphire black scrambler with K and 5 in the number plate. We think it might be legally on the road as the police haven't had reports of a bike matching that description reported stolen. There have been four murders so far and this picture indicates that Brian and his old lady and her daughter's family are the next targets. This picture was taken at a family event that I also attended. So, the implications are that Sophia and I are also targets. Also by further association he has no respect for the club, which I guess is why we are sat here in front of the man. This is a warning from a murderer and we can best support the biking community by removing him before he drags us down. The police, I am told are releasing the video evidence as the start a public manhunt for a church going Station Master. The damage to all bikers will be immense. We don't want that, do we?"

"So what do you think they want from us?"

"To assist in locating the rogue using the bike. If we can, it would be better PR than a hundred toy runs."

"Thank you Andy, enjoy your evening." The two took the hint and left the room to return to the table to see two very relieved ladies.

"Don't worry both the blokes said in unison they are thinking about helping with locating the bike."

"Well, it is true then," the three looked at Pat with wonderment as she continued, "the best way to get a message to the whole universe it to mark it secret and tell those who know, not to tell anyone."

There was an uneasy laugh. "When this is over I can't see me being allowed to continue. At best it will means sacking, at worst it will mean prison time."

"You're joking, right?" Sophia looked alarmed.

"No, no joke, if this goes tits up then I am in the firing line without a friend."

With that sobering thought, Andrew ordered a round of drinks at the bar. The Sgt at Arms walked over and stood next to him. "We will see what we can do for you," and walked away. The encounter was so brief that no one noticed it. So when Andrew returned he was able to update them. It came as a bit of relief for them to hear the news.

"What will they do?" Pat asked.

"They will speak to all the right people in the right way."

"But we do that."

"Yes but they know you need a warrant and you have rules of behaviour whereas the club isn't bound by those rules."

"Christ, I didn't hear that Andrew and you certainly didn't say it," Pat protested.

It wasn't long before last orders and the friends split to go their own ways.

Pat was driving the car and turned to Brian. "If the job be damned will you still be around?"

"Silly question babes, I am in as long you want me around. Pat I sought you out because I wanted to be with you. I am not a stalker, so if you say enough is enough, I will be upset but I will abide by it. You are, so far in my life, the best thing ever to happen and I am truly batting above my limit.

But here's the thing Pat, you are a copper, an honest one, not one of those bent bastards that try to fit people up to the crimes for the sake of a result. We need honest police more than ever in these troubled times.

As I see it, you haven't broken any law, you have been trying to protect your friends and family and can even put your hand on your heart and say neither you or I have asked the Local MC for help, because we haven't. Andrew has, because he isn't bound by the same rules as you and me by proxy.

Look I know you and Jane are close, so that gives you an ally at work. But then let's face it, only a dishonest copper would be going on without a conscience."

"Thanks Brian, that's just what I needed to you say, you're a love."

By now they had arrived back home. Pat said, "I am driving round the block just to check out I am not being followed." She couldn't see anyone following or acting strange. So after parking on the driveway, she gave everywhere a second look before she would let Brian alight from the car and go into the house.

Once inside she went straight to the computer and checked the monitors on fast forward to see if there was anything suspicious. Brain let her get on with it as he realised this was going to be the new Pat until the killer was apprehended. He went into the kitchen, made a hot drink for both them and waited for her to settle down.

"Sorry darling but I had to check," she eventually said.

"Don't worry babes, I get it."

She asked him to give her a cuddle and that was it for a while, as it made her feel safe enough to retire to the bedroom.

The following day Pat was unable to settle. She was sat by the live cameras watching them in case there was something suspicious. There was a car parked for a little more than ten minutes and she was just going out to challenge them when the neighbour's children ran out and got into their friend's car.

She was relieved to be able to stand down as she felt just a little bit foolish, but Brian was there and it helped her feel safe or safe as can be. "Do you want me to stay with you until you arrest the bastard that put you in the cross hairs?"

"Would you, please, I would feel so much safer, than being on my own. I was going to ask my daughter but I would prefer you and I think so would she."

"Settled, darling, I think that discretion is better part of safety. It is important not to show any major changes as it will alert him that you are making changes. But then we can look at tweaking your security. I am sure that Charlie did his job well but get your colleagues from Crime Prevention to do give you a few extra hints. It is important you have these just so that you can trust coming home. Luckily, I'm currently on days so I can stay on those again until the matter is resolved. Perhaps it might be useful for Charlie to get involved with your daughter as well and give her some advice."

"Yes, not bad idea," Pat agreed as they settled in for the night.

Monday morning came and at work, Pat kept her word by keeping things away from the top brass. She provided a very basic brief of the plan to the chief, who wisely didn't push it as he suspected the same. That problem was a job for the Independent Office for Police Conduct to deal with. Pat didn't inform the chief about the help from the Local MC, she felt he would frown upon it.

Now she had bigger problems. She had to restart her case from scratch and to do that she needed to chat with Jane. But first she arranged with the Crime Prevention Unit to assess her and her daughter's homes for weakness.

"Come on Jane, let's get out of here, I don't trust anyone at the moment lets go to Baristas coffee shop." So the two ladies left for somewhere more private.

As they went Jane asked, "What's going on with the boss?"

"What do you mean?"

"You are falling to bits your as jittery as Hell. You have shut the station out, what is going on?"

"Jane I can't trust anyone. I have asked Brian to move in, not because I want him but because every sound sends me to the window checking out what is going on. I am the target and so is my daughter. Yesterday I nearly arrested two kids for getting in a car. I can't speak to the boss as I know one of them is bent, I feel trapped."

"Pat, I love you to bits but is this, this isn't right. This isn't you. I need you to get this under control. The only way we stop it is to find the bastards that are doing this to you and me. We need to do it fast now. We have four victims and now we have been added to list, as well as the good Christians.

Pat I need you at your best. Now!"

It was now that Jane's phone pinged. She looked at it. "The Gov wants to know what is going on?"

"Tell the bent bastard to fuck off." Pat was angry because of what she was becoming.

"John isn't bent Pat and you know it, this goes much higher than him, I don't know where but IOPC are on the case. They will find out how it is. Let them do their job, let us do our job.

Jane do you think I should go on the sick or resign?"

"NO FUCKING WAY BITCH, you got me up here, you promised you would stick by me keep it. Pat I am a bag of nerves.

We are amazing detectives on our own but together we are team and fucking brilliant. Why do think they have kept us together for all this time? Trust me as cute as your ass is, it ain't that good and we know that both you and John had a thing for each other. You said yourself, 'If he wasn't married' and he doesn't want to upset you which is why I know he won't knowingly betray you. It is also one of the reasons why we are kept together. So, get your bony ass shit together!"

"Wow Jane, that's told me!"

"Pat I don't do self-pity and babes, boss, bestie you need a slap and I am the only to get away with doing it for a reason."

They were now approaching the Baristas coffee shop and as they went in, Pat looked at Jane puzzled.

"And that is?"

"You know I am right, coffee?" Jane asked.

"Latte please."

"Pat, grab the table." Pat claimed the table by sitting down and she was shortly joined by Jane, just waiting for the order.

"By the way there is also a bacon butty on its way, my treat."

"Thanks babes, you're a love." After a few minutes the waitress brought over two coffees and a tea and two bacon butties. Pat turned to Jane "Who's the tea for?"

"John! And we have enough time to scoff these butties without sharing." came the reply.

It wasn't long before as predicted, Chief Inspector John Haydon arrived. "Ah, ladies, cleaned out the bacon butties I see, but at least there's a brew. Thanks." He poured out his tea and added the milk. "Now ladies, nice to meet you here, how are things Pat?"

"Sir?"

"Your briefing this morning was a load of crap and reports are shit…… I am guessing that the case is affecting you more than what you care to admit."

"Sir, what do you base that on?"

"The fact that a really rubbish doctored photograph was delivered and the Crime Prevention asked me to confirm your address which means you are worried enough to have your home security upgraded. Your case fell apart. Each of these are bad enough on their own but to have them both together would affect even the best of us and you believe one the Chiefs isn't playing fair. Is that a fair summation?"

"Yes sir."

"IOPC are looking into your fears and you have been interviewed already, I have supported it. So I and the chain of command will be looked into. I have nothing to hide, the rest will have to look to themselves. If they are honest they won't have anything to worry about. I have told them I will support you no matter what, but Jane is your friend, if you prefer, she can take the lead to help you, by taking some of the pressure off you. Besides it will do her a world of good stepping up for her promotion after this case."

"No way are you promoting me sir, I am happy being a sergeant and I told you both, leave me out of this. I will support Pat to the ends of earth but sir if she goes I will go, pension be damned."

He was taken a little aback with this so he softened his tone a little bit. "Ok, may be a bit hard but you have my full confidence both of you. Your original theory was a sound one based on the evidence in front of you, if I was given that evidence I would have come to the same conclusion, one hundred percent. The important thing is, we are not on course for a miscarriage of justice despite the Carters being guilty of lot more, yet to be proved. Nobody deserves to be fitted up."

"But sir, I have been on this case for six months and I am back to square one, now with a target on my back. One which we know the others have had and sir, I am scared not for me sir but my daughter."

"Ok, would it help if you go over and see your daughter and sort out any issues on our time. You take Jane, she can keep an eye out on you.

Just stay away from the office for today. Chat girlfriend and mother daughter talk but not work and come back tomorrow with a plan. Talk to me and I will pass on the minimal to keep the high-ups off our backs, ok? I need you to solve this case, four murders and you and God knows who else are targets. I want that bastard behind bars and not on my patch, nice tea."

With that John got up, and with a wink to Pat, walked back to the cop shop.

"Looks like we have a free day, but let's do what he says and have a rethink over daytime TV at Michelle's."

It wasn't long before they both arrived in their own cars at Pat's daughter's home.

"Mum, Jane, what are you doing here?"

"We've been given leave just to come over and check you're safe."

"Yer, your mate Charlie came around, scanned the place and stuff, we were clean and like for you he set up the cameras." She showed them off to her guests.

Jane asked, "Pat do you still have that picture with you?"

"Yes, why?"

"Come on, let's go outside and see where it was taken from."

So the three went outside. Jane held up the picture and positioned Pat and Michelle in the same positions as in the photograph. Then after a few minutes saw it was only a couple of parking spaces away.

"Ok Jane, you have found out where the pictures were taken from!"

Jane turned to Michelle, "Darling just check that you can see me on your monitors."

Michelle disappeared and reemerged moments later to confirm that indeed she could see Jane on the monitor.

"Good, now see if any neighbours overlooking this spot have CCTV or one of the newfangled door cam thingies."

It didn't take long as a quick knock on the door and a flash of their warrant card soon yielded results. One house had a security cam. It only showed the front half of a white car which arrived a minute after Pat and Brian in their car and left immediately afterwards. Although only the bonnet showed while parked, when it moved off, they could see in fact it was a small car-derived van. As the image was looking out of a window, it only captured the side of the vehicle and not the number plate.

"Pat, download the footage onto your computer and can we print off an image?" Jane was on a roll.

"Er, Michelle can we?"

"Yes mum of course." The three thanked the owner and returned their memory card.

Once back in Michelle's home, Jane said, "Right Pat, we know that he didn't just randomly turn up, so he must have followed you from your home or how else would he know to be here. Now at the time we didn't know what we were looking for but now we do. But here is the thing we know the route you took, can trace it on the map and draw a timeline. Then we map all the public and shop CCTV on the route and we can use your car as a marker and then we only have to look a few minutes after for a white van and we can keep going through all the different footage till we get a viable image of the driver and number plate."

"The Chief was right, we needed to come here to get ourselves back on track, hey Jane?"

"Yes, so if Michelle is ok with it, first we take a print of your route on the street map. Then we go through 'Satellite Maps UK' and spot all the street CCTV on the route and mark them on the map. There's also shop webcams. We might have to go around the shops but more importantly, we have a way back into the case and finding your stalker."

"Sometimes, but only sometimes, it is a pleasure to know you Jane."

"Bugger that, put the kettle on, I think we have earned a brew, don't you Michelle?"

"Ok, Jane, looks like I am making every one a brew." She didn't mind because she had seen her mother go from really upset and miserable to reinvigorated in the case.

Meanwhile Pat followed the plan, printing off the street plan and then following the time line of her journey from her home to her daughter's, marking it out with a fluorescent pen. Using the street view she drove slowly virtually along the route looking for CCTV and traffic cams for further scrutiny. This was laborious and painful but she had to stick with it as it was her only hope. She also marked out possible sites where privately owned camera's might be sited.

"Jane, as you said, we can go tomorrow and we can drive along the route for confirmation even call into the shops to see if they might have video evidence. So it is going to be a bitch of a day. But the real bitch is going to be trying to work out where the bastard went to afterwards because we just don't know the route and he could have gone anywhere."

"See Pat, it is all part of the plan of life just as one door slams in your face another opportunity disappears."

"Yes and how did John find out where we were having our bacon butties, eh Judas?"

"Boss, he texted. I can't ignore a direct order, so I had to reply."

"Phone now, hand it over now."

She saw a text that basically said *'Pat is having a meltdown currently at the Baristas coffee shop. please help.'* and the reply *'on my way.'*

"Ok snitch I forgive you,"

"Look no matter what boss, it was the right thing to do and you said it yourself he wouldn't shit on you as he fancies you too much to do that. So yes, I took a chance and yes, he chose to call around and let's face it babes, we are closer than ever to finding our villain."

CHAPTER 13

The following day, Pat went to update John.

"So what happened yesterday Pat?"

"Temporary loss of direction sir, plus the knowledge, me and my family are being targeted. Thanks to you, I was able to regain the initiative. We are looking for a white van. I will have a better idea when we have checked the CCTV footage.

Yes sir, a white van. There is a good chance it was the one seen in the Joyce Grey murder up at High Force. We don't have a registration number, but I am hoping that will change. This guy hasn't made to many mistakes. It is why we are here wondering what happened and why."

"Do you need any help?"

"We could use a DC or a PC sir to help with the CCTV footage, we have twenty cameras to check on the route."

"The route?"

"Yes sir, the one mistake this guy has made is posting this photograph to us, I guess he thought I would be discredited and thrown off the case but in fact it pinpoints a known point that could only be arrived at by following me. I know the route and the time. I now know the vehicle because a neighbour had security CCTV hidden. I know what I am looking for and I will find the bastard. Sir, I still want to know how he found out I was on to him and how he knew to target me, this investigation hasn't been made public."

"Pat, yesterday you had me worried, I wasn't surprised: but you stood up to your challenges and turned them into a strength, well done and respect for that."

"Yes sir, the hunted is definitely the hunter." With that Pat got up and left the room.

Pat and Jane were discussing the logistics of the CCTV review when a young lad turned up. "Ma'am, DC Ben Gough. I have been asked by the Gov to come over and give you some help with your CCTV search for a car."

"Well you are welcome, pull up a pew, young Ben. Have you had a brew yet?"

"No ma'am," he smarty replied.

"Great, so two lattes with sugar and whatever you are having." She handed over a crisp £10 note.

"OK, back in five," said Ben as he left the office. He returned promptly with the drinks and sat down. Pat began the briefing.

She showed him the picture of her silver Beetle and another with the white van. She also showed him the route with the CCTV camera positions and the time of the journey, both arrival at Hazlerigg and departure at Westerhope.

"The silver Beetle is mine with the reg and the white car-van is your target vehicle. I need its registration number and identity of all the occupants if possible. The hard part is the trying to work out where he went afterwards, which I guess would be easy with a registration number, any questions?"

"No ma'am, it the usual drill and not a problem."

Ben was still in his early twenties and hasn't had much life experience. He was a high achiever and on leaving school went straight to university to study Computer Science. He had achieved a 2:1 with honours and then joined the police force as a detective. He had been in post for six months and was starting to be pigeon-holed for computer work. His main role was as a technology analyst which was ok with him, as he didn't have to deal with the public, remaining in the background but still be a crucial part of the team.

He knew that this task was going to be laborious, but he was prepared for that and slowly got to grips with the job in hand.

"Do you need anything to help Ben?"

"Some choccy biccies wouldn't go amiss," he rather cheekily replied to Jane's request.

"Oo, you'll go far with that cheek." The two ladies left the office going to the car park.

"Where's your car Jane?" a puzzled Pat enquired.

"Oh, I got a new one over the weekend. It is the black Captur over there."

"Even better," Pat remarked, "the stalker knows my car but hopefully not yours, so can you drive?"

"That's decent of you, but of course."

The two drove to the starting point which was Pat's home. It would normally take ten minutes to drive the five miles to Hazlerigg. The first camera was the Community Centre camera.

They pulled into the car park and walked into the centre. The caretaker was cleaning the hallway when he looked up to see the two detectives standing there. After the preliminary introduction, they showed him their warrant card and then asked if the CCTV was switched on. He agreed to show them it as it was operational on the Saturday two weeks previous. He scrolled forward to 3pm and quickly found Pat's car.

They studied the footage for the next few minutes. When they saw the white car-van the quality wasn't the best as it was angled to the car park and not on the road. He agreed to forward the section of film to the Jane's police email.

The next stop was a set of shops. Once again there was nothing other than to confirm the white van was still following Pat but it could have been any other van as far as the courts were concerned. Jane had it forwarded to her work's email just for continuation of evidence.

They were now on the main carriageway. "Well, we know that we can pull the bus video footage on this route if we need it."

"What do you mean 'IF'? Jane I think we will. This case is getting frustrating. The number of resources we have had and we are nowhere near finding out a motive or a culprit and when we do, I want this murdering bastard banged away for life." Jane continued to drive knowing the commitment to the case.

"Well the analysis can do that."

By now they were driving along the A1, "At least these babes should be fruitful for us to see a number plate if nothing else." Pat muttered pointing at the monitoring camera.

They eventually arrived at Hazlerigg where once again they were frustrated once again at the shops. They managed to get side views of the van passing by. One outstanding feature they had seen on previous video footage was a small mark on the passenger side of the van. They had dismissed this as a mud stain, which was quite reasonable as there were mud stains around the van as clearly hadn't been cleaned for quite a while. The footage from the newsagents clearly showed the side of the van and they could see more detail of the mark. It now appeared to be a scratch where the van had come into contact with a wall or another vehicle.

With that thought in mind they returned to base for a much-needed break.

It was now midafternoon and Ben was working hard on the computer. By chance he looked up to see his assigned DS and DI walking towards him. "Ma'am, just in time."

"For why?" replied Pat.

"If you go to the printer there is an image of the van driving behind you, two significant features the number plate and a scratch on the passenger side and a partial image of the driver. Clearly it is a middle-aged man. He is wearing glasses, a baseball style cap, possibly a wig and a short beard. He is clearly aware of the road cameras and done his best to disguise his appearance. If the number plate genuinely belongs to the van, then it is registered to a Robert Hite of Bury St Edmunds. I say that but, it hasn't been reported as stolen. It may have been cloned given that it is a working van, so far away from home. It has been registered to this chap for five years or more accurately the last registered change of ownership was five years ago. It is taxed and insured to the same address, so to all intent and purposes is road legal, the only question is, is the person driving the van real?"

"Is there a driving licence in that name?" Jane asked.

"Yes, but it is still an old one in the paper form as it was last issued in 1998 just before they became compulsory for photocards. So we haven't an image of him on that system."

"Any other vehicles registered to that address?"

"I did check, but no there isn't."

"Damn," Pat added, "thank you for your hard work Ben."

"So boss, does this mean tomorrow..."

"Yes, tomorrow we are paying a visit to Mr Robert Hite of Bury St Edmunds. Jane can you pick me up at seven tomorrow morning?"

"Ben, I need you to go through the notes and see if there are any patterns we need to know about, work your magic. But most of all I would like to know where the target van went to before he parked outside my place and where he went to after he left. You now know what we are looking for so see if you can track him on the cameras because at the moment you are the best bet we have to find him and also put a monitoring alert out for this van. If he wants to play, we can."

"Yes boss."

"My guess is that whoever it is has had this van for five years, will be using it for just criminal work, hiding it undercover and there will be a central point where the vehicle is stored, probably a factory unit. By the way, can you contact DS Mark Monroe from the British Transport Police Drugs Investigation Unit and pass him the van details. He is working on a different aspect of the same case. Use my name and he should know what to do with them; in fact, when he comes back to you, he might be able to drum up some more work for you so work with him."

"Ok boss"

"Good, then it is all arranged. I update the boss and you lot can all bugger off. Ben, tomorrow early turn ok." With that Jane and Ben disappeared. Pat went and briefed the chief inspector. For the first time she was gaining a bit more confidence over her case after it had been shattered by not being connected to the drugs barons.

The following morning Jane called around at Pat's home and they went to Bury St Edmonds. It was a long journey so they broke it up with a rest break at Blyth Services before continuing down the A1, then onto the A14 which took them all the way to their destination. They had made good time. It was just gone twelve and the satnav took them to a block of flats. After a few minutes searching, they found the right number and knocked.

It was answered by a lady in her early sixties. She was quite surprised to see them. But she agreed to let them in and chat in private.

"Hi. I am DI Pat Nottage and this my colleague DS Jane Richards. We are from Northumbria police. You are?"

"Mrs Hale, please call me Stella."

"Stella, we are investigating a murder in the Newcastle area, so thank you for inviting us in. We're trying to trace a gentleman who has a vehicle registered here."

"Can we ask, how long you have been living here please?" Jane followed up

"Oh, five may be six years now I rent it from the council."

"Oh really. Do you know anything about the tenants prior to moving here?"

"No, Sally Godfrey did, she lived next door. But she passed away last year. Quite sad really, she was the same age as me but had a heart attack. I was friends with her and she did talk about them in passing as I think there was a bit of a scandal, something to do with the police, I think. A married couple, she was in the police and he worked for a housing association. I wasn't really listening but I do believe he went to prison and that is why they split up, with her being in the police and all. Well, you know the rules better than I."

"Do you remember the couples name being mentioned?" the DI asked.

"No, she just referred to them as the Lewis's."

"Has anybody registered her car here?" Jane insisted.

"Well no, why?"

"Have you had any problems with identity theft?"

"No, nothing, just me. I don't do the internet thing I prefer the local shops. There is plenty in the markets around here and they take cash."

"Ok thank you for your help." Jane finished hand writing the questions and answers on a note pad. She then asked Sally to read, sign and date it, which she duly did. The two ladies left and drove to Bury St Edmonds police station. Pat took the lead once inside.

They went to the desk, produced their warrant cards and asked to speak to the inspector.

"Hi, I am Inspector Roslyn Land." She was now in her late forties and had joined straight from university as a WPC, as it was in those days, and progressed through the ranks. She was tall with flame red hair and deep brown eyes. "How can I help our colleagues from up north?"

"Hi, we are investigating a murder on our patch and we had a car registered here in Bury to a Robert Hite. We have reason to believe the car was involved at some point in this crime, so we are anxious to get in contact with him."

Jane continued the conversation. "It seems to be a ghost address. We spoke to the occupant who had told us the previous tenants called Lewis had split up. The wife was a police constable, does she still work here as we would like to see what she has to say from her point of view?"

"Indeed she does work here, she's the Desk Sergeant this afternoon."

"Is it possible for a quick chat with her to see what she knows?"

"Yes not a problem. We have a small canteen upstairs. You are welcome to wait with drink and I will send her up when she arrives." They thanked her and did just that. It was wasn't long before she arrived with the inspector."

"Hello, this is Sergeant Cassandra Lewis." They all greeted each other with hellos and handshakes.

She was smartly dressed and was five foot ten in height with greying blond hair, sparkling green eyes and a pleasing smile. She still had an athletic figure although in her fifties.

Pat repeated herself verbatim from earlier.

Cassandra confirmed she had lived at that address.

"At the time I was at the address, it was seen as a temporary staying point for me and my ex-husband. We had met in the RAF. We were both in the military police and married after a couple of years. Sometimes we were deployed apart while we were courting, but the RAF allowed us, once married to be posted together it kept us in the UK, although we were both deployed to Afghanistan separately.

It was after the Afghanistan deployment, Bill had had to deal with an IED, sorry improvised explosive device, and the aftermath. It was awful, the device took out a patrol and an Afghan family. They had to secure the immediate scene, collect forensic evidence for the British Coroner and glean military intelligence from what was left and where it was left.

He was upset by having to retrieve body parts of the children. Bill changed, he started drinking and gambling. Eventually he was time served and left the RAF and the police. He took up work for Bury Council Housing and I joined the police with my experience they snapped me up. We had bought a house but it needed extensive building work we went for it as it came with a little land and was going to be our retirement pad. We moved into the flat for a year to give the builders free rein. They were doing a fantastic job, taking a shell of a barn to a modern efficient house.

But what I didn't know was Bill was stealing money from the council. It turned out he had gambled all our money away and having spent that, he was now gambling with the council's money. Of course, they did an annual audit as routine and found there was a £180,000 missing. After an investigation it was proved that Bill was stealing the money. He was maintaining the lie about our money, saying he was paying for the building work with it but still heavy gambling. Although I knew something was wrong, I had no idea what was going on as the builders were being paid on time.

Despite the criminality of what he was doing, the house was in joint names so when he was caught, I was dragged down with him. As the law is, I was responsible for half the housing debt but ended up paying for everything. The only saving grace was I managed to keep my job. I lost gratuity from the RAF and I have just finished paying off the debt. Luckily the courts cleared me from wrong doing. Although Bill was made responsible for the money, everything was seized. I was left with the clothes on my back and my uniform.

The strain separated us and we divorced. He was sentenced to two years inside. I believe he served half that. I never made contact with him again. I heard later that he was sent back to prison. This time it was for scamming people online, but had died on release. I have never heard from him since indicating it may be true. In fact if it wasn't for my police wage and upcoming pension I would be having a pretty sorry time of it."

"I am sorry to hear what he put you through and glad to hear you made a good go of it. Have you heard of a Robert Hite?"

After a moment of thought she replied, "God, I haven't heard that name for a while. He was a friend of Bill's. I think he died in the early nineties."

"So would it surprise you to know he still has a driving licence and owns a car registered to your flat address?"

It took a moment, but Cassandra understood the implication of what was being said. "My God! No, no, no, no, no, no, please God no, that bastard is still haunting me."

Jane was moved and sat next to her giving her a reassuring hug and tissue.

"Do you have a photo of Bill we could have please?"

"No," she replied shaking her head, "when I lost everything, I burnt what was left. Try the military records at RAF Cranwell." She wrote down his military number and date of birth and handed it over to Jane.

"Are you going to be alright, you have had a bit of a shock?"

"Yes," she replied, "I am ok, I am on the desk."

"Ok, if you can help with anything, here is my mobile number, anytime day or night, please don't hesitate and thank you. You have helped a great deal, I'm sorry we brought a bit of a shock to you. It might be wise to check you are one hundred percent divorced, just to be sure. I would hate to think something has gone wrong and if he is alive then you may have more problems, worth thinking about."

As before Jane had been taking notes and Cassandra read and signed it.

As she left for the desk, the inspector came in and asked, "Did everything go ok and is there anything she needed to be aware of?"

Pat informed her that at the moment it was but advised her that Cassandra had had a bit a shock and she should keep an eye on her.

Back in Jane's car, they sat there for moment, "Right, time for a dinner." Pat agreed. They drove to the fast-food mall and chose a chicken dinner.

"Ok, so if he is dead and not just anecdotally, there has to be a record. It's one thing to say some one is dead if they want to disappear and no one would check it out. There should be a death certificate if he is. If he is still alive, is he still collecting his pension? There would a paper trail even if there is identity theft. He could be using a PO box where he can access post whenever he wanted to."

Jane photographed the piece of paper and sent it to Ben with instructions to check with the births and deaths register and also with the RAF, he was a military policeman. Also, the same with Robert Hite, no details, but death overseas in the early nineties possible starting point would the RAF.

"Looks like we're back in the game eh Pat?"

"Yes Jane it seems so, but remember we have been here before."

"PO box, if there is one, could reveal a regular pattern to him collecting his mail and the CCTV in the post office will give us an image of our Quarry. That would give us a chance of finding him."

"Yes Jane, and its thanks to Cassandra Lewis, poor girl. Fortunately for her, she is divorced but imagine if she had remarried, what a nightmare that would be if she was still married and the hell she would have to go through. Yet we still don't know for sure that he is our Quarry, but you know what? I feel lucky."

After they had finished their chicken dinner, they called into the coffee shop, picked up two lattes and returned to the car.

With a long drive back, they set off to Newcastle calling at Blyth Services again. It was seven by the time Jane got home after dropping Pat off.

It had been a long exhausting day, with a nine hour round trip and then two interviews. So they arranged the following day for an extra hour in bed.

Pat, when she got in, scrolled through the entire day's CCTV footage, just to see if her car had been messed with, but the only visitor was the postman.

CHAPTER 14

They arrived at their office at nine in the morning, refreshed and ready to go. DS Mark Monroe from the British Transport police was there with CI John Haydon.

"Good morning Pat, how was yesterday?"

"Morning sir, potential result."

"Good morning ma'am, how was yesterday down in Essex?"

"Morning, Mark. As it happened it was very interesting."

"Can I make it more interesting?"

"Go on mark."

"We have had a hit with the van on the CCTV in the car park, in fact we currently have three hits, all outside the station. All with the driver sat inside, no pick up or drop off just parked there for hours on end. I have my team looking back over the last three months for the van, it was there all along. It seems that it was parked in a blind spot so we only got a partial view but we have the number plate. As soon as we have a visual on the person, I can get a search on any platform activity and train movements. I understand it's an alias he is operating under."

"Thanks Mark, it is yet to be proved. Firstly, we need to confirm he is alive as we believe he is. He has a military pension which I bet he is still claiming, if he is, we can link him to the van. We can also prove he is driving under a false name. When you get the image of him it is your job to link him to the murder of your Station Manager Andy Reid, that is your baby, do that and you're at the table with a seat for the 'kill' deal?"

"Deal." They shook hands on the plan.

"In the mean-time we have a lot of hard work to do to build a case before we can even interview him. He is ex-Military Police with form for embezzlement and fraud. He is surveillance aware, trained to look for this shit and he knows what we are looking for. Well we kinda profiled that earlier on, just went down the wrong track, excuse the pun with the train thing.

Just a thought, now you know the van and we know he is following me; do you think you can tie the van into Carl Mills death? If so, that will make us fifty-fifty partners and proudly working together. We still need a motive and hard evidence because he is a clever bugger or he likes to think so. When we reel him in, we need the oven up to temperature, the sauce ready. We just need to skin and gut him, that will be the confession and the motive, because this has been going on too long and I am his next target."

"It will be a pleasure and may be put him in the oven for life."

"Boss!" Pat turned to see Ben, "I can show at the time of the Grey death, the van was parked outside the pub nearby. We have the CCTV from the pub car park, it still doesn't show the number plate but the passenger scratch mark is there."

"Why didn't we pick up on it earlier?"

"We weren't looking for it, that is why boss. Also, for the first year she was classed as a disappearance."

"Sir, what are the chances of the same van being seen at two possible murder locations and seen outside the investigating officers home?"

"I ain't a mathematician but I am guessing remote, so what do you want to do Pat?"

"Sir, can we tag it so that if it goes passed a camera, we know about it, but at the moment I only want surveillance not apprehend? We are not ready for that quite yet. When we are ready, I will pull him in with a full week's dinner menu in front of him with guests and their attire. He is a smug bastard who thinks he can get away with murder and an ex-copper so he knows how to wriggle and I want him bang to rights."

"Ok Pat, your call."

"Sir, about that, the top brass and your report. I can't ask you to lie but can I ask you to describe it as Classified? Something isn't right when information goes beyond your desk, and I am the next mark for this lunatic because of this leak."

"Your way Pat."

"Sir, just to be clear, I still have trust in you and I believe that most of the bosses are honest but there is one rotten apple. It may be accidental; it may be corruption but IOPC will determine that and I don't want to pay the price for the error."

Just then Ben appeared to deliver a message. "Ma'am, Mr John Faith is downstairs and requesting to speak to you and you alone."

"Ok, thanks Ben."

She turned to John, "Sir can you excuse me?"

He nodded. Pat went to the front desk and seeing John Faith, she beckoned him, they went into a small room and Jane joined them.

"Ok John how can we help you?"

"Let's be clear, I hate grasses but favours need to be repaid and I am free thanks to your fair judgment."

"Go on, what you tell us will remain between you, me and Jane. You won't be called on as a witness, the information will be used only as background intelligence and I guarantee it won't appear on any report."

"I have heard on the tom-toms that over the last couple of years someone behind the scenes has been increasing and rewarding petty crime. There is something like a reward scheme for robberies and muggings but now it has ended and gone into reverse.

It is bizarre but there was a Fence who would pay folk £500 over the odds, payment for him to fence the stolen gear, in and around the local area up to Christmas last. But it was invited members only and the crime had to be in the papers."

"It pays to advertise," Jane quipped.

"They were known prolific blaggers only, some of them made a good living at it for the two years, some even managed to move up the food chain."

"Any names?"

"Let's be clear, I ain't a grass, this is information only. I am clean and under licence and I intend to remain free and stay straight but then some of them apparently would quote Shakespeare, 'render unto Caesar' they would say."

"Thanks, John we are grateful," Pat encouraged, "do you know what happened to the stuff that was brought by this new and generous fence?"

"No, that is just it, with a glut of stolen gear, the stuff never reappeared, it just vanished but there was a rumour it ended up in eastern Europe. Now that takes money."

"Thank you John, is there anything else you would like to know?"

"No, please don't tell anyone, except my parole officer but only on the QT, a few extra brownie points don't go amiss."

"Sure John, this conversation will be logged as a follow up from the previous complaint, when you were cleared, Ok?"

"Thanks, can I go now."

"Yes thanks once again, Jane will show you out."

Jane escorted John out of the station security gate and returned to Pat who was now in the office.

"Render unto Caesar!" Jane quipped.

"Yes I was thinking about that. Why would you pay over the odds for stolen gear, that and insist it is high profile?"

Jane turned to Ben, "Can you produce an annual graph of crime data over the last ten years, looking at the different categories of crime to date and any unnatural spikes."

"Yes, shouldn't take too long."

Pat turned to him, "Ben we are asking a lot from you, how are you coping with the work load, alright?"

"Yes, if I wanted a quiet life I'd be working on the deck chairs in Spain."

"Good on you, have we heard back from the MOD yet?"

"Yes, he is still collecting his pension and it is registered to a PO box in Cambridge. The post office don't keep records of the time when they are opened but I have asked them to monitor and inform us when it is next accessed."

"Great! Check him out with the DVLA, see if it throws up any vehicles and licences. We are after an image of this guy, also any social media contacts with groups associated with the RAF and any military. He has also been to prison for stealing money from the council, so there might be a news article. Ben, I want his picture on this wall chart today! Make it happen."

"Ok boss."

"Based on the lack of evidence and method of operation this guy is screaming out surveillance aware and he is a convicted criminal. We can tie the white van to two murders and a deceased alias known to Bill. So I am making him the suspect on all four murders and other crimes pending," Pat paused,

"I need to know about this guy, his full history, that's his past. I also want his present. Once we get that, we can link him with evidence and build a rock-solid case against him, because all the false trails he has led away from him but paradoxically, still lead us to him. The picture he painted for us to see only stands up to a casual glance but it is counterfeit and counterfeits do not stand up to scrutiny.

Ok team let's see what we can do but at a guess he is showing us Suffolk and Essex but I bet he is active here below the radar."

The information came through. Pat shared it with the team along with a summary so far.

"William Lewis born 06/03/67

Joined the Royal Air Force Police age 18

Served between 1985 – 2008:

RAF Halton 1985-1985

RAF Newton 1985-86

RAF Decimomannu 86-87

RAF Gütersloh 1987-90

RAF Lyneham 90-97

RAF Wattisham 1997-2008

2006 Awarded two medals, the Medal for Long Service and Good Conduct and the Operational Service Medal for Afghanistan.

He was trained in forensics and electronic surveillance.

On being discharged he worked for the Bury Council, where he stole £180,000 over eighteen months to fund a gambling addiction. This spiralled out of control and he was losing money hand over fist. He was sentenced to two years imprisonment at HMP Hollesley Bay. After one year he was granted early release due to him seeking treatment. However, his criminal life continued and he was sent back to HMP Hollesley Bay for three years for running an online scam, serving eighteen months.

His divorce became absolute in 2011, but his ex-wife believed he had died. She hasn't been in contact since his first stint in prison. On release in 2013, he used the identity of a friend who had died, Robert Hite. Guessing from what Cassandra his wife said I bet he was RAF too.

Ben, do your magic, military, birth, deaths, oh and passports, we have his driving licences."

"Boss, we have his picture from his passport, driving licence, police record and prison."

"Great, send them to Mark and me and our team. Do we have a current location on him at the moment?"

"No boss."

"Right, that is our priority, find out where he lives and we need to strengthen our case because at the moment it is all circumstantial and will be thrown out. What happened after he followed me, Ben did you trace him?"

"Only to your house boss, then he disappeared from the cameras."

"So, what does that tell us? It tells us that he is using a lock up or similar to hide the vehicles when not in use. It can't be a small domestic one as he has at least two motor vehicles there. The van and the bike and possibly a civvy 'non crime' vehicle. Again, after he sent that picture, he would know we would be looking for him, just because of the photograph. So, where are these vehicles hidden? Once we find them, we will find our evidence.

One final thought is Cameron Wood. Was that a real suicide or was it staged for our benefit, taking advantage of the poor guys work situation. We are going to have look into that Ben, are you ok with that?"

"At last Boss, something meaty to get my teeth into, but just one thing boss, if I can find the link do I get the credit for it?"

"Yip."

"Give me a day on it."

"Here is the file. By the way, that white van, can we search for its movements?"

"It is easy, time consuming in one way but AI tech does the business. Once we have the vehicle number plate the computer does the work in minutes for what a poor DC analysing it took hours, if not days."

"Good, I bet it turns up at Cameron's address at some point, we have four people all devout Christians going to the same church. They all lived in the same general area of Cramlington.

First was Carl on the 12th May 2018, Carl Mills he died, when he was knocked over crossing a road, stoned on dope and six times over the drink drive limit.

Second, on the 10th September 2018 Cameron Wood. He strung a wire around a pole and hung himself in the stairwell after drinking a bottle of whisky and having problems at work.

Sadly, we have our third victim, Joyce Grey. She was a forty-five when she disappeared on the 13th June 2019 after a day out a beauty spot.

Finally, we have the fourth victim, Andy Reid, who was attacked and killed last month. It made to look like he had tripped on the tracks, but drone footage shows it was a vicious assault.

So, we have two things in our favour. Firstly the drone footage, which he doesn't know about, and the second is the mistake of sending the stalking picture, leading to the van being partially identified from domestic CCTV.

Re the Essex diversion, he must be operating locally, secretly, as the travel time makes it untenable from his native Essex and Suffolk.

During this time, apart from the Pandemic, we have an increase in burglaries fuelled by an active fencing programme that was limited in time and receiving media attention. Which in itself is bizarre as most burglaries want anonymity to get away with their crime but now a drop in the crime as it has stopped being funded by persons unknown.

Is it coincidence or is it connected?"

"Don't forget with the Essex connection boss, there is the argument, the missing memory stick and documents which fuelled the blind alley, and also the Chimera effect." Jane reminded Pat.

"Yes, I haven't forgotten that, caution is needed when it comes to DNA. However, I think it will be a valuable tool as this will show contact with the victims.

It is essential we find that van, it is the key to solving the crimes. I believe it has been used in all the crimes and will hang around the murders like an Albatross."

The three broke for lunch. On their return Ben, who had been away, returned with a big grin.

"I have four hits with the van at Cameron's address. I can tie the van with Cameron, Carl and Joyce's addresses. the AI programme can't spew the hits out fast enough and even Andy has a hit, but there is a problem!"

"Oh and what's that Ben?"

"There are no hits leading to a central point indicating a physical home address of the van. The hits suggest that the vehicle is local to Cramlington, which is fine but then there no hits from Cramlington to Durham for Andy."

"So how is it getting from Cramlington to Durham unnoticed?"

"Yes, but I thought we talking about storage units?"

"Yes, but I have a problem with that."

"Ok. Talk to me."

"Well, if there is a storage unit, there will be paperwork, rental, something that is auditable and ID's required. So, if the whole premise of the murders is to remain out of sight and as untraceable as possible, then it can only happen if it is kept on the owner's premises. But that still begs the question, how does it disappear after your trip and again to Durham?"

"What about disguising the van?"

"Possible, it is a blank canvas. A few magnetic stickers and a change of number plate simple and easy but, unless he puts the sticker over the door scratch he would still be detected by me when I carried out the initial search."

"Go on Ben, you are making sense, so what are you suggesting?"

"I'm not sure but the army make tanks look like buildings and guns like trees, you know camouflage.

What if the small van looks like something else until it is required to do the job? This guy is RAF so he will be aware about disguising and camouflage. So he could be hiding in plain sight, like he was before the picture, covering his tracks."

"You mean he was still covering his tracks post mortem, knowing if there was a post attack search and we were looking for the van, that it needs to disappear in a way not to leave any trace, like Hansel and Gretel," Pat interjected, "Camouflaged, you say tanks like a building, small vans like big vans, hiding in plain sight? What about on the back of a transporter, like a recovery van?"

"Yes, but only if it had a tarpaulin covering the van again to hide the scratch."

"The tarpaulin might hide the van type and colour but not the shape, so to a casual observer no problem but a waving red flag to a deliberate search. No, he would have to change the shape of the vehicle in such a way as to not draw attention," Pat surmised.

"Ok so not on the back of a recovery van, what about inside a bigger van?"

"That would do it Jane, but so very 70's crime robbery films," Ben confirmed.

"But that means we would have to have at least three vehicles involved in the crimes, the bike, the car van and now a bigger van. Does this guy have a warehouse at his disposal or something?"

"Email just through from the MOD/RAF."

"Go on."

"Robert Hite born 16/09/68.

Joined the Royal Air Force Police age 18 years

Served between 1983 – 1995

RAF Halton 1983-1983

RAF Honington1983-85

RAF Newton 1985-88

RAF Leuchars 88-90

RAF Buchan1990- 1992

RAF Lyneham 92-95

1990 - awarded the Medal for Long Service and Good Conduct and the General Service Medal 1962-2007 with a Northern Ireland clasp.

His death is recorded as accidental, as the result of a road traffic accident. He was the passenger; the driver was our friend Mr or Sgt Lewis. They were on duty and a drunk driver swerved into them," Ben read out,

"So we can tie this guy into being the owner of the vehicle and that's how he managed to use the ID of Rob Hite."

"This is being a most productive afternoon. Well done Ben, as a newcomer to the team you really have changed our fortunes, so a big well done from me and keep up the good work."

"So all we need to do is find his lair. How the hell are we going do to that I wonder?" Jane pondered the question.

"Well my friend, that is the hard part. All of his official documents go to a PO box, if we catch him using it in Essex, we will then lose the vehicles and all of our evidence trapped in them." Pat replied.

"Well, if the post office is going to ring us when his post is collected, then we get his vehicle details and track him home on the traffic network cameras. That will get us close but not close enough," Jane was on a roll.

"Fine Jane but we know he has contacts in the area, so we might find that an innocent friend is posting his mail up to here, which is okay but if it is going to another PO box up here, then we're going to be stuffed again."

"We don't have to catch him there or even wait for the post office to ring, although that would be useful."

Both Pat and Ben looked at Jane really hard. "Explain."

"Sorry Ben, this is more your thing but we know he collects his mail on a regular basis and we know the PO box number and address."

"Get on with it," Pat insisted.

"Well my first thought was to drop my mobile phone in his car when he collects his post. But then I thought it was going to be difficult and we couldn't pull it off because of the five-hour drive. Why not post a tracker to him?"

"Jane sometimes it is almost a pleasure to know you, you're a genius."

"But there is a problem, first we can't send Junk mail, there is a good chance he doesn't get junk mail, so it would stand out and that brings us on to the next problem. We need him to keep it, so he returns home with it in his possession and not bin it. We know he is a cautious type and we know he won't make mistakes. So the tracker will have to be in the letter he needs to keep with him and from someone he has given his postal address to."

"Won't he have a pension?" Ben chipped in, "so we can bug a letter from the MOD?"

"Yes and as he is a military man and it will be the RAF, so will he get circulars from them?" Pat was thinking about her own pension statements and other official police circulars.

"I am going to have to have a serious chat with the boss on this one, so let me think on it and I will brief him tomorrow. In the meantime you all disappear and be here first thing, bye."

So the team dispersed with the task to think about for the following day.

The next day, Ben sought out his boss to brief her. "Boss I have been looking at the computer file for Cameron Wood, it appears a clue has been overlooked."

"Oh and what is that?"

"The murder weapon!"

"Did you say weapon?"

"Yip I did, we have been talking about a 'WIRE'."

Pat confirmed that.

"Well wire is available to most domestic houses; rope is less obvious."

"Go on Ben," Pat encouraged.

"Well the rope might be a tow rope but it isn't, it might be a climbing rope but it is not. The report here lists it as rope, notably bailing twine which is only available through farm suppliers."

"Well done Ben. Can you look into his computer activity and see if he is operating any online scams. He has been convicted once already and he may be up to his old tricks."

"No problem boss."

Pat went to see John, her boss, to brief him away from where they could be overheard. She told him they could link the suspect to all four crimes, (although the Andy Reid case needed the Transport Police to provide stronger evidence), they could also provide evidence for the false trail that links the suspect to the false ID. But the location of the suspect was now tied to PO box and the plan to post a tracker to him.

"Tracker. What if he has someone collect his post and send it up to him? A simple trick."

"Sir that means sharing his ID with someone else and I am betting he wouldn't risk that because it means if the guy is intercepted he would give him up through innocence or criminal guilt. No sir, I bet he makes few but regular trips down there.

This guy doesn't make easy mistakes, lucky for us he has made mistakes or things haven't gone to plan. We need to know that he will keep the letter and take it home. I have a plan. We get the MOD to send the tracker and hope he takes it home."

"Really, and where do get the tracker from?"

"I think the National Crime Agency or GCHQ have the technology."

"I will make a phone call Pat and see what we can get, serial killers do attract a bit of motivation to catch the killer."

Jane then appeared. "Boss, Mark from the Transport Police just rang. Darren Hilton is coming into the office this afternoon, if we want to be in on the interview."

"You're busy Pat, I will see what I can do but I think your team needs you."

"Sir," and Pat returned to her team.

"Ben did you actually check out the forensic evidence?"

"No boss just, I just read the online inventory."

"Right, come on then. Jane liaise with Mark and go to the interview with Darren. He needs to be warned but don't give any details, I am going to look at the physical evidence.

Ben we are going to look through the evidence boxes of the three victims we have. That excludes Andy Reid because the Transport Police are dealing with him, so let's see what we have."

First they pulled out the box on Joyce Grey and found nothing but clothing that had been weathered and damaged. There were no effects left to speak of, most likely they were washed away.

The next box was Cameron Wood, it was a bit more revealing. Pat found the rope that was described in the inventory and agreed it appeared to be bailer twine.

"This needs to be sent to the crime lab for further analysis."

The final box was Carl's effects. Like the other boxes it was mainly clothing but there was his wallet. The contents were taken out and bagged. There was a bulge it.

"What is this?" Pat opened the bag using a gloved hand. After a few minutes squeezing the wallet a small memory stick popped out.

They looked at each other.

"Get this down to forensics asap get it cleared for handling and then get it downloaded and sent for analysis Ben. If there is anything on it, I want to know."

Ben and Pat spent the whole afternoon going meticulously through the evidence questioning its relevance.

Jane returned to the office later on, after the meeting with Darren. She reported to Pat, "He was a bit shaken with the news that Andy was killed and he was a likely target. But he has agreed for BTP to keep a close surveillance on his home. He is aware of the two vehicles, a white van without markings and a black Triumph motorbike. I didn't give him too many details but I made him realise there was a secret operation under way to catch the suspect. With him being ex-services he understood.

He has been given a mobile number from Mark to text or ring if he sees any of the guy's following him. He appears to a sensible chap and I think he is a good asset to have on the team."

Pat then updated Jane about the memory stick found and it should be available for analysis the following day.

CHAPTER 15

The following day started with a bit of buzz.

Ben was working on the memory stick and Jane was working through evidence that was in the boxes.

Pat returned from seeing the chief inspector and called a team meeting.

"The boss came through, the letter we requested will be sent today, the tracker is hidden behind the stamp. Curiously the National Crime Squad have assisted us with the tracking device, they will be monitoring its location in and around the UK. It will be sent as a service recall from Glasgow (military records). We now await Mr Lewis to collect his mail and his fate and hopefully before me or Darren Hilton end up as his next offering to 'Mars or Aries' the God of War."

Jane turned to Ben, "What's going on with the memory stick data, Ben?"

"Tricky." he replied, "it has been encrypted. It is a commercial encryption, so the trick is to work out which one. Two uncoded words are 'Jericho file'."

"Ben, top priority, I want to know what is on the stick, and a full forensic examination on the stick."

"Yes boss."

"Well that is cryptic, keep on with the decoding Ben it is important, it is almost as good as a confession."

"Jane, as soon as this guy shows his face on the plot, I want him followed. The arrest must be at his home address. If it is a farm, then it is there were we are going to get all the hard evidence."

Jane was still thinking about the name of the file.

"What's up Jane?"

"Nothing, I was just thinking, the name Jericho and why Jericho? Wasn't that from the Bible when Joshua led the Israelites around the city walls, blew their trumpets, the walls came tumbling down and it was captured?"

"Or an operation by the RAF to free the French Resistance during the second world war," Ben chipped in.

"So does this mean that Newcastle is a city under threat from terrorism?"

"Could be boss, Newcastle still has city walls, well the parts that haven't crumbled to dust or a blast from the Trumpets, or Semtex but clearly the problem isn't from the Jews these days but China Town. Doesn't that run close to the wall section, so you think it might be an attack on the Chinese?"

"Anything is achievable, but this has been going on for three, maybe four years, so I don't believe that it is possible. I know this is something more subtle than a terrorist action but to be honest I can't rule it out, but just to be sure I will flag it up along with my analysis, pass the buck upwards so as speak."

Just then the phone rang, Jane answered and relayed the message. "It is from the Forensic department, they are saying no DNA on the Joyce Grey clothing and two DNA profiles on the clothing from Cameron and Carl; which matches up to a Robert Lewis with a known criminal record, who served two prison terms. Thank you, yes, we will look out for the report and thanks for telephoning."

"I didn't think we would get Joyce's DNA it had been in the river too long but we have two positive hits and now we are just waiting for our colleagues to advise us, did Mark say anything to you yesterday Jane?"

"Yes, there is a forensic review of Andy's clothing for DNA, I'll get in contact with Mark and check what is happening with that, I think they use the same labs we do, so it must be due."

"Ok Jane chase it up with Mark, and appraise him of the situation with the tracker."

Just then, the chief came into the office. "Pat, the Nation Crime Agency have just rung me, since the urgency of the situation is crucial, they have had a letter printed off from the MOD as we requested. They have put the letter with a tracker in it and it is currently in his PO Box. as they will be conducting the tracking of his journey on our behalf, they have logged into the cameras so if he drives to Bury then they will have him even if he parks around the corner, they will also let us know the vehicle and reg number so we can have eyes on him when he comes into our patch."

"Thanks boss."

"Further to that Pat, Mark has just rang and forensics have confirmed that the DNA from Robert Lewis is on Andy's coat and the nature of the blood splats stands a good chance of being on Lewis's clothing."

"Boss, Cameron, the lead up to his murder or the premise to his suicide was his motorbike was stolen and a split up with his girlfriend?"

"Go on Jane."

"Up until now we have treated Cameron's death as a suicide brought on by events in his social life. We didn't react to it as suspicious because we thought that it could be just one of those things. We interviewed his ex-girlfriend just to confirm that they had split up and nothing more. The investigation at the time was merely to confirm suicide, she said he was cheating on her even though he denied it."

Jane continued, "Well who is to say that the motorbike our suspect is riding isn't Cameron's and the evidence the girlfriend was a trick designed to make him look like he was cheating. He did the same to you with the photo he sent here, to try and discredit you."

"So Jane what you are suggesting is that the poor guy was driven to suicide?"

"No boss, I am saying the pretext of suicide was a *ruse de guerre. So a murder could take place in plain sight.*"

"Jane, find this woman and speak to her but, be ready to drop everything I want you here on the bust."

"Should be easy as she is in the same church group."

"I am going to work on an arrest plan so we know what we are searching for and get it processed asap. Starting with the white van and the motorbike and then any other vehicles we find. Ben, you need to standby to work your magic because we will have seventy-two hours to formally charge him I want a pack with all the exhibits prepared and numbered and allocated to each of his victims. We have the DNA but we need to convince him that we have everything because if he experiences doubt or we have any doubt, he will wriggle out of it, so he needs to think that we know what he knows."

The following day the chief came into the office early with a message for the team. "Our man showed up at nine on the dot. As soon as the post office opened, they confirmed he has the tracker with him and is currently on the A14. He will come into our target area around midday and estimate that he will back in his home area on or around fourteen hundred hours." John handed Pat a piece of paper with the vehicle details on it.

"Good hunting," Jane remarked and left.

"Right boss, so can we have the snatch squad ready for 1pm with warrants and SOCO prepped and standing by. I want all the vehicles on site to be impounded and sealed for forensics and a team to be ready to go through his clothing. We have three definites and one possible to link to this guy. He is a convicted scammer and embezzler, into the hundreds and thousands and now he has upgraded himself to murder." Ben announced.

"Thanks Ben, how are we getting on the Jericho file?" Pat asked.

"Still working on it, I am going to search the dark web to try out a few ideas there, it isn't a standard hackers programme it is a bit more sophisticated and not as simple as changing the font from New Times Roman to Wing Dings."

Then after a few minutes of thinking about the problem he turned to Pat, "Boss, there is a group of us who can geek the night through, they are friends from Uni, may I show them a paragraph out there on the group's site and see if they can come up with a programme to translate the code?"

"Yes Ben, but no more than a paragraph."

"Ok boss."

"Wow, it has been another high-powered day, see you all tomorrow folks," Pat finally announced.

The following morning, Jane had already gone to the ex-girlfriend's home address and introduced herself.

The girl introduced herself as Valerie Peterson, formerly Lion. She had moved on and married again since Cameron's split with her and his death. She confirmed the reason they had split up was due to him cheating on her, recalling she was sent a series of photographs of him in a full embrace with another girl but didn't know who had sent them.

She had thrown the photograph's away after she had confronted him with the evidence along with anything else of his. Jane wrote out the statement and she signed it.

By the time Jane was back to the office it was dinner time.

John had come in to inform the team that Lewis had collected his mail at nine and was on his way up with the letter and tracker still in place. He also told the team that he was traveling in blue Mini with a Union flag on the roof, the number plate was registered to a company with the address at the PO box.

Shortly after Jane had returned, DS Mark Monroe from the British Transport Police Drugs Investigation Unit arrived.

"Great, the full team is here, Ben has the blue Mini arrived into our camera patch yet?"

"Yes boss, he is on the A1 just past York."

"Right so that means he is an hour or so away. I want to know when he gets to junction 63 or if he turns off before then I want to know. I am going for some dinner with Jane and Ben you go as well I suspect it will be a busy afternoon."

She called into the Chief's office. "Sir, it will be about an hour before he gets onto our patch can we task the helicopter once he arrives so we have eyes him on first hand?"

"Wheels in motion already."

"Ok boss, we are off for some dinner."

With that, Pat, Jane and Mark went to the canteen and grabbed a chip butty, a latte and sat at a table together.

"Got the helicopter as well Pat, really pulling out the family silver for this one." Jane mused.

"For a four times murderer and at least two more to boot and I am a target. To bloody true but we still don't know what it is all about and that is what I intend find out." The half an hour past quicker than they expected.

Ben arrived. "Ma'am the helicopter is in pursuit. The suspect left junction 63 and is now heading the A693. There are two ground units in pursuit with orders not to apprehend until the word is given."

"Good, Jane, Ben and Mark, I am getting a police car to get us there as soon as possible."

"Ma'am I have a marked car, if you can suffer 'British Transport Police.' on the side."

"Come on Mark, you're driving." The three got into the Audi A4.

"Jane, do you have the radio handset?"

"Yes boss."

"Right then, let's go."

As soon as Mark left the car park he put on the blue lights and very quickly they were heading down the A1.

The message crackled over the radio from the helicopter, "Suspect car now stopped at the Mile Grange farm. There are two buildings, a main building and a small house next to it."

Then, "Suspect now entering the small house. Officer's cars now stopping in the lane leading to the farmhouse, no other road entrances available, read excess to fields only."

"Eta Mark," he had just adjusted the satnav and they were heading towards Stanley.

"Five minutes from current location, go for it".

"All units this is Bronze control, arrest suspect Robert Lewis on suspicion of having a stolen vehicle."

The two police cars accelerated into the farmyard and ran into the house. A middle age man stood there with a cup of tea in his hand. "Hello officers can I help you?"

"Are you Robert Lewis?"

"Yes."

"Sir, do you live here?"

"Yes."

"Do you own the place sir?"

"No way, I couldn't afford to live here. It is a live in job, I am Chef and occasional chauffeur and any other job I am required to do."

"Robert Lewis, we require you to assist us with the theft of a motorbike, and the murder of four people"

"Well there is a motorbike in the barn, it isn't mine. Is that the one you are looking for and as for murder, I don't know what you mean?"

"Can you show us the bike please sir."

"Ok." He led them to the barn and straight to the bike.

"Who owns it sir?"

"Dunno, it isn't mine, I think the owner rents the space out."

Just then the car with the three detectives arrived.

"What is going on?" Robert asked alarmed at the arrival of the BTP car.

Mark got out and looked at Pat, "Go ahead Mark."

"Robert Lewis, I am DS Mark Monroe from the British Transport Police Drugs Investigation Unit, I am charging you with the unlawful murder of Andy Reid, the Station Master at Durham railway station. You do not have to say anything. But, it may harm your defence if you do not mention when questioned something which you later rely on in court. Anything you do say may be given in evidence. Do you understand this caution I have read to you?"

He acknowledged the caution.

"You will now be taken to Newcastle Central Police Station where you will be questioned by myself. Do you have anything to say in your defence?"

"No," he replied.

Mark put the handcuffs on Robert and escorted him to the car. He got in the backseat sitting next to Ben, Mark returned to the driver's seat and Jane in the front passenger seat. Pat returned in the other police car as she wanted to keep her distance at this moment in time because she didn't want him to become suspicious of her presence.

Once they arrived at the police station he was taken to the desk sergeant, who collected the required details including he did not have any health issues. He also elected to have the duty solicitor present but required no one to be informed. He changed into a police issue sweater and trousers, as his clothing was required to be submitted for forensic examination.

Once done he was fingerprinted, photographed and DNA swabbed before he was taken to the police cell.

He requested a cup of tea which was provided.

DS Mark Monroe then entered the cell. "Robert, I am informing you that a search warrant has been issued to search your premises and also a warrant for the vehicles in the barn, they have been seized pending forensic examination. I am currently waiting for the duty solicitor to arrive to commence the formal interview."

"Thank you, sir." Robert muttered.

It took the solicitor about thirty minutes to arrive and the desk sergeant gave him the brief on the case.

He was then introduced to the suspect in the interview room.

Shortly afterwards DS Mark Monroe and DS Jane Richards entered the room, Mark switched on the recording tape.

"Good afternoon, this interview is being both audio and video recorded on the 15th November 2022 at 1530hrs. Currently present is DS Mark Monroe from the British Transport Police and DS Jane Richards representing Northumbria Police. Also present is the duty solicitor?"

"I am Leslie Woodard and I representing....."

"I am Robert Lewis."

Turning to the suspect Mark addressed him, "How would you like me to address you?"

"Bob will be fine,"

"Bob, first I must remind you that you are under caution and that still is valid. Do you know of Andy Reid the station master at Durham railway station?"

"No."

"Have you ever been to Durham railway station?"

"No."

"Have you ever owned a motorbike?"

"No."

"Have you ever been to prison?"

"No."

"Have you ever been convicted and given a non-custodial sentence?"

"Bob, have you served in the military?"

"No."

"Do you live at Mile Grange farm near Stanley?"

"Yes"

"You told the desk sergeant that you work there as a chef and chauffeur, is that correct?"

"Yes"

"Who is your employer?"

"I am self-employed."

"Who provides you with work?"

"Liam Staveley, the Police and Crime Commissioner."

Mark remained composed, "That is ok Bob, I represent the British Transport Police and Mr Staveley doesn't have any bearing on us, we are responsible directly to the Department of Transport and not the Home Office. Now Bob, would you like to start again?"

"No!"

"Ok, I am now showing the suspect exhibit RL 101.the military service record of former RAF Police officer Robert LEWIS. Do you still deny being in the Armed forces?"

"Yes."

"Ok, I am now showing the suspect exhibit RL 102 this is a communication sent at our request from Military records to Robert Lewis, the letter found on your person."

"It was intended for another Bob Lewis."

"Ok, I am now showing the suspect exhibit RL 103 the contract with the post office for the PO box you have in Bury and the address of the PO box appears in the MOD address, care to comment?"

"I am the person who served while at that address but I had a horrible time so I was trying to forget that I was in, losing friends does that you know."

"Ok, thank you Bill but I notice you are still in receipt of a military pension. Never mind, I am now showing the suspect exhibit AR 100 please look at the screen this drone footage taken at the time of the assault on Mr Andy Reid by a young person not involved in the incident and recorded by chance."

They watched as Andy was hit over the back of the head and then was laid on the tracks.

"Would you like to comment Bob?"

"That is totally not me, any fool can see that."

"For the recording I have frozen the frame showing the back of the person dressed in black. Ok, I am now showing the suspect exhibit AR 101 a print off from that video RL 106 and RL 107, photographs of clothing recovered at the suspects home address.

"That could be anyone."

"Yes Bob it could, but this is a black hoody and black trousers that corresponds to the video footage. It contains blood splash patterning corresponding to a rear attack. These items are currently with the forensics to determine the origin of the blood.

I am now showing the suspect exhibit AR 102a. This is a photograph of a tyre mould taken near the scene approximately ninety-five feet from the assault on Mr Reid."

"Would you care to comment?"

"Not really"

"Ok, I am now showing the suspect exhibit AR 102b this a statement linking the motorbike seen by the farmer who tried to engage with the motor biker, stating he saw a black Triumph scrambler would you like to comment?”

“Common bikes, plenty of them about.”

“Ok, I am now showing the suspect exhibit AR 103a, a photograph of the motorbike as identified by the farmer in the AR 102b. Please note he described the bike as a Triumph 900 black scrambler with K and 5 in the number plate.

Comparing that to the number plate in the photograph, the letter K appears and the number 5 appears on the bike recovered at the barn.”

“I am now showing the suspect exhibit AR 103a, a photograph of the motorbike as identified by the farmer in the AR 102b and RL 108, the forensic report hot off the press stating that the wear patterns on the tyre tread are a match.”

“Bob?”

“You will have to speak to the owner, he is the one who rents space out.”

“And the owner being Liam Staveley, the Police and Crime Commissioner?”

“Yes.”

“And you are trying to tell me he is responsible for the bike?”

“No”

“I am now showing the suspect exhibit RL 101 a log book, this bike is registered to a Robert Hite. Do you know a Robert Hite?”

“No”

“I am now showing the suspect exhibit RL 101a, you will see it is a statement from your now divorced wife stating that you do ride a bike and that you were friends with Robert and that you found his death hard to take. I am now showing the suspect exhibit RL 101b, the service record of Robert Hite, there are at least two postings where you worked on the same team.”

"So it was traumatic time and yes, I was trying to protect his name."

"Bob it is best if you tell us the truth. I am now showing the suspect exhibit RL 102, a photograph of a rock. This was recovered at the scene, five feet away from the body. It has traces of the victim's blood and hair on the rock with also fibres matching those used in motorcycle gloves, Any comment Bob?"

He shook his head, saying "No."

"Can you account for where you were on the 30th September around 2pm or 1400hrs give or take thirty minutes in the afternoon?"

"I was at the farm preparing the nights tea for the boss."

"Are there any witnesses to confirm that?"

"No, but I had my mobile with me."

"Don't worry we believe the mobile phone was at the farm, but we found the second 'pay as you go phone', both are being forensically examined as we speak."

"Well, how is that fair, you are going to fit me up."

"No, we wouldn't do that Bob. You see, the forensic trail is independent. Also Bob, as I said the bike is currently being examined by the forensics lab as well, they are independent; they are now looking for fibres and any blood stains. We now meet the test for charging you with murder. 'Robert Lewis, I am charging you with murder: Robert Lewis on the 10th October 2022 you did murder Andy Reid contra to common law. You will remain here pending the forensic reports on the clothing and motorbike we seized and further investigations."

"Can I have some time with my client before he is returned to the police cells, please?"

"I will inform the desk sergeant."

Mark switched off the recording devices and the two DS's got up and left the interview room.

They met up with Pat, Mark saying, "Over to you Pat."

"Great because that now means we have time to build up a forensic case against him for the other three murders."

"By the way, he tried to shake me by telling me he worked for Liam Staveley, the Police and Crime Commissioner, but I had great pleasure announcing that we were responsible to the Department of Transport and not the Home Office, that threw him. By the way, I didn't mention the VIN number on the bike is wrong."

"Thanks, but I have to go and speak to the boss, he is going to shit a brick when I tell we have arrested the PCC's chauffeur and cook."

They both gave a grim smile of satisfaction to the climax of the charge.

"It's enough for him at the moment, I will deal with him tomorrow,"

CHAPTER 16

The following day Pat made straight for the chief's office.

"Ah, please come in Pat. I have had the PCC on the phone all night complaining that you have arrested his cook and chauffeur."

"Yes I did, he is a serial killer and a bit of a high cockalorum. We are waiting for the forensic link to make everything water tight. Mark from the transport police has already charged him with the murder of Andy Reid. He was good to go with that one, but because we need the forensic link we can't proceed. I let him go first as he can buy us a day or so while the boffins come up with the goods for our charges. So, in fact we have had nothing to do with the initial arrest."

"That will make the top brass happy, ok, good hunting."

"Don't make them too happy sir because we will probably need an extension, and once the papers get a whiff that a member of a politician's personal staff is a serial killer, all hell is going to break loose.

Sir, at the moment there is no reason to suspect the PCC, so as far I am concerned it is just a coincidence but if he puts pressure on us in any way, shape or form, I guarantee he will be held accountable for the mayhem and his career in politics will be buried forever, job be damned. So it would awfully decent of him as a law-abiding citizen to volunteer to make a formal statement to confirm he knows nothing."

"I will pass it on."

Pat returned to the office where Jane was working.

"Pat, the Triumph motor bike is linked between Cameron Wood, Rob Hite and Robert Lewis."

"How?"

"We already have the Rob Hite and Robert Lewis connection via the registration document and the bike was found at the farm. Well, Bob swapped the number plates from another similar bike, but he didn't change the VIN number, which still linked it to Cameron Wood. So with that and along with the bailing twine found at the farm….."

"What bailing twine?"

"Didn't you know boss, SOCO found it and is a brand match for the twine found at Cameron's home."

"So Jane, you are telling me that we have Robert matched for two of our three, plus the BTP murder, so three out of four. Brilliant, now all we have to do is connect him with Joyce and we have got him for the full house."

"Also on the forensic side, we have a match for Andy's blood on the seat of the bike, it must have been carried on Bob's clothes. We are waiting to see what the van reveals. By the very nature of the vehicle, it is going to take a while but again he has been overconfident. For the record, we have the large van that has been modified to take a small vehicle inside, as we suspected. There is a mud match from the tyre marks inside the large van and on the small van."

"What vans are they Jane?"

"The small one is a white Peugeot Partner 1000 1.5 HDi 100 Van and the large van is a white Renault Master LM35dCi 135"

She showed Pat the photographs of the two vans the small van, the mark on the side of the van and the inside of the Renault. It showed a reinforced floor and a small winch to pull the van inside. It also showed, stowed inside, two ramps to allow the vehicle into the back of the van.

"So that was how it could disappear from the cameras and reappear from different directions."

"Yes boss. We are still awaiting the forensic evaluation of both vehicles and the suspects clothing. I have told them to concentrate on clothing that matches up with the video first making the assumption that he wears it like a uniform on duty."

"I like that Jane, but we still need a full profile eventually of all his clothing, but I agree, for the moment let's concentrate on the red flag clothing, I want to link him to the crimes by person."

"Right, when is Mark next due to speak to his prisoner?"

"After dinner, the solicitor is the delay."

"Good, when he is finished, if we have time, I want to have a go. Unless we can tie him to Joyce, although we know we have the van, we are going to have problems. We'll ask SOCO to look for souvenirs in his room, that might help us with the other two but we will be lucky for Joyce without a confession."

"Where is Ben?"

"He has organised a trace for the Renault on the cameras, working with his geeky friends, also he is saying something about a double encryption on the memory stick."

Mark turned up with the solicitor, Leslie Woodard, Mark stopped to speak to Pat. Leslie went to collect his client, and spoke to him in the interview room. After a brief chat they were joined by Mark and Jane.

Mark activated the recording equipment. They all acknowledged their presence for the recordings.

"I must remind you that you are still under caution. But first are you well and rested Bob and had something to eat?"

"Yes thank you?"

"Bob, since we last spoke there has been an update. I am showing the suspect RL 112. This is the forensic report on the motorbike. We have Andy Reid's blood and your skin cells on the bike, so I would like to give you an opportunity to offer an explanation before you go to the Magistrates Court for proceedings to send you for a Crown Court trial."

"I have nothing to say."

"Ok Bob, have it your way, I am now going to leave the room and start the process for you to go to trial." Mark stopped the recording, got up and left the room but within the minute. Pat walked in.

Pat activated the recording equipment. They all acknowledged their presence for the recordings.

"Robert Lewis, I am DI Pat Nottage, I am with Northumbria Police. I work with DS Jane Richards, who you have seen sitting in on the last two interviews with DS Mark Monroe from the British Transport Police. I have a lot to cover with you so if you require any breaks, please let me know. I have no intentions of playing games with you. I will first go through your background and that of your victims, one at a time.

I am interviewing you about the unlawful murder of Carl Mills, Cameron Wood and Joyce Grey. You do not have to say anything but it may harm your defence if you do not mention when questioned something which you later rely on in court. Anything you do say may be given in evidence. Do you understand the caution I have read to you?"

"Yes," he replied.

"I am aware of your military service record as a former RAF Police Officer and your contract with the Post Office for the PO box you have in Bury St Edmonds.

I am also aware that you have served two prison terms for theft and running a scam operation. I am now showing the suspect exhibit AR 102a, a photograph of a tyre mould taken near the scene approximately ninety-five feet from the assault on Andrew Reid;

AR 102b, a statement linking the motorbike seen by the farmer and who tried to engage with the motor biker stating he saw a black Triumph scrambler;

AR 103, a photograph of the motorbike;

RL 101, a registration document for a bike registered to a Robert Hite;

RL 101a, you will see it is a statement from your now divorced wife stating that you do own a motorbike and that you were friends with Robert Hite and you found his death hard to take;

RL 101b, the service record of Robert Hite. There are at least two postings where you worked on the same team.

So Bob, we have already established the motorbike is directly connected to you. Something that has come to light is the Vehicle Identification Number on the bike is wrong for the registration mark. We checked it out and it appears the motorbike was cloned. When we found the VIN number, we found the original owner was a gentleman called Cameron Wood.

Do you know Cameron Wood?"

"No."

"He had his bike stolen; we know this because his ex-girlfriend told us.

I am now showing the suspect exhibit CW 100, a photograph of the ligature used in his death. Do you recognise it Bob?"

"No, it looks like an ordinary bit of string to me."

"It does to me, but here is the thing, it is made in Hanover Germany, we know that because it is a match forensically with the roll of twine found in your barn, would you care to comment."

"Anybody can buy that; it is so common."

"Yes, you are right Bob, but there are micro changes in the weather that effect the production and it shows up in the chemical signature of the twine, a very similar process to the ice cores they take in the Antarctic. More importantly as a former police man in the military where two different fabrics come into contact there is an exchange of fibres. This is the forensic report of the twine, exhibit CW 101, showing fibres from a material used in motorbike gloves. On its own it doesn't mean much but when we look at your gloves with your DNA on, highly magnified, it shows the cut marks made by the twine are shown in exhibit CW 102, a picture of the glove.

I am now showing the suspect an exhibit CW 103, a forensic report of Cameron's clothing, it shows a DNA match with your profile, taken at the time would you like to comment?"

"No, I have nothing to say."

"Would you like a break for a hot drink?"

"Yes please."

Pat paused the recording equipment.

They took a five-minute break, all had a hot drink provided.

Pat turned on the recording equipment and continued, "Mr Robert Lewis: so far my colleague has shown the Crown Prosecution Service that the test for prosecution more than meets the test for the murder of Andy Reid. They also agree the same for Cameron Wood."

Bill remained motionless then dipped his head and drank some of his tea but remained quiet.

"I am going to discuss with you Carl Mills."

"Do you know him?"

"No, how the heck would I?"

"I don't know, I think you do, but the matter is immaterial as I think you do and I intend to prove it."

"Good luck," he replied unjustly.

"I am now showing the suspect exhibit CM 100, a picture of the white van seized at the farmhouse, with a scratch down the side. Would you like to tell us how it got there Bob?"

"How should I know?" he replied indignantly.

"Are you aware that Carl was being monitored by the British Transport Police?"

"What?"

"Yes, DS Mark Monroe was investigating him for drug offences, I guess you didn't know he was a main supplier to railway staff and was under their watchful eye while trying to build a case on him. So, Mark has kindly given us footage of your van driving into him."

"I said it isn't my van," but Pat ignored him.

"He was involved with a major drug cartel and they were trying to get him to expand his repertoire but you cut that short, his prosecution that is."

Jane showed Bob the footage marked BTP/CM/101. It lasted for a full minute. When it showed the driver, it looked clearly different to him.

Bob struck while he could. "That isn't me!"

"No Bob, I agree it doesn't look like you, but Scenes of Crimes Officers found this wig and dark glasses in the glove compartment in the van, exhibits CM 102 and 103, which surprisingly has your DNA on and is documented as indicated in reports exhibits CM 104 and 105,

"Bob, we can link you forensically to the van and to the picture of the scene, so the charge is failing to stop and causing death by dangerous driving."

He gave a wry smile.

"Is something funny?"

"No not really, but hearing a driving offence being read out after a murder charge is."

"Yes but it isn't just a driving offence is it? It still represents the death of a person, we can't at this point prove premeditation."

It was then that the Leslie spoke up. "We have now been talking for a couple of hours. May I have some time with my client, and is it a good time to break for lunch?"

"Certainly, we will break for thirty minutes, no er, one hour, returning at two o'clock, I will inform the desk sergeant that you are having some client time."

"Thank you"

The two detectives left the interview room after switching off the recording devices.

Ben was waiting for them outside. "Ma'am just updating you on the memory stick, we have cracked the first layers of encryption and now working on the second layer."

"Good work, keep it up," Pat praised him.

"Nottage!" came the shout, "here now!" It was from the Chief Inspector.

"Sir."

"What the hell is going on? Why have I got the PCC shouting and screaming at me that he can't get into his home."

"Sir, the farm is now a crime scene, a forensic treasure trove and until it is cleared by SOCO, it is out of bounds to anyone. The suspect, Robert Lewis has been charged by BTP with the murder of Andy Reid and is soon to be charged with the murder of Cameron Wood, also the murder or unlawful killing of Carl Mills. We are trying to find evidence for the fourth death, Joyce Grey, the one which started this investigation. The PCC has money to go elsewhere and isn't he supposed to be on our side?"

"Ok Pat, just remember, he is a politician with money, he is somebody not to upset."

"Sir! We have evidence that Bob was at the Carl Mills scene but nothing for murder. I am still trying to link him to the death of Joyce Grey. If he gets off due to lack of evidence for her death, tell the PCC I will hold him personally responsible, let's see him get re-elected after that; assuming that employing someone who was convicted for theft and now being charged with murder isn't going to make it difficult enough. I do require him to come in and make a statement as a matter of routine."

"Ok Pat but be careful."

Pat left the room to go straight into Jane. "Yes?" she snapped, "sorry Jane, what's up?"

"We have some of Joyce's hair, found in the corner of the van door." She handed over the forensic report. The two returned to the interview room where the suspect was waiting with his solicitor.

Jane turned on the recording equipment, took the lead. They all reintroduced themselves, confirming they had had dinner during the break.

"Robert Lewis, we have so far discussed two people, I would now like to introduce a third person, Joyce Grey."

"Who? Never heard of him."

"HER. She disappeared in 2019, her remains were discovered early this year. Have you ever been to High Force?"

"Nope, never."

"This is exhibit JG 101, footage taken in 2019 by the public house nearby and shows a white van with a scratch down the side, similar to the scratch on the van we retrieved at the barn with your fingerprints and DNA attached." Pat played the video.

It showed Joyce in her blue Fiat 500 pulling up in the car park, getting out and walking toward High Force, she had a camera over her shoulder. The footage showed on the edge of the frame, a white van with a scratch down that side.

"What have you to say about that?"

"Must be another van!"

"I am showing the suspect exhibit JG 102, the forensic report of the van. I would like to draw your attention to paragraph 5. A hair follicle with a DNA match with Joyce."

"It's mistaken," Bob continued.

"Robert, you were a time served policeman in the RAF, what would be your response to a suspect who had just made the same remark you have just made to me?"

"No comment."

"I am now showing exhibit JG 103, a picture of a Canon camera. The strap and the battery pack compartment on the camera had dust, the DNA showed a positive match for Joyce. The battery itself still had her fingerprints on it. This camera was found during the search of your accommodation. How do you account for that?"

"I think it was left by the previous tenant."

"If you notice the forensic report on JG 102, paragraph 6 states it includes your DNA, how do you account for that?"

"Yes, I found it and used it, so what?"

"Finally, you have admitted to doing something Mr Robert Lewis."

"I would like to confirm purchase from an online shop with matching serial numbers in the name of Joyce Grey, but more importantly, I would like to draw your attention to an image found on the camera, do you recognise this?"

"No"

"It is a picture taken of me outside my daughter's home. Why did you take that picture and send it to my boss?"

"Again, I didn't!"

"I interpret this at best as trying to pervert the course of justice, at worse intimidation, but we are drawing a link between the two crimes. The question I have is why?"

"I didn't send it."

"Oh, I believe you did, but no matter the second question why me?"

"Good question when you know let me know please."

"So far my colleague has shown the Crown Prosecution Service that the test for prosecution more than meets the test for the murder of Joyce Grey." Jane gave Pat a nudge and took the lead.

"We are now taking a break from the interview; I will send someone in to offer you both a hot drink and you give time for some reflection with your solicitor."

The recording equipment was turned off. The two ladies stood up and left the room.

As soon as the door shut Pat turned to Jane, "Jane what the hell is going on?"

"The memory stick has been decoded – you really need to see and speak to the boss."

"Ok, where is Ben?"

"The interview room next door."

"I'm intrigued."

They both went in to see Ben sitting at a table with a pile of papers and a computer. He looked up and was white.

"The memory stick shows a motive for the murders if it ended up in someone else's hands." Ben explained.

"The file named Jericho details payouts for items stolen and receipts and links to the criminal underground. It refers to Gaius Julius Caesar and Marcus Antonius."

"Thank you Ben."

Pat started looking through the papers she had been given.

"So I am guessing we are looking for a leader and 'Render unto Caesar'." Jane quipped.

Pat then had a look of horror on her face. "No no no no no please God no."

"Boss?" The two other detectives looked confused.

"Nothing. You discuss this case with nobody DO NOT EVEN BREATH A WORD I am warning you."

She then disappeared smartish to talk to the Chief inspector.

He took one look at her face, by now it was drained of colour.

"Pat come in, what's up?" He was expecting a family death or something.

She showed him the papers that she had picked up. He too realised the impact of he what he was reading.

"Who knows about this?"

"Just my team Ben and Jane. I told them to keep shtum."

"Good, because I have officially just shat a brick and you lot have just caused it." He paused for a moment in real thought. "Pat, do you trust me?"

"Yes sir."

"Good answer, NOBODY IS ABOVE THE LAW and that should be executed without fear or favour of this noble Kingdom including its princes and princesses; but at the same time there are ways and means of applying it to suitable people. I don't want it to cause a shock to the public. You shall apply the law to the full, but I wish to discuss it with my bosses and to boot your bosses as well. I will brief you in the morning on this matter. Is this the only copy."

"Yes sir and the memory stick as well?"

"Can I have it please?"

"Yes sir but may I have a receipt for it please?"

"Yes of course Pat." He immediately wrote out a receipt and handed it to Pat.

"Ben has it on his computer."

"It must not leave this station and I insist it is locked up and the desk sergeant keeps an eye on it and free from interference. Do we understand each other? Trust is the key word here."

"Ok sir."

"Brief the others to the fullest extent and keep it away from your suspect as well, so no hidden messages can escape."

Pat returned to the interview room and passed on the instructions.

The two detectives returned to the interview room where their suspect was waiting.

The recording equipment was turned on again, Pat continuing, "Interview to recommence, so far you have been charged with the murders of two people and causing the death of the third.

We have shown you the path that leads to this conclusion and you have been charged, as such now I want to discuss with you, under that caution, this photograph.

I am showing the suspect exhibit PN100, a photograph of me and another person outside a private address have you seen this before?"

"No."

"How come it was taken and sent to my boss?"

"I really don't know."

"So it wasn't sent as a warning to back off then?"

"How should I know?"

"I am now showing the suspect exhibit PN 101, a still from a video filmed outside the same address clearly showing the van we recovered at your address with the telltale scratch, please comment."

"If it was me then I was just passing and checking the satnav."

"This is exhibit PN 102, a still from the Westerhope Community Centre car park. On the left is my car and on the right of frame your white van showing the scratch, please comment."

"Coincidence."

"You have so far denied any contact with the crimes we have discussed. Can you account for your location if you claim you weren't there?"

"I was at home, check my mobile phone!"

"But we have and I can confirm we did that as you would expect us to. Each time there was a ping from the masts making it impossible for your phones location to give you an alibi. Well, assuming we believe you did or did not have your phone with you, I am now the suspect exhibit

BT100, phone records showing your location near the farm. Your Mobile exhibit BT 101 making it impossible for you to be at the scene on time."

"See I told you so!"

"Yes but the ping was made by a pay as you go phone with different numbers. When searched the barn we found your pay as you go phone and the relevant sim cards, exhibits BT 102, BT103, BT 104 and BT105. So instead of clearing you it implicates you even further, any comments?"

"Never seen the phones or the sim cards before."

"I am now showing the suspect BS 101,2 and 3, statements from your bank account saying you did purchase them.

You have now been held in custody for two days the superintendent has just given us an extension for thirty-six hours so we have time to speak to you tomorrow. Ten ok for you Mr Woodward?"

He acknowledged it would be. "Yes, can I have a few moments with my client?"

"Yes sir. Robert, I will hand you over to the duty desk sergeant and I suggest you consider your situation very carefully."

CHAPTER 17

The following day Pat reported for duty at the chief's office.

"Come in Pat." John was very stern and his normal glow of confidence had disappeared.

"Everything has been arranged for you. Let me make this quite clear, no one is above the law and we take this very seriously. Can you text me as soon as you have made the charges so I can inform the Home Office. You can consider the only order on this is, and I do insist, maximum security. The top brass are all briefed and ready the second you charge him with all the murders you can. We are going to face a political and media shit storm, ok?"

"Ok sir."

On returning to Pat the office, she briefed the team with her orders and what the chief inspector wanted. It was now coming up to 10am.

The two detectives Pat and Jane arrived in the interview room to find the solicitor and suspect sitting there.

Pat went through the preliminaries. "Due to the nature of the offences, I will be formally applying via the courts for the maximum 96 hours. So I may extend the forensic search. To make this happen, today will be formally dedicated to the meeting the administration demands. This is to facilitate a proper search for more evidence. Do you wish to say anything."

"Yes, I am an RAF veteran and I have served this country as a military policeman. I admit the evidence may appear convincing but then it has been wrongly interpreted and you have to show beyond any doubt I did this. It frankly belongs in the realm of fantasy.

Once a policeman always policeman and I would never threaten a civvy colleague or harm a member of the public from what appears to me as accidents. All the DNA shows is that these poor people have been in contact with me in some innocent manner and not as a result of criminal action. The van is registered, legally on the road but not to me and I am entitled to drive it. I have my own insurance on own my car, the Mini Cooper, that is fully comprehensive allowing me to drive other vehicles on third party cover. It is also not illegal to find items and look after them until the proper owner can be located.

You have shown no motive for these alleged crimes that stands up and as for the drone footage that could be anything. It certainly doesn't implicate me. It also isn't illegal to strengthen a van up so it may carry other vehicles inside. Motorhomes do it all the time. So, as sad as it is for the families of the those departed whose family members met with a tragic end, I was not involved in their demise. Again, once a policeman always a policeman and now I even provide security for the Police and Crime Commissioner such is my commitment."

"Yes, but does an honest policeman embezzle hundreds of thousands of pounds which you were convicted of stealing from the council while working for the rent collection office? According to your prison record at HM Prison Hollesley Bay or the Colony, a Category D men's prison, you were signed up for gambling addiction. A couple of years later you were there again for more treatment when you were sentenced for three years for embezzling and running a computer scam. Your veteran friends are a pretty conservative bunch aren't they, how do you think they will react to you when they find out you are not only a thief and a reckless gambler but a murderer? I think you have failed the service test, don't you?"

"Yes but then I was sick with mental health issues and addicted to gambling. I got treatment for that while I was inside, so it is no longer a problem. I am back on the straight and narrow and working hard as a chauffeur and chef with a bit of personal protection for your boss."

"Yes we know, he is here checking up on you. Here is the thing, you created a Pepper's Ghost crime but now the trick is revealed. I am betting he will ditch you. Remember he was in the government when they burnt the Liberal party. I am guessing when he makes his statement, as he will shortly, you will be thrown under the bus and by the way what is the going rate for close protection these days?"

"50k per annum plus generous expenses."

"I was talking in years in prison but then shame, if convicted you won't get to spend it."

"I won't get convicted on what you have."

"We will see. Mr Lewis, one thing I don't understand, is why would you increase a crime wave were there isn't one and then let someone else take the credit for solving it?"

"I don't know what you are on about."

"Why would you increase a crime wave by funding criminal activity, surely that isn't policing with a remission of £500 and over the odds pricing we know about Jericho."

"I don't know what you are talking about, but any increase in crime is my boss's job to reduce it, that is why he was elected, is it not!"

"Ah, so that is it, ok sir we will type that up I would like you to sign it as a true account of this interview. Just one thing Mr Lewis, I would take a long good look at yourself and think further about your level of cooperation it might help you in the future."

The statement was printed off. He read it with his solicitor and signed his most recent statement.

"Thank you, Mr Lewis, interview terminated pending a magistrate review."

The recording equipment was turned off and the two detectives left the room.

On seeing Ben, Pat asked, "Ben any fresh news for us?"

"Nothing stands out, just more forensic hits and camera hits on all the vehicles but nothing conclusive. We can add to the weight of evidence."

It was just then that the Police and Crime Commissioner arrived. Pat and Jane greeted him and showed him into the interview room."

"Right sir, thank you for agreeing to come in and make a statement with regard to your employee."

"You are welcome."

"Sir, I am going issue a police caution so that anything discussed here meets the legal requirements due to the nature of the charges against your employee. You do not have to say anything. But, it may harm your defence if you do not mention when questioned something which you later rely on in court. Anything you do say may be given in evidence. Do you understand this?"

"Yes detective I do."

"Sir do you require a solicitor?"

"No."

"Can you explain the nature of the relationship between William Lewis and yourself?"

"He is my chef and chauffeur; I have employed him for eight years."

"How did you meet him?"

"I put an advert in situations vacant when I was an MP in Essex."

"Were you aware he had just come out of prison?"

"Yes, that isn't a crime, is it? He served his time and I do believe in rehabilitation, don't you?

I asked for an ex-military person with personal protection training to act as driver and you can't get better than a policeman from the air force who knows both sides of the fence."

"Was there a formal contract?"

"No, he was self-employed, I paid him monthly. It was a live-in job; he was able to take it up as he had just been divorced."

"Can you confirm that as a chauffeur he had access to all your vehicles and they were in a legal condition?"

"Yes, I insisted on it as in my position being high profile I need to be seen as legal and above board."

"Do you have a close relationship?"

"Yes, well sort of as an employer, he cooks and drives for me as and when required."

"You are aware the reason he has been to prison twice is he has had major gambling debts."

"And I believe that was sorted why?"

"You see sir, when somebody in financial difficulties, he is easily bought and then controlled with the lure of money."

"What are you implying DI Nottage?"

"Oh nothing. Ok sir, I think that is it for the moment if you would just wait a minute while my colleague finishes writing your statement and when she is ready will you sign it please?"

"Thank you detective, how long will it be before my employee is released from police custody?"

"Sir, I have been granted an extension to question Robert for a further twelve hours."

"Render him unto Caesar me thinks."

"What was that sir?"

"Sorry, product of a classical education, I'm afraid, it is Shakespeare," he sneered.

Pat got up as if to make for the door, but this was a rehearsed manoeuvre intended to throw the Police and Crime Commissioner off guard. She returned to her seat as if there was an afterthought.

"Er actually sir, I am aware of the Shakespearian quote."

Pat turned on the recording equipment. They all identified themselves on tape, Pat repeating the caution.

"We have something I would like you to look at. It is the memory stick currently being load on my colleague's computer."

The gibberish appeared then translated into plain text on Jane's laptop.

"Sir, it did give us some real problems to understand what was on it. As you can see to any casual observer it is pure gibberish. Once you clear the first and second level of encryption with a decoding program it is quite revealing, titled Jericho with subtitles Caesar and Marc Antony. Strangely enough, we were arresting quite a few professional criminals who were being paid over the odds for fencing their stolen gear. They were all saying the same thing, that they were being paid a minimum of £500 plus an inflated cash price, no questions asked. The thing is, when asked who was paying for the gear they merely replied 'render unto Caesar.'"

"Detective what are you implying?"

"Nothing sir, should I be, but I can't help noticing that the documentation lists all the money given out. It corresponds with the mini surge in burglaries. All the professional burglars realised they were onto a good thing and the only clause was it had to be documented in the local rag.

Sir, didn't you run your campaign for Police and Crime Commissioner on the reduction of burglaries? Which did happen and it coincides with the last recorded entry on the log sheet.

I am quite sure there is a documented audit trail, but we will find out as there has been a court warrant granted for examination of your bank account for the period in question and also your henchman."

"Henchman, what do you mean?"

"Sir, a group of ten Christians with one out of the four who died, finding your money, documents and the memory stick I have just shown you. Why are all four of the people now dead by the hands of your staff member, please respond?"

"I had no Idea of his alleged actions."

"This is a camera linked to the murder of Joyce Grey by serial number and DNA, but that isn't what I want to discuss with you. Why is there an image of me on it! Can you explain this?"

"No, you will have to ask the guy who took the picture."

"I did," Pat replied, "but I want to know Liam Staveley as the Police and Crime Commissioner how you had access to knowledge about ongoing investigations, you even asked me about it?"

"Limited but no details."

"Did you inform him that I was assigned a cold case investigation that involved Joyce Grey?"

"Of course not, how ludicrous."

"It arrived shortly after you asked me about my investigation, strange isn't it?"

"Pathetic is what I think."

"I don't really care Mr Stevenly, sorry Staveley isn't that what you do?"

"What do you mean constable?"

"It's DI and you see sir, that if you are aware I was investigating one death, only the one guilty of all four deaths will understand the significance of the one. So now I am talking to you about four murders I am investigating and you have access to that information. So, it seems strange that someone you have employed has used that information in an attempt to intimidate me to leave the case."

"That's a bit of a leap but your evidence is light."

"Not really, we found a manifest of a company you own with all the items matching the stolen items from numerous of burglaries logged in on it. Also that the company Staveley Eastern Transport, ships out regularly to eastern Europe, including all the stolen property from the UK, chasing the money from the Russians with cheap imports. Sir, would that be just to reduce some of your losses so you could rig the election for the Police and Crime Commissioner and be impossible to trace?"

"Rubbish you little conniving cunt."

"Sir! Please your language, but I don't think so, therefore I am arresting you for conspiracy to burglary and conspiracy to the murders of Joyce Grey, Carl Mills, Cameron Wood and Andy Reid also known as Cy, contrary to Common Law.

I am also charging you with perverting the course of justice and interfering with a police officer carrying out the course of her duties.

Conspiracy to threaten a police officer in the course of their legal duty, also Handling stolen property against common law.

You see Sir, the coal mines, the railways, the steel works and the NHS, you run them down then sell them off cheap to your party donors.

Then you solve a problem that you caused, I believe to increase your chances to get elected and rig the process. You engineered and distorted crime issues by funding criminal activity and then appeared to solve it by withdrawing funding; then when the evidence was lost, you financed and supported the murder of four churchgoing people who innocently stumbled on artefacts of crime. I am sure I would have appeared on that list so, please don't insult me anymore. I will inform the Parliamentary Committee on standards and the election committee of my thinking; they will also be investigating you."

There was a moment of silence.

"You must be mad you little pleb."

"Yes sir, I am from the plebeian class and not the equestrian class, yes I know the Latin social classes from ancient Rome."

Liam was even more frustrated at this, what he considered a social insult, as he like to lord it over people.

"This is a career ending move for you detective, just wait until after I speak to your bosses about this!" he shouted at the two detectives.

"Sir, again, Detective Inspector if you please, and do you honestly think that I am so stupid to arrest the Police and Crime Commissioner without evidence that has not already been seen by all those in the chain of command independently and they all came to their own conclusion. I must warn you sir that there is a press conference taking place shortly announcing the arrest of your driver in connection with the four murders and we are also announcing that you are linked with the four murders and other offences and have been arrested and charged."

"WHHHHAAATT that is disgraceful, how dare you?"

"Sir, please don't shout, would you now like to have a solicitor?"

"Sod off and stick your solicitor up your bony ass."

A message flashed through on Pats mobile.

Pat terminated the interview, turning off the recording equipment, saying, "Excuse me, I have someone really important to speak to and yes another pleb class."

They left the interview room taking the Police and Crime Commissioner, smarting at the way he was being treated, to the desk sergeant to be processed.

The detectives walked into the other interview room. Waiting for her was Louise and Dennis Grey. They all sat down.

"Hi, I am glad you both were able to come in. There is a bit of unusual activity here and in part it was started by your Joyce."

"How do you mean?" Dennis asked

"Looking into her passing we came to speak to you and you put us in contact with the church group. We found they had unwittingly stumbled into a crime scene. Sadly, because of that they were targeted to maintain secrecy of the crimes. The group were unaware and what is ironic that their deaths were meant to appear innocuous but it had the opposite effect and brought our attention to them."

"So what are you saying?" Louise asked.

Jane picked the conversation. "A politician created a mini crime wave and then appeared to solve it. He then tried to cover it up."

"Why would he do a thing like that?" Louise looked puzzled.

"He was a rising politician and was kicked out of Parliament because of allegations of misbehaviour, this was his way of returning to politics by appearing as a successful Police and Crime Commissioner. He would use it as a springboard to returning to Parliament, but things, as always, started to go wrong. Thinking he was discovered by the group he arranged for them to have accidents and that was the important part, it was the unusual pattern of accidents that brought him to our attention. He would have got away with it, if it wasn't for your Joyce and I wanted to tell you before you see on the tonight's tv news."

"So he killed Joyce to win an election, is that right or am I confused."

"Yes you are, sadly that chap is so rich and arrogant that he doesn't live in our world, he isn't interested earning enough to retire on as he has that, he is after power; being number one is all that counts. He was selling an illusion of being in control with ability to his former colleagues. Well no matter what happens he will no longer be welcome anywhere but prison and he will find out how fickle his friends are to hanging around murderers."

Dennis Grey spoke, "Thank you for Joyce's sake, we know you did her proud." Dennis and Louise stood up to leave, Jane escorted them out.

Pat and Jane were summoned to the chief's office, where Ben was already sitting.

"Well done, the forensics did come through and a great bit of detective work by you two and Ben. Just the press conference to do and then get on with the rest of the processing for the courts but it has been a busy day enjoy the weekend break you have earned it."